P9-CBP-431

JY 09 '96	DATE DUE		
JY 11 '96			
JY 27 '96			
AG 3 '96			
AG 19 '96			
SE 04 '96			
SE 13 '96			
SE 24 '96			

DISCARD

HEART
TROUBLE

HEART

A CALLAHAN GARRITY MYSTERY

TROUBLE

*Peabody Public Library
Columbia City, IN*

KATHY HOGAN TROCHECK

HarperCollins*Publishers*

HarperCollins books may be purchased for educational, business, or sales promotional use. For information please write: Special Markets Department, HarperCollins Publishers, Inc., 10 East 53rd Street, New York, NY 10022.

FIRST EDITION

Designed by Ruth HN Lee

Library of Congress Cataloging-in-Publication Data

Trocheck, Kathy Hogan.
 Heart trouble/Kathy Hogan Trocheck.—1st ed.
 p. cm.
 ISBN 0-06-017638-5
 I. Title.
 PS3570.RR587H43 1996
 813'.54—dc20 96-6554

96 97 98 99 00 ❖/HC 10 9 8 7 6 5 4 3 2 1

*This one is dedicated with love to
Mary Kathleen Trocheck, who is mostly Katie,
sometimes Smoochie, formerly the Tiny Dainty Princess.*

ACKNOWLEDGMENTS

ACKNOWLEDGMENTS

This is a work of fiction, of course, and any resemblance to real life occurrences is strictly unintentional. But the author wishes to thank the following individuals for their time and advice. Any errors in fact or judgment are my own fault and none of theirs.

Lori Evers, CPA; Bill Hankins; Rober Waller; Leslie Fuller Secrest; David Secrest; Jim Walls; Lt. Don Hardman of the Dekalb Arson Unit; Bob Davies; Roy Staples of Jackson, Ga.; Lib Groves Brennan and Anne Groves Morris; John C. Villines; John D. Cantwell, M.D.; Susan Hogan, RN; Amy Schwartz, M.D., and the Rev. Jackie Jenkins.

The usual suspects: Sallie Governeur, Eamon Dolan, and Tom Trocheck.

1

"CALL THIS FATBACK?"

Miss Sister Easterbrooks held the plastic-wrapped slab of pork up close to her Coke-bottle-thick glasses. The milky brown eyes took a long, educated look. She sniffed disdainfully. "Don't look like fatback. Don't smell like it neither."

Her sister, Miss Baby Easterbrooks, nodded in agreement and clucked her tongue. "Couldn't find no pig knuckles at all. Sorry. That's what. The Auburn Avenue Curb Market got all cleaned up and fancy. Too good for itself, that's what I say."

"I know that's right," Sister said. "Can't make no mess of greens with fatback smells like a shower curtain."

Baby and Sister are technically employees of The House Mouse, our cleaning business. "Older than dirt" was the only age either one would admit to, although we guessed they were closing in on eighty. Baby is as close to deafness as Sister is to blindness, but the two of them manage to clean maybe one house a week, working as a team.

1

They had been carping about the downfall of the Auburn Avenue Curb Market ever since the Atlanta institution on the corner of Auburn and Butler was renovated a few years ago. Health inspectors had demanded sneeze guards and hairnets and plastic gloves. Soul had been sacrificed for sanitation, and Baby and Sister were still mourning the loss of their favorite vendors. They would have no truck with meat they couldn't view up close and personal.

Baby recited the menu as she unloaded the grocery sacks.

"Fried chicken. Collard greens. Sweet potatoes. Biscuits. Apple cobbler. Now, Callahan, it ain't fancy, but your mama, she'll be ready for some home cooking. Ain't that right?"

It was Edna's coming home dinner. She'd gotten a bad cold in September, and it had lingered and worsened until her racking cough had led me to bundle her into the car and deliver her, wheezy protests and all, to our family doctor. An hour later she was admitted to Piedmont Hospital, diagnosed as having pneumonia, and put on oxygen and intravenous antibiotics.

I still shudder when I think of the way she looked in that hospital bed. My larger-than-life mother shrunken with illness and fatigue, blue-tinted hair matted to her head, her face the color of unwashed sheets, eyes ringed with dark circles, tubes everywhere.

Edna had had a double mastectomy years ago, but I was a kid then, and my father was still alive, and with the invincibility of youth, I thought of her hospital stay and recuperation back then as a minor inconvenience to the family. Five years ago I had my own brush with the C word: a lump on my right breast, followed by a lumpectomy and the happy news that my cancer was early and noninvasive. Since then I've tried to be a good little girl. I eat my broccoli and cauliflower, drink bottled water, cross my fingers at mammogram time, and try to avoid stepping on the cracks in the sidewalk.

My mother had been smoking three packs of cigarettes a day since her early teens. Nothing anyone said or did could detach those long slender fingers from her filter tips.

Now it was all I could do to stand by the bed and hold her hand while Jeanne Payne, our family doctor, ranted at her about her smoking.

I'd known Jeanne since we were in Girl Scouts together. She could probably still fit in her Brownie uniform. Five foot two, slender, with thick, wavy dark hair, she somehow managed to cut an imposing figure in her white lab coat. Maybe it was the bifocals she wore on the bridge of her nose. Or the fact that she'd finished Emory Medical School at twenty-six, first in her class, youngest, brightest, shortest.

"You've got a spot on your right lung, Edna," she said, getting right to the point. "Your pulmonary capacity is roughly that of a tubercular ninety-year-old coal miner. All your symptoms point to the early signs of emphysema."

Edna winced and squeezed my hand. "You want me to quit smoking."

Jeanne shrugged. She could be merciless if circumstances merited it. "Only if you want to stick around for another few years to spend your kids' inheritance."

Edna tried to laugh, but the chuckle disintegrated into a spasm of coughing.

"There's a woman your age in a room two doors down here," Jeanne continued. "She's being discharged tomorrow, same as you. But she's going home with a portable oxygen tank. Going to be hooked up to a breathing mask and a canister of oxygen twenty-four hours a day. That's the best we can do for her."

She looked sternly down at Edna. "Is that what you want?"

Edna sighed. "No. No oxygen tank. I'll try. Okay?"

Jeanne crossed her arms over her chest, hugging the clipboard with Edna's chart. "Trying's not going to make it this time, Edna," she said, her attitude softening just a smidge. "The pneumonia has weakened your heart muscles. We're going to release you tomorrow, but I want you back in my office next week. You're a good candidate for those new nicotine patches, and I've also got the names of some smoking cessation progams I can give you. Later on, when you're stronger, we want to run some more tests on that heart of yours."

"I can go home?" Edna leaned her head back on her pillow and closed her eyes. For the first time I noticed the blue veins in her lids, the tiny network of wrinkles radiating out from the corners of her eyes. When had she gotten so old?

"Tomorrow," Jeanne said. "You've been here a week with no cigarettes. So you've got a head start on quitting. Right?"

"I never liked you," Edna said, not bothering to open her eyes. "Go away and let me sleep."

I followed Jeanne out into the hallway.

"She's really sick, huh?"

"She's a lot better than she was," Jeanne said. "But I meant what I said about the smoking. You live with her. Can't you get her to quit?"

"How long have you known us?" I asked.

Jeanne pursed her lips and thought about it. "Second grade, right? More than thirty years." She grinned. "You're right. Nobody makes Edna Mae Garrity do anything."

"She's scared this time," I pointed out. "You notice she didn't say she wouldn't quit. That's a first."

That had been on Friday. Now it was Saturday. My sister Maureen and her no-account husband had volunteered to bring Edna home from the hospital. My brother Kevin had been transferred to San Diego in September. And Baby and Sister had arrived with all the makings for dinner.

Maureen had installed Edna on the living room sofa, swathed her with quilts, and was now lining up her array of medicine bottles on the coffee table.

"Can't we put those somewhere else?" I asked, irritated that Maureen had once again taken over my house.

"She needs to see her medicine so she can remember to take them all," Maureen snapped, plumping a pillow behind Edna's head.

Steve, Maureen's husband, who had ensconced himself in my favorite overstuffed chintz armchair, nodded rapidly in agreement, holding the remote control out at the television, flipping rapidly through the channels.

"I'm not helpless," Edna snapped. "Put the damn pill bottles in my room, Maureen. We're not setting up a clinic in here."

"I'm just trying to help," Maureen said, tears rising in her eyes.

Home fifteen minutes and we were already in round two of *Family Feud*. I walked quickly into the kitchen.

Baby stood at the kitchen counter on a footstool, whacking away at the chickens with a giant meat cleaver, while Sister was at the stove, dumping some evil-looking piece of meat into her bubbling pot of greens. The sugary smell of baking apples and yams mingled with the sharp vinegar smell of the collards and I suddenly felt myself relax for the first time in days.

"Can I help?" I asked timidly.

Sister rolled her eyes at Baby. "You the cleanup crew, Callahan," Sister said, wiping her hands on one of Edna's aprons. "Go on and stay out the way now."

It amuses all the girls, which is what I call the House Mouse employees, to think that I'm helpless in the kitchen. Like all the women in my family, I'm actually a pretty damned good cook. My macaroni and cheese makes you want to

smack your mama, it's so fine. But when Edna sold her house in the suburbs and moved in with me here in Candler Park, part of our agreement was that I'd stay out of the kitchen and let her do the cooking. It didn't take much arm-twisting to get me to let her have her way.

Edna's playing cards sat in a neat but dog-eared stack in a corner of the worn oak kitchen table, near her empty ashtray. I slid open the drawer in the table and stashed the ashtray inside. Out of sight, out of mind. Then I dealt myself a hand of solitaire. Like cooking, and putting our noses in other people's business, solitaire is a Garrity family habit. We play it when we're tired or worried. To calm down, or take our minds off whatever troubles nibble at the corners of our subconscious.

No telling how many hands I played at the kitchen table that afternoon. Edna was napping and Maureen and Steve were probably plotting some fresh assault on my nerves, and Baby and Sister hummed church hymns accompanied by the sizzle and pop of a skilletful of frying chicken. Maybe I dozed a little too. The next thing I remember is Baby standing over me, shaking me by the shoulder. "Come on, honey!" she hollered. "Supper's on."

Everybody else was already seated in the dining room by the time I straggled in and seated myself. The table was covered with food: platters of golden, still steaming fried chicken, a casserole of pecan-topped candied yams, a big bowl of collard greens, a basket of biscuits, and at each place a tall glass of iced tea.

Edna sat in her usual place at the head of the table. She was a little wan, but her eyes were positively twinkling, and she had a huge grin pasted on her face. Maureen had her head ducked, making that sniggering noise through her nose, and Steve's face had gone crimson with embarrassment.

"What's the joke?" I started to ask, reaching for the napkin

to put in my lap. The question died on my lips as I looked at that napkin. It was thick and narrow, with a blue plastic peel-off strip on one side. Maxi-strength Kotex.

I looked down the table for an explanation. "What's this for, Miss Sister?" I asked.

"Dinner napkins," she beamed. "Good and thick. Ain't that nice?"

2

MONDAY WAS UNUSUALLY HECTIC. Word was out that Edna was home, and every one of our regular clients called to welcome her back, inquire about her health, and complain about how I'd screwed up the schedule during the two weeks Edna had been out sick.

"I know," she sighed into the phone, "She's got these books so messed up I may never get 'em unsnarled."

I flipped her a bird and then went back to the stack of bills I was working on. I really had let things slide while Edna was sick. Now it was time to get back to business.

The House Mouse is only six years old, but Edna and I have slowly built it up to where it turns a tidy little profit—most months.

If you'd told me back in my college days that I'd be a glorified cleaning lady when I grew up, I'd have suggested you switch to a better brand of dope. Back then, I thought I would end up a lawyer—three-piece suit, high-rise condo in Buckhead,

was unhappy with his housekeeping service, had heard of The House Mouse, and wanted to know if I'd like to bid on that business.

I was going over the material he'd faxed me about the place. Sixteen units, all but four of them two-bedroom, two-bath. The other four were three-bedroom, two-and-a-half-bath units. All the units were fully furnished, with tile kitchens and hardwood floors; they even had fireplaces. The manager wanted a bid price by Wednesday. I scratched my jaw and scribbled on my legal pads.

Cumberland Oaks could be a nice piece of business. Most of the tenants would be single. No pets. Minimum mess, which meant we could probably do each unit in two hours apiece, but all the new business would put a huge strain on our man-power situation. We'd need to hire two, maybe three new mice.

And that's what was making me squirm. Over the years we've hired and fired probably a dozen employees. It's my least favorite part of the business. Well, that and mildew. The thing about clichés is, they're mostly true. It *is* hard to find good help. Lord knows our girls aren't perfect. Far from it. But their quirks and faults are ones Edna and I can live with. Laugh at, even.

When it comes down to it, all the girls are hardworking. They like what they do, they take pride in it, and they've developed their own code of ethics. And they are loyal to a fault.

The same couldn't be said of the would-be mice who've wandered in and out of our lives over the years. Some drank. Some had drug problems. Or they were lazy. Or unreliable.

I must have been scowling, because Edna glanced over at me and laughed. The rasp in her voice was nearly gone. "When you were little I'd tell you your face might freeze that

the whole yuppie package deal. I'd gotten accepted to law school too—a fact I remind myself of when I'm feeling low. Instead, though, I'd read in the paper about the entrance exam for the Atlanta Police Department. After fifteen years as a cop, I'd found myself stuck in a holding pattern on the property crimes unit. Not a bad place to be, but it was never going to be the homicide squad.

I got out of police work as suddenly and unexpectedly as I'd gotten in. Quit the day my private investigator's license arrived in the mail and picked up my Callahan Garrity & Associates business cards the next day.

Somewhere around the house I still have that box of cards. After six months of staring at a phone that didn't ring, Edna talked me into buying The House Mouse. I tell myself I'm out of the private investigation game—tell everybody else that too, but in reality I can't seem to get away from my fascination with crime. So I keep my license current and a box of ammunition for my Smith & Wesson nine-millimeter tucked in an oatmeal box on the top shelf of the pantry.

Nancy Cook says that my need to right wrongs comes from the same part of my psyche that finds housecleaning a satisfying occupation. "It's a need to impose order," she tells me. "You want the universe to be neat and tidy, but unlike most folks, when things go wrong you are willing to step in and clean up other people's messes."

I really was trying to mind my own business. For once I had all the girls out on the job. Neva Jean's car was working, Ruby's blood pressure was normal, and Jackie had dropped Baby and Sister off at a job in midtown.

The week before I'd had a call from the manager of Cumberland Oaks. It's a small, ultra-exclusive residential-suites hotel in Buckhead. They cater to corporate types staying in town on short-term leases, up to six months. The manager

way," she said. "Now you'd better just be worrying about wrinkles."

"It's this Cumberland Oaks job," I admitted. "I dread the idea of hiring more people."

She nodded. "What about Jackie's cousin? Antoinette?"

"I'd forgotten about Antoinette," I said, brightening. "I'll ask Jackie about her when she comes in."

Antoinette had done fill-in work for us a couple of times. She was shy, but quick and efficient. I looked at the bid again. Could we get by if we got Antoinette full-time?

The phone rang as I was massaging the numbers.

"House Mouse," I said.

"You should change that name," Nancy Cook said, not for the first time. "People don't associate rodents with cleanliness. It's psychologically off-putting."

"It costs too much to change the name," I said, same as I always do. "And people don't care what we call the business, as long as we do the job. It's not a restaurant, you know."

"Fine," she said. "Ignore the advice of a mental health professional."

"I do," I told her. "All the time."

We both knew that was a lie. I'd been seeing Nancy as a patient for the past eighteen months. We'd become friends too. And she was a House Mouse client. I swap headshrinking for housecleaning. Everybody wins.

"You sleeping any better?"

"Some," I said cautiously. Nancy had taught me some relaxation exercises, "sort of meditation" to combat the insomnia I'd been battling.

"I can give you a mild sedative," she offered. "Nothing habit-forming. It might help."

"I'm okay," I repeated. "Edna came home from the hospital this weekend, so that's a big help."

"I'm glad," she said. "How's the smoking coming?"

"Let me ask her. Ma, the shrink wants to know how the not smoking is going."

Edna made a face.

"She says it's going great," I said. "What's up?"

"I've got somebody I want you to meet," Nancy said.

"Forget it," I broke in. "I don't do blind dates. And I shudder to think about who you would think an appropriate match for me."

"It's not a date, you twit," Nancy laughed. "Why would I find you a man when I can't find one for myself? Besides, all the single men I know are even more messed up than you."

"How comforting."

"This is a woman. A potential client."

"Tell me she doesn't want Fridays," I said, reaching for the appointment book. "Everybody in Atlanta wants their house cleaned on Fridays."

"Not this woman," Nancy said. "It's not The House Mouse she wants to hire. It's you. J. Callahan Garrity and Associates."

"No way," I said quickly. "I'm up to my ass in alligators here, Nancy. We're bidding on a job and it looks like I'm going to have to take on a new hire. Sorry, but there's no way."

"Just meet her," Nancy said, suddenly insistent. "Hear what she has to say. She really needs your help, Callahan."

"Who is she?"

"I'll let her tell you that," Nancy said. "Can I tell her you'll at least talk to her? She needs to see you right away."

"How soon?"

"I told her about the Yacht Club," Nancy said. "Don't ask me why, but she's fascinated with the place. I told her you'd meet her there tonight, about nine."

"You take a lot for granted," I groused. "What if I'd said no?"

"Then I'd have to push some more buttons," Nancy said cheerfully. "I'm your shrink, remember? I know your weaknesses."

"I should report you to the state board," I told her. "What's this woman look like? And remember, I'm only agreeing to talk to her. It doesn't mean I'll actually take her on. In fact, you can tell her right now. I definitely will not take her on. Save us both some time."

"I'll tell her," Nancy said. "But she'll want to talk to you anyway. And don't worry, you'll know her when you see her. She's definitely not standard Yacht Club material."

3

THE EUCLID AVENUE YACHT CLUB is not a place of quiet contemplation. But when I walked in that Monday night the mood was strangely subdued. A dozen or more regulars were seated at the bar, their eyes trained on the big color television mounted in the corner, and Tinkles had his back turned away from the door too. When I took a closer look at the television, I knew the reason for the silence.

Final Jeopardy.

"The category is World Geography," Alex Trebek announced, his salt-and-pepper mustache quivering slightly.

"The answer is: 'The capital of Burkina Faso, once known as Upper Volta, this city had a 1990 population of five hundred thousand.'"

"Burkina Faso?" Tinkles shouted at the television. "Burkina Faso? Who the fuck cares about Burkina Faso, Alex? Get a life for Christ's sake."

"Wait a minute." The guy at the end of the bar, burly, with

dark curly hair, held up a hand. He wore a set of green surgical scrubs with GRADY MEMORIAL HOSPITAL stenciled in bold letters across the front. "Shut up!" he shouted. "I'm thinking, man. I know this one. It's . . . uh . . . "

"Ouagadougou," came a woman's voice.

Heads swiveled. She was sitting, alone, in one of the booths by the wall. She was beyond petite and into itty-bitty. Her white-blonde hair was cut short and feathered becomingly around a tanned face. Bright blue eyes squinted from the smoke that arose from her cigarette.

"*What is* Ouagadougou?" she corrected herself.

Young Dr. Kildare, otherwise known as Bucky Deavers, my buddy from the Atlanta P.D. homicide division, shook his head violently. "Nah. That's not it. It's . . . "

The others looked back up at the television and at Alex, who was congratulating the returning winner, a dorky-looking computer programmer.

"That's correct, Allen," Alex said, beaming. "The correct question is 'What is Ouagadougou?' Which brings your weekly total winnings to sixty-seven thousand dollars."

Tinkles pointed the remote control at the set and the screen went blank. "Beer or bourbon?" he asked me.

"Jack and water," I told him.

"Ouaga-fucking-dougou," Tinkles muttered, handing me my drink. "Where the hell do they get these questions?"

"Hey," Bucky called. "I'm still the last correct questioner. Right? So I win—right?"

"No way," Tinkles said, glancing down at a bar napkin with numbers scribbled all over it. "You blew your wad on Final Jeopardy, Deavers. You ended up with squat."

"What?" Bucky's face fell. "That ain't right. I must have had three or four thousand."

"You know the rules," Tinkles said, setting a glass of red

wine in front of a young sleepy-eyed black woman sitting two seats down from where I was standing. "Everybody bets everything on Final Jeopardy."

"You didn't give me a chance," Bucky said. "I was gonna say Ouagadougou. Right when she said it. It was on the tip of my tongue."

I stepped behind Deavers and whispered in his ear. "It's only a game, Bucky. Don't be a crybaby."

He put his arm around my shoulder and squeezed hard. "There's a hundred dollars in the pot, Callahan. It should have been mine."

I looked at Tinkles in surprise. "A hundred bucks?"

He shrugged. "We gotta bet on something."

I took a drink of my Jack Daniel's. Sweet and smoky.

"Oh yeah. I forgot. The boycott."

When the baseball players went out on strike in 1994, Tinkles took it hard. And personally. The next year when the baseball season started, he canceled his subscription to *The Sporting News* and gave up the Yacht Club's season tickets. Not even the Braves' first ever World Series title could soften his heart toward the team he called the Millionaire Babies. Tinkles was also upset about the way Atlanta's Olympics were shaping up. He'd sent away for five hundred dollars worth of tickets for women's gymnastics, beach volleyball, and synchronized swimming.

"Four fuckin' months they keep my money," he raged. "Then I get a postcard tellin' me I'm S.O.L. And I *still* gotta file a form for a fuckin' refund."

He'd programmed the Yacht Club's television to black out ESPN, and the regulars knew better than to discuss the "O word" around him. Now the bar's TV was mostly tuned to Nick at Nite. Instead of sports trivia the regulars amused themselves by making lewd suggestions about what they'd do if they were shipwrecked with Ginger and Mary Ann.

I glanced over at the blonde in the booth. She was sipping a drink, trying not to stare at me.

"Was she playing *Jeopardy!* with everybody else?" I asked Tinkles.

"Nah," he said. "She came in a little while ago. Walked up and down the place, looking at all our shit like it was a sale at Lord & Taylor. Sat down and ordered iced tea. You get the feeling she's in the wrong place?"

"Not this time," I said.

I walked over to the booth and slid onto the scarred wooden bench. "I'm Callahan Garrity," I said. "Were you looking for me?"

From a distance her size made her look younger, more vulnerable. I'd figured her for twenty-five, tops. Up close I saw the crow's-feet radiating around her eyes, the slight sag under her chin, a hint of dewlaps around the mouth. She was pretty and well preserved, but she was in her midforties. And she looked familiar.

She took a puff of her cigarette and cocked her head to one side. "Figure it out yet?" Her voice was high, with a slight lisp.

"Have you cut your hair recently? The person I'm thinking of had the same hair color, but it was chin length. And of course, you're not wearing makeup tonight, are you?"

She shook her head. "That photo the *Constitution* runs was taken years ago. At some horrible charity thing." She struck the pose and I knew who she was.

Of course. The color photo showed a woman in midlaugh, chin held high, a diamond necklace around her throat, the strapless ball gown showing just the right amount of cleavage, and the all-important detail, a highball glass in her hand.

The other photo, the one that accompanied every news account, was a school picture. It showed a little girl with tightly braided pigtails and a shy, gap-toothed smile.

Their names were inextricably linked. Whitney Albright

Dobbs, arrested for vehicular homicide, driving under the influence, and leaving the scene of an accident. Faneeta Mayes, second grader at PineHills Elementary School, dead on arrival at Piedmont Hospital.

Faneeta Mayes had been buried in her frilly pink Easter dress. Whitney Albright Dobbs sat across the table from me, a cynical smile on her pale thin lips.

I took a deep breath and did what I usually do. Said the first thing that crossed my mind. "I can't help you."

"Probably not," she agreed. "It was Nancy's idea." She stubbed out her cigarette in the ashtray, picked up her leather billfold, and took out a five-dollar bill. She hesitated a moment, took a napkin from the metal dispenser on the table-top, mopped up the damp ring her glass had made, and only then put the five on the table.

"Thanks for coming," she said, getting up.

I took a sip of my drink. "That was pretty amazing. Ouagadougou, I mean. I thought it was a made-up name."

"It's my daughter. Alison. She's a sophomore at Bryn Mawr. Sometimes she's so much like her father it's scary. She goes on these kicks. In third grade she memorized all the presidents and vice presidents of the United States. In order. Another time it was world capitals. We'd practice in the car on the way to school. Of course all the African ones have changed since then, so Alison sends me postcards to keep me updated."

"Did Nancy tell you I run a cleaning business? Full-time?"

She looked down at me in surprise. "Yes. She told me you were too busy, too. It's okay. It was a long shot anyway."

I'd hardly touched my drink. The ice hadn't even melted. And Steve and Maureen were back at the house, hovering over Edna. I decided to stay and listen.

I sighed. "Why don't you go ahead and tell me about what it is you want me to do that I'm too busy to do?"

4

TINKLES BROUGHT A BOWL OF BAR NUTS and another glass of iced tea. He slapped the glass down, deliberately spilling the cold tea on Whitney's lap, then tossed a dirty bar towel at her before he stalked away. She bit her lip and dabbed at the tea. I got the feeling she was used to this kind of treatment.

If you'd been living in Atlanta for the past six months it would have been hard not to recognize Whitney Dobbs. Her face, and that of her eight-year-old victim's, had been front-page news since May. Schoolkids wore these big round lapel buttons featuring Faneeta's picture for months. Every black-owned business in Atlanta had a poster in its front window of the blown-up color photograph of Whitney, the one with the cocktail and the glassy-eyed grin. NO JUSTICE was all the caption said.

The trial had been over weeks ago, but the racial tensions exacerbated by the trial's outcome would take years to cool.

Everybody in Atlanta had an opinion about the case. You couldn't blame them. It was a tragedy in black and white.

Whitney Albright Dobbs. Old Atlanta money, married to new. Debutante, socialite, wife, and mother. Carson Dobbs, her husband—or was it ex?—was one of the top cardiologists in the South, a boy genius.

I'd read about the divorce in the newspaper too. Not pretty. Divorces seem to get uglier in proportion to the amount of money involved, and there was a lot involved in this one.

The facts of the accident were pretty cut and dried. Whitney and her girlfriends had been having après-tennis cocktails at the Piedmont Driving Club late one afternoon in early summer. In addition to the four or five Tanqueray and tonics Whitney had after her tennis match, she'd admitted to taking antidepressants prescribed by a sympathetic shrink. There had been some kind of trouble over her bar bill, and she'd left the Driving Club in a fury, nearly mowing down two valet-parking attendants. Coming out of the club, which sits at the edge of Piedmont Park, she'd made a wrong turn, then another, and ended up on a restricted access road inside the park.

Faneeta Mayes had been in a group of children brought to the park by their mothers to Rollerblade on the gently rolling bike paths.

At the trial, parts of which had been broadcast live, the district attorney called Faneeta Mayes's mother to the stand. She told, in a faint, halting voice, how Faneeta and her friend, an older child, had skated off the bike path and onto the access road, to go to the rest rooms two hundred yards away. From nowhere, Janie Mayes said, clutching and unclutching a worn family Bible, a red Jeep had come roaring down the access road. The other child had managed to get off the road and onto the shoulder. But Faneeta's skates were new, and she was

unsteady on them. She'd tripped and fallen down on the bumpy asphalt. And the red Jeep never slowed. The Jeep had been easy to trace. Vanity tags read L84AD8. Late for a Date.

Whitney Dobbs never took the stand. Instead, her lawyer, a young hotshot named Zack Alexander, called a string of experts who testified that all of it had been somebody else's fault.

The bartender at the Driving Club, an elderly black gentleman who'd been a fixture there for forty years, admitted that yes, he thought perhaps Miss Whitney had been drinking too much. But it wasn't his place, he thought, to tell a club member she'd had enough.

A professor of psychology from Duke University testified that Whitney Albright Dobbs's messy marital problems had left her psychically damaged, as battle-scarred as a Vietnam vet. He'd even had a name for the sickness that afflicted her; Domestic Dysfunction Syndrome, he called it. One local columnist suggested that Whitney could be the new DDS poster child.

Another defense witness was the old friend who'd prescribed Whitney's antidepressants. The doctor admitted that she never actually saw Whitney in her office. When Whitney called to complain about her symptoms, she simply called the prescription in to Whitney's drugstore. And no, she hadn't specified a limit to the number of refills. Or cautioned Whitney about drinking while taking the drug.

The battle was won at the last minute by a prosecution witness, making a chance, unsolicited remark.

The Atlanta police officer who'd stopped the weaving red Jeep a few miles from Piedmont Park was testifying. Whitney had repeatedly asked him to call her husband, the officer mentioned. It was all Zack Alexander needed. On cross-examination he got the cop to admit that yes, Whitney had identified her hus-

band as a physician. And yes, he believed her to have been clearly intoxicated. A danger to herself and others? Yes, the cop readily agreed.

Denying medical aid to a suspect, Alexander charged. Two weeks into the trial the judge ruled Whitney's arrest illegal and threw out the vehicular homicide charges.

Early that evening, a group of black college students staged what was supposed to be a peaceful protest march, from the steps of the state capitol to the Fulton County Courthouse three blocks away. But when the students arrived at the capitol's newly mown lawn, they were met with a jeering mob of shaved-headed, club-swinging Aryan youths. Ringing them, wearing riot helmets and carrying bulletproof shields, was a hastily assembled squadron of Atlanta cops, Georgia State Patrol troopers, and Fulton sheriff's deputies. It was a toxic mixture.

The crowd swelled and festered, tossing bottles and bricks at police cruisers and passing cars. Shots were fired. It could have been a starter's pistol. Thugs rampaged through the nearby streets, smashing what was glass, burning what would ignite, striking out at anything in their path.

It would have been worse except that one of Atlanta's famous summer storms descended on the city an hour into what the *Constitution* delicately called "the racial disturbance." The storm's slashing rain and ear-popping thunder-and-lightning display literally swept the rioters out of the streets and into shelter.

Edna and I watched it all on the news at home, wide-eyed and terrified at the hate-fest simmering just a few short miles from our bungalow. It was early summer and the rains brought a welcome coolness, but we could hear the police sirens and the fire trucks roaring down nearby DeKalb Avenue toward the capitol. That night we closed and locked all the windows and turned on the air conditioning. The barricades were up.

"Animals," Edna whispered, watching the footage of a group of bare-chested black teenagers darting out of a ruined liquor store, cases of beer under each arm.

"They're angry," I tried to tell her. "If Whitney Dobbs gets off, it's the same thing all over again."

Her face when she turned toward me was stiff and unyielding. "Look what they're doing down there. Destroying people's property. Their life savings. Whitney Dobbs didn't own that liquor store. They ought to lock those animals up and throw away the key."

Whitney Dobbs's jury stayed out just an hour. The judge's rulings on Zack Alexander's motions had stripped the list of charges against his client down to almost nothing. The jury foreman, a thickly built black man the newspaper identified as a career postal employee, was stone-faced as he handed the jury's verdict to the court clerk. The clerk read the verdict in a toneless voice. Whitney Albright Dobbs was guilty of reckless conduct. A misdemeanor. The judge had given her sentence: a one-thousand-dollar fine and one hundred hours of community service. No jail time.

It was hard to sit in a bar with Whitney Dobbs and not think about the wreckage she'd left in the wake of that red Jeep. Whitney was sipping her tea, watching my face.

"My lawyer says I'm the most despised person in Atlanta," she said calmly. "Do you believe that?"

I gave it some thought. A few years ago, the cabdriver who struck and killed Margaret Mitchell as she was crossing Peachtree Street to go to a movie died of cancer. With him gone, I thought Whitney Dobbs might have a shot at the title, at least the female half. The male contender is definitely the guy who owns the local pro football franchise.

"You wouldn't win any popularity contests in here tonight," I pointed out.

Her eyes swept the bar, and as she did so, people turned their heads hastily back to *Bewitched*. It was one of the episodes with the original Darrin. Everybody in that bar knew who Whitney Dobbs was. And their hostile stares said they didn't care for her company.

"I'm curious," I said. "How does Nancy Cook think I can help you?"

"You know about my divorce?"

"I read about it. Is that what this is about? Because I don't do divorce work. Ever. I'm surprised Nancy didn't tell you that."

"She did." Whitney tapped a cigarette out of the box and toyed with it. She had long ringless fingers, the nails bitten down to nothing. "I thought you might change your mind."

I got up and went to the pay phone at the back of the bar. The Atlanta Yellow Pages are divided into two volumes. We're a big city now. I brought back the M–Z book and put it on the table in front of her.

"There are four pages of listings of private investigators in here," I said. "Most of them consider divorce work their bread and butter. Maybe one of them would be glad to take your money."

She shook her head. "I talked to one of those guys." She shuddered delicately. "He does work for my lawyer. A horrible man. He had tattoos on his arms. No. I need someone like you. A woman. Someone who isn't . . . "

"A lowlife?" I looked down at my own blue chambray work shirt and jeans. "I'm not interested, Mrs. Dobbs."

"Whitney," she said automatically. "Whitney Albright. There's a new Mrs. Dobbs on the horizon, you know. As soon as the divorce is settled."

"I thought it was final."

"Oh no," she said bitterly. "Carson filed for legal separa-

"Shouldn't have been," Whitney said. "But clear thinking hasn't been a way of life for me up until recently. And I was still under the illusion that we might get back together."

"You didn't know he was involved with somebody else?"

"Not until Alison told me," Whitney said, chewing her lower lip. "He took Suzanne, that's the girlfriend, up to see Alison at school over the summer. We thought it would be better if she stayed up there, what with the trial and all. Carson thought Alison and this . . . woman should be good friends. Alison was horrified. She wouldn't talk to the woman. Apparently she threw quite a scene."

"That's pretty tough stuff, what with your trial and all," I said.

"Alison was devastated," Whitney said. "After that, we both began seeing Nancy. At first Alison wouldn't say a word. Nancy finally got her to open up and talk about it."

I winced. All during the trial I'd ached for Faneeta Mayes's family. It hadn't occurred to me that the pain was contagious.

"You mentioned that your lawyer thinks your husband has been hiding assets. Is that why you want to hire me?"

She nodded. "He says he's broke."

"The most famous cardiologist in Atlanta? Broke?"

"He claims that Ben Dwyer, who was the business manager for his medical practice, ripped him off for more than three million dollars. Carson says he just found out about it a couple months ago. They were going to fire Dwyer, have him arrested for fraud, but Dwyer supposedly got wind of it and skipped town without a trace."

"How are they claiming Dwyer stole the money?" I asked.

"Something about phony payments to vendors and some kind of insurance scam," Whitney said. "I don't understand it myself."

"Do you believe any of it?"

tion eighteen months ago. He just got around to filing for the divorce after the trial. How convenient of me to give him grounds. Right?"

She had me hooked and she knew it. Besides, Edna would be fascinated with this. She'd followed the trial religiously, declaring it better than any of her soap operas. As far as Edna was concerned, Whitney Dobbs was a victim, the older wife traded in for a newer, shinier model.

"Go ahead," I said. "I'm listening."

"He moved out right after Christmas, it'll be two years in December. Told me he just needed some space, but that he'd always love me and Alison, and of course he would take care of us."

"Did he?"

"Of course. Carson is pathological about doing the right thing. He even paid for my lawyer."

"That's odd."

"Not when you know that my lawyer's mother was one of his patients," she said. "Ex-lawyer. When I figured out his game I fired him. But in the meantime, my first lawyer got a separation agreement, and Carson was paying all the bills, the mortgage, car payments, Alison's college tuition, everything. Very generous. Very decent." She nearly choked on the last word.

"Was?"

"Zack says that Carson delayed filing for divorce in order to give himself time to hide the goodies. Naturally, I wasn't eager to end the marriage." She smiled sadly. "It was a nice life. Or so I thought at the time."

"And when you were arrested he dropped the dime," I said.

"That's a quaint expression," she said. "I've got to remember that one. He filed for the divorce the same week."

"You couldn't have been surprised," I said.

"No way," she said quickly. "Carson's too smart to let somebody get away with anything like that."

"Even smart people get ripped off," I said.

"You don't know Carson," she retorted. "He grew up dirt poor. Went to med school on a full scholarship. He's got the first nickel he ever made and he trusts one person only: Carson Dobbs. He'd never turn full control of his finances over to anybody. Not even a business manager."

"So you think he's hiding assets."

"I know he is," she said. "I need you to help Zack prove it. His lawyer is asking the judge to sell the house. My house. And divide the assets from it. He's also refusing to pay Alison's tuition. He claims she can get just as good an education at a state school. The bastard."

"I don't know anything about this kind of stuff," I told her. "And I don't want to know. You need somebody who specializes in white-collar crime. I know a guy. He's a former FBI agent. Clean cut. Has an M.B.A. from Penn State . . . "

"I want you," she said stubbornly. "Carson's been planning this since the beginning. He sold the town house he and his girlfriend were living in over in Ansley Park, because he says he can't afford it now. They're renting some pathetic apartment out in Sandy Springs. Alison went there once, before she realized he wasn't living there alone. She left as soon as the girlfriend walked in the room. But I know that's not where he's really living."

"Let me guess. You want me to find his real home."

"And the money."

What she was asking was hopeless. It had been interesting, hearing her story, but that was all.

"I'm sorry, Whitney," I said, looking her straight in the eye. "It does sound like your husband is hosing you. But there's nothing I can do."

"It's because of the child—isn't it?" she asked, her blue eyes unblinking. "God help me, if I could take that day back, I would. I wanted to plead guilty, go ahead and do the time, but Zack talked me out of it."

She grasped her glass with both hands, and the ice cubes rocked gently in the tea. "Zack said I'd been given another chance. To get my act together. And there was Alison to think of. She's already lost her father. She needs her mother, even one as screwed up as the one she's got. Did I mention? Carson's girlfriend is pregnant.

"The minimum sentence would have been fifteen years. Alison would have been middle-aged by the time I got out. With a jailbird mother and a father who's more interested in his new baby. So I let Zack do it his way.

"He's very clever, Zack is. But he's so busy. He needs somebody to help him."

I got up from the table. "Not me."

Bucky grabbed me by the sleeve as I was hurrying toward the door. I was afraid if I stayed any longer I might start feeling sorry for Whitney Albright Dobbs.

"What's Mrs. Drunk Driver want with you?" he asked, loud enough for everybody at the bar to overhear. Tact is not Bucky's strong suit.

"She wants me to help her catch her husband with his hand in the cookie jar," I said. "I told her no."

"Damn straight," Bucky said approvingly.

He patted the bar stool next to his. "Sit down and let you buy me a drink."

"Can't." It was getting late, Steve and Maureen would have left by now. I was still uneasy about leaving Edna alone.

"Aw, just for a little while," he said. "Look. *The Patty Duke Show*." He pointed with his beer bottle at the television, where Patty was doing a mean frug and demonstrating how

she'd only seen the sights a girl can see from Brooklyn Heights.

"I've seen 'em all," I told him.

"Which one do you think is cutest?" Bucky asked, gazing lovingly at the set. "I like Cathy best. You know, 'cause she's got that cute English accent."

I shrugged. "They're both the same. I never gave it much thought, Bucky."

"No," he said. "Identical cousins. See, Cathy was raised in Europe, or someplace like that. And Patty, you know, she's from New York."

"They're both Patty Duke," I reminded him.

"What?" He looked confused.

"It's why it's called *The Patty Duke Show*. Because she played both parts."

"You shittin' me?" Bucky looked hurt.

"No shit," I assured him. "I've got another flash for you too. That is *not* Mr. Ed's real voice. It's an actor."

"Hell," Bucky said, taking a swig of Rolling Rock. "I knew that. Everybody knows that, Garrity."

"Just checking," I said, giving him a playful punch on the shoulder. "See you later."

On the sidewalk outside the Yacht Club, I glanced back.

Through the bar's open door I could see that Whitney Albright Dobbs was still sitting in the booth, sipping her iced tea and staring intently at the television.

5

"NANCY COOK CALLED," Edna announced when I got back from running errands Tuesday morning.

"She did, huh? I need to call her and tell her to take me off her referral list."

"Nancy told me about Whitney Dobbs. What a rat that ex-husband sounds like. She wanted to know if you'd agreed to help Whitney. Did you?" The hopeful note in Edna's voice said she was dying to hear all the details.

"Absolutely not," I told her, unloading the bag of office supplies I'd bought. "She's not as bad as I expected. I even felt sort of sorry for her. I thought Tinkles was going to kick her out of the Yacht Club last night. But her kind of problems are the last thing I need."

"We could help her," Edna started to say.

"Forget it, Ma."

I spent the rest of the morning tracking down Jackie's cousin Antoinette.

"Last I talked to her, she was stayin' with her boyfriend," Jackie said. "No tellin' where she is now."

"That kind of boyfriend, huh?" Warning bells go off with me when I hear about boyfriends. According to Jackie, Antoinette specialized in men who were terminally unemployed.

I finally found her late in the day. She'd dumped the boyfriend and moved in with her sister in an apartment in Marietta.

"I got me a good job," she told me proudly. "Jackie wants to spend her time doin' nigger work, that's her problem."

"Nigger work?" I felt as though someone had slapped me across the face. "Jackie makes damn good money," I said hotly. "She's driving a new car, all paid for. She makes her own hours, gets benefits. I don't call that nigger work. What kind of job do you have, Antoinette?"

"Office job. I sit at a desk, answer the phone. I wear nice clothes."

"Making what?" I prodded.

She paused. "Two-thirty a week, if it's any of your business."

I laughed rudely. "That's take-home?"

"Uh. No."

"Never mind," I told her. "My girls make a minimum of seventy-five dollars per house. Good days, they do two, maybe three houses a day. They want to work five or six days a week, it's up to them. I clean houses myself. See you around, Antoinette."

I hung up. Edna looked up from the appointment work. "She turned you down?"

"Antoinette has gotten above cleaning houses," I said. "She's got one of those good office jobs now. Minimum wage, but she gets to wear panty hose and heels every day."

"Got any more ideas?" Edna asked.

"I'm fresh out," I admitted. "Think we should run an ad in the paper? Maybe I can stall the Cumberland Oaks people a little longer."

"You want to put me back in the hospital? You know the kind of response we get when we run those ads."

I did know. People with no references. People just out of jail, or mental institutions. People with no cars. People who wanted to take their children to work with them, or worse yet, leave their children with us.

I had my hand on the phone, ready to call the manager at Cumberland Oaks and tell him no thanks, when Neva Jean walked into the kitchen, her eyes red-rimmed and swollen, a damp and crumpled handkerchief pressed tightly to her nose. She collapsed into the nearest chair and sneezed loudly.

"Is this about some soap opera again?" I asked suspiciously.

She sniffed, then blew her nose hard. "What?"

"Something happen on *The Young and the Reckless*? Dr. Saint-Germaine lapse into another coma?"

"Dr. Saint-Germaine's dead," Edna said. "Landslide. Back in September, right after he didn't get his contract renewed." She put an arm around Neva Jean's shoulder. "What's wrong, honey?"

Neva Jean snuffled and said something unintelligible. It sounded like "yoo-hoo."

"Run that by me again?"

"Emus," she said, wiping at her streaming eyes with her shirtsleeve. "I'm allergic to emus."

"What's that?" Edna said.

"It's a crossword puzzle word. E-M-U. Flightless Australian bird," I told her. "You always see it in the easy puzzles. They're like an ostrich, only smaller. I saw something about them on the Discovery channel one night."

"Those new people over on Hardendorf keeping emus in the house?" Edna demanded. "If I'd known that, we would have charged them twenty-five dollars extra." She grabbed the appointment book and started to make a notation of it.

"It's not the Marinos," Neva Jean wheezed. "It's Swannelle."

I gave her two of my antihistamines, and after some consideration, Edna gave her a puff off her new inhaler. When Neva Jean could breathe and talk without sniffing, she explained.

"We got a flyer in the mail," she said. "You know how Swannelle's always sending off for free stuff in the back of magazines he steals from the barber shop?"

I nodded. Swannelle's lust for easy moneymaking schemes was never-ending. Since I'd known him, he'd dabbled in time-share telemarketing, mail-order vitamin sales, and an Amway distributorship.

"Emu ranching's a real big thing now," Neva Jean explained. "Bigger than catfish farms. Swannelle wanted a catfish farm real bad, but it takes at least an acre of land. Then he found out about this emu deal."

She blew her nose with such force it would have knocked a daintier woman off the chair.

"You know what a breeding pair of emus costs? Eight thousand dollars!"

"For a pair of birds can't even fly?" Edna asked. "That's some pricey poultry, Neva Jean."

"Where'd Swannelle get that kind of money?" I wanted to know.

She sneezed again. "He says his cousin Rooney loaned him the money. As a silent partner."

I remembered Rooney. He was the one who'd gotten Swannelle involved in an ill-fated bass boat acquisition. "And where's he keeping the emus? Aren't they pretty big?"

"They're as tall as me," Neva Jean cried. "And he's got 'em in a pen he built in the backyard. I come home from work last night and he'd fenced in the whole damn thing. Ripped up my flowers and took my plaster jockey-boy and flung it in the side yard like it was nothing. And these damn giant birds spend the whole night running up and down the yard, till I thought I'd lose my mind. I started in sneezing at two in the morning and I ain't quit yet."

"Eight thousand dollars, huh?" Edna couldn't get over the money part. "What do they do with these emus makes 'em so expensive?"

Neva Jean sneezed three times. "You sell the eggs to other breeders," she said, dabbing at her eyes again. "Swannelle says a good female will lay thirty-five eggs a season. And they sell for a hundred dollars apiece, easy. Only now he's thinking about hatching the eggs too, and selling the chicks. They go for five hundred dollars. He's thinking about turning the garage into a hatchery."

"That's bad," I said. "Especially if you're allergic to them."

"I told Swannelle they were making me sick," Neva Jean said, crying real tears now. "He just told me to take some pills and quit sniffing. I hate those damn birds."

Edna got up and got the bottle of antihistamines. "Here," she told Neva Jean. "Looks like you're gonna be needing these."

I called Reg Vaughn, the manager of Cumberland Oaks. "I'm sorry, but I can't bid on the job," I told him. "We just don't have the manpower."

"Well now, that's too bad," Vaughn said. "We've heard good things about your people."

"I appreciate that," I said. "Can I call you if something changes?"

"We've got to find somebody right away," Vaughn said.

"But yeah, you know how things happen. Gimme a call."

I hung up the phone and started doodling on a yellow legal pad.

"You're worried," Edna said.

"Kind of," I admitted. "We're busy, but unless we hire some extra help somehow, we're just not going to grow like we need to."

"Something will come up," Edna said.

There was a knock at the back door. We were having a busy afternoon. It was C. W.

I threw the door open all the way so he could maneuver his walker inside.

"Hunsecker, you're doing pretty good with that thing," I said.

"Not good enough," he groused, letting himself down into one of the kitchen chairs and giving the walker an ungracious shove.

Edna got up and brought him a glass of iced tea. "How's the smoking going?" C. W. asked innocently.

She put the glass down with a bang. "Fine. I only want one every time I draw a breath. Why does everybody have to ask about my smoking? I quit, okay, what more do you want?"

C. W. held his hands up. "Sorry I asked. You feeling better otherwise?"

"Just dandy," Edna said, softening a little. "How's the therapy?"

"It could be going better," C. W. said. "These fool therapists over at the Spinal Center keep trying to slow me down, tell me I got plenty of time. They don't seem to realize I've got a one-year-old at home who walks better than I do."

"Little Wash didn't take a bullet through the belly or have his spinal cord nicked," I said, regretting the words as soon as I'd spoken them. It had been more than a year since the shoot-

ing, and C. W. and I had still never discussed that night in the parking garage.

Linda, his wife, did our discussing for us. He told her he'd been injured in the line of duty, his first in a thirty-year career as a cop. It was nobody's fault, a risk every cop took. I told her I should have waited, shouldn't have insisted that we charge into that parking garage after a woman I knew was mentally unstable. The woman had fired at C. W., hit him in the belly. I fired back, killed her in front of her fourteen-year-old son. I watch a lot of late-night television these days when the sleep won't come, but I seem to have lost my taste for westerns and police dramas.

"That Wash is the cutest thing I've ever seen," Edna said quickly, trying to cover for me.

"Fastest thing you ever seen is more like it," C. W. said. "I don't remember Kenyatta being into everything the way he is. If he's not playing in the cat box he's pulling everything out of the kitchen cupboard. I tell you, that boy is a mess."

"How old were you when Kenyatta was born—nineteen? Twenty? And how many jobs were you working?" Edna asked.

"I was twenty-one," he said, smiling ruefully. "I worked the day shift downtown, and a second job as a security officer. I get the point. I was at work, the wife was home with the baby. Different kids, a different wife, different times."

He cleared his throat. "Did, uh, Linda tell you I've been thinking about making some changes?"

Linda had told me he was miserable at work, confined to a desk job, juggling crime statistics and trying to keep his head down in the midst of the political upheaval that constantly surrounds the Atlanta Police Department.

But policing was the Hunsecker family business, had been ever since the department had deputized its first "colored" officers in the 1940s. C. W. was a third-generation cop, a cap-

tain in the homicide division who'd always managed to survive departmental politics.

"She mentioned it," I said cautiously.

"Aw, y'all tell each other everything," C. W. said. "Anyway, I came by to show you something." He pulled some papers from his shirt pocket and handed them to me. I read them with disbelief. "Disability leave? You're serious?"

He nodded. "We may starve, but Linda talked me into it. I finished up the paperwork this morning, got out of there before somebody tried to give me a party or something."

"Well, that's great, C. W.," I said. "But don't tell me you're going to stay home and be a Mr. Mom."

Even he had to laugh at that notion. "No, I'm going into business for myself. I've been thinking about it for a long time."

"Doing what?" Edna said in her usual blunt manner.

He took another piece of paper out of his breast pocket and handed it to me. It was a business card.

HUNSECKER & ASSOCIATES, it said in flowing gold script. Underneath were the words SECURITY CONSULTANTS: INDUSTRIAL-CORPORATE-RESIDENTIAL-PERSONAL.

"What do you think?" he asked anxiously.

I flexed the card. "Nice weight paper," I said. "You get a good deal on the printing?"

He snatched it away from me. "Seriously, Garrity. What do you think?"

"What kind of security? Like rent-a-cops?"

"Yeah, we got about six, eight guys," he said. "I bought an existing business. Did you ever know Lou Gowcher? He was a desk sergeant down at the Southside precinct for years. He and a buddy started it years ago; now the buddy's dead and Lou's ready to retire and move to Florida. It's consulting mostly. We've got some convenience store contracts, two or three office parks, a shopping center. We hire out the guards, install surveillance

monitors and security systems. It's a decent little business."

"Wow," was all I could think to say. "Sounds like you're set pretty good."

He nodded. "Looks like we'll get a piece of the Olympics too. The guy in charge of security in the athlete's village? We were in the Academy together. He says he can use all the qualified people I can supply."

"Yeah," I said sarcastically. "Just try finding qualified people."

"You got personnel problems?" C. W. asked.

"Micepower shortage. It's impossible to find competent people who want to make housecleaning their life's work. It's not exactly politically correct these days."

"Never thought about that," C. W. said.

He grabbed for his walker and struggled out of the chair. I had to resist the temptation to offer a hand. Another matter of political correctness.

"At least you've still got your private investigator's license," he said.

"She's got a big new case she don't want to take," Edna began. "I told her . . . "

"Never mind," I said, giving her the look.

C. W. raised his eyebrows at me.

"Divorce work," I said hastily, opening the back door for him. "Tell Linda to call me and we'll go to dinner."

"We could make it a foursome," C. W. said.

I knew who he had in mind for a date for me. Mac.

"I'd love a foursome," I said smoothly. "But does Wash eat solid food yet?"

"You're a hard woman, Garrity," he said.

"The hardest."

6

EDNA'S FINGERS FLEW OVER the adding machine. Usually she loves to add and subtract figures. She's a bookkeeper at heart, and without her I don't know how our business ever would have gotten off the ground. But today she had a stack of papers beside her, and she scowled with each figure she entered.

"What's up?" I asked, sitting down beside her at the kitchen table. After our discussion the day before I didn't want her stewing about the business. We'd make it somehow. We always had.

She swept her hand toward the stack. "Doctors' bills and hospital bills," she said, breaking into a coughing fit.

I moved the bills away. "You just got out of the hospital," I told her. "We've got insurance. They'll pay for the bills. You just take it easy. You know what Jeanne said about stress."

"That's easy for her to say," Edna said, coughing again. "Look at these charges. "Four hundred ninety-one dollars for

radiology. Two hundred twenty-one seventy-five for emergency services. What emergency services? All they did was listen to my chest and tell me I was sick as hell. I coulda told them that for nothing."

"The insurance will cover it, Ma," I said, but she was on a roll now.

"Respiratory services, five hundred seventy-two dollars." She stabbed the bill with her finger. "Here's a one-hundred-seventy-dollar charge for a visit from a doctor I never heard of and never asked to see. Why should I pay for that?"

I looked at the bill. I didn't recognize the name either, but I seemed to remember that Jeanne had asked a pulmonologist to look in on Edna. She was coughing again, her face getting red. I got her inhaler out of the kitchen drawer, shook it, and handed it to her.

She puffed twice and inhaled. I took the bills and put them in the folder and put them on top of the refrigerator.

"We've got to pay the deductible, you know," Edna said, her breathing coming easier now. "If they don't get paid they'll come after us. Then I'll really get sick. I'm about damn sick and tired of all those other money-grubbing doctors and hospitals charging me eight dollars for a couple of Tylenol."

I was entirely in agreement with her. I knew we'd have to wrestle with all the insurance companies and doctors and all the rest of it, but right now we both needed something to take our mind off her sickness and my worries.

"Maybe I could put a help-wanted ad in the paper," I said, sighing. "It might be good comic relief."

Her long bony fingers played with the empty ashtray beside her on the table. She spun it around and around, fingering the groove where the burning cigarette should have been, and she smacked her ever-present wad of gum.

"I think you should take the job working for Whitney

Dobbs," she said evenly. "I know you don't like divorce work, but this is different. It's like a treasure hunt, isn't it?"

"Except this time I'd be working for one of the bad guys," I said thoughtfully. "She killed a kid, and got away with it, Ma. I still can't get over that."

Edna nodded her head. "I know. Doesn't seem right she got off with nothing. I know you think different, but I still don't see how this is race-related. If Faneeta Mayes had been white, do you think people would have carried on and rioted and looted like these hooligans did? Whitney Dobbs got off on a technicality. The cop that stopped her was black. The judge was black, most of the jury was black. You tell me how that makes for a white conspiracy."

"It works the other way too, Ma," I said. "If Whitney had been black and hit a white kid, what do you think would have happened? Her butt would be in prison right this minute. Instead she's driving around free, just like you and me."

"I don't buy that," she said stubbornly. "This isn't the Georgia I grew up in. Times are different. Anyway, you know my theory, Jules. What goes around, comes around. I've got a feeling that gal is living through her own hell right here on earth."

"Maybe," I said.

"Charge her double," Edna said. "That ought to help your white guilt. And pay all these goddammed doctor bills."

I picked up the phone and managed to get Jeanne Payne by having her paged.

"Is Edna all right?" she asked quickly.

"Fine. Nervous as a cat in a room full of rocking chairs, but she hasn't smoked, and the inhaler seems to be helping her breathing."

"Good. What can I do you for?"

"Do you know Carson Dobbs?"

"Sure," Jeanne said. "Who doesn't?

"He's telling the judge in his divorce case that he's broke. You find that credible?"

"Dobbs?" She laughed. "Tell me another one. He's just cheap, is all. Drives a beat-up gray sedan, and his clothes always look like he bought them out of the Sears catalog. But times can't be that tough. He and his partners just moved into a new building."

"Do you ever refer heart patients to him?"

"Sometimes," she said slowly. "He's supposedly a genius. A little too intense, if you ask me. But I've never heard anyone question his expertise."

"So he's not broke?"

"I know you think all doctors are rich, Callahan, but this guy really is," she said. "He's got not one but three satellite offices, one over in Athens and one down in Peachtree City at that new regional hospital they just built. What's your interest in Carson Dobbs, Callahan? If you're not happy with Edna's care, we need to discuss that, you know."

"Oh no, Jeanne," I said quickly. "You're wonderful. I, um . . . well, this is confidential, but I guess I can trust you since you're the family doctor and all. Whitney Dobbs wants to hire me because Carson's claiming he's broke. He says his business manager ripped him off with some kind of phony insurance scam or something, and she thinks he's lying."

"That's interesting," Jeanne said. "I knew about the divorce, of course. His girlfriend supposedly works in his office. I hadn't heard about the business manager thing. Usually that kind of thing would be all over the hospital grapevine. But Carson plays things very close to the chest. He's sort of a loner. Are they going to prosecute the business manager?"

"I don't know. Listen, Jeanne, would you ever consider referring Edna to Dobbs?"

"We want to do a cardiac cath later on, but I'd planned to refer Edna to Patricia Soong. She's just as good as Dobbs, and I think she's better with women patients like Edna. More understanding."

"It's just a thought," I said. "But it occurred to me that to get a good picture of the office and how it works I might try to get Edna an appointment with him. As a patient. That wouldn't actually hurt anything—would it?"

"I guess not," she said reluctantly. "Just one office visit, right? Carson Dobbs likes invasive procedures. He's a little too cozy with the surgeons for my taste. He thinks the answer to every patient's problem lies behind the operating room door."

"No, no," I said, horrified. "Nothing like that. She goes in for a visit, scopes the place out, and that's that. I won't even let her fill one of his prescriptions."

"I should hope not," she said pertly. "Is Edna feeling up to all this?"

"Are you kidding? She loves to snoop. Especially on doctors."

"I'm keeping that in mind," Jeanne said.

"Could you call and set it up? Tell him the family's really concerned."

"I can try," she said. "But if he's like most other cardiologists in town there's a three-month waiting list. Wait. I know. I'll tell him she's my darling auntie."

"Why do I think you're enjoying this?" I asked.

"I'll let you know when the appointment is," Jeanne said. "In the meantime, you tell Edna I said to behave herself."

"Fat chance," I muttered as I hung up the phone.

✳ ✳ ✳

"I'm charging you double my usual rate," I said matter-of-factly. "Will that be a problem?"

Zack Alexander didn't look surprised. He made a note to himself. "Shouldn't be. Whitney's grandmother left her a small inheritance. That's what's funding my work. And if you help me prove the doctor's a crook, we'll get the court to pay your fees and mine both."

He pushed an inch-thick file folder across the desk toward me. "That's everything we've gotten out of the good doctor during discovery. It's good reading, if you like fiction."

I picked up the file. "You don't believe any of it."

"Not a word."

He sat back in his chair. I'd expected someone older, stodgier, the whole leather-suspenders, Gucci-loafers, power-tie divorce lawyer protective coloration. Zack Alexander apparently hadn't read the dress code. He wore an olive green corduroy shirt with a wool plaid necktie that screamed Eddie Bauer. His graying brown hair was parted down the middle and hung below his shirt collar and he had a thick, wicked brown mustache that obscured the corners of a mouth that looked perpetually amused. He was attractive in a sort of urban terrorist way. I wondered fleetingly if he and Whitney Dobbs had conducted their own interpersonal discovery. That's the kind of smutty mind I have to work with.

"Dobbs fired Ben Dwyer, the business manager, a month ago. Told him to clear out his office on a Friday. But he never filed any charges until we started asking questions about his finances. His excuse was that he didn't want his patients alarmed."

I brought out my notepad and started writing. "How's it spelled?"

"D-W-Y-E-R," Alexander said. "It's all in the file. He's skipped town. Cleaned out his condo and his bank accounts and nobody's seen him since."

"Be nice if we could talk to him, or somebody who knew him," I said. "Who's supposedly investigating?"

"Tillie Foster, in the Fulton district attorney's white-collar-crime unit," he said. "Her business card is in the file, but I wouldn't sweat that right now."

"There's a lot of work in here," I said, tapping the file. "Did your private investigator do all this?"

"Bollinger?" he laughed. "Hell no. Whitney took one look at Bollinger and decided he was a reject from the chain gang. No, that was the work of Barry Lewis. He was a summer associate. He has a wonderfully suspicious mind. But the dumb fuck thinks he wants to do municipal bond issues. He's back at school in Virginia now, finishing his senior year."

I leafed through the file. Barry Lewis was a very thorough worker. Maybe this wouldn't be so tough after all.

"I told Whitney I've never done divorce work before," I said. "I've got some general idea of what to do, but why don't you tell me specifically where you want me to start?"

"The house," he said promptly. "Dobbs sold a three-bedroom town house out at Windward for eighty-eight thousand dollars. The exact same unit on the other side of the lake sold for three hundred thousand dollars two months earlier. Dobbs said he had to get his equity out to satisfy creditors. I say it's bullshit."

"Who was the buyer?"

He nodded toward the folder. "It's a corporation. Barry looked them up at the secretary of state's office, but I could have told him what he'd find."

"And what was that?"

"Corporation's name is Paradox Properties. Registered agent is ETS Services."

"And they are?"

"Professional agents of record. That's all they do. You pay

them a fee, they set you up a dummy corporation with them as the agent of record. Your corporate address is their corporate address. It's a blind box. Check the listings in the secretary of state's office sometime. They're agents for hundreds and hundreds of companies."

"What about the corporation's board of directors? Don't they have to list them somewhere?"

"It's in the file," Alexander said. He reached across, took the file, and paged through it until he found what he was looking for. "Johnnye B. Adams, V. R. White, and J. F. Farmer."

"And we have no idea who these people are?"

"People with generic last names," Alexander said. "You can see why Barry hit a brick wall."

"Whitney said her ex is living in a little one-bedroom apartment in Sandy Springs," I said. "That's quite a comedown from a three-hundred-thousand-dollar town house."

"Even more of a comedown from the house on The Prado. It's been appraised at two point three million," Alexander said. "That's why Carson is leaning on her so hard to make her sell it. Alison told her a little bit about the apartment, but she was only inside for a minute. And she was in an emotional state. He won't let Whitney near the place. That's another reason we suspect it's not his real residence. If you could gain entry to the place, photograph it, that could tell us a lot."

"And get me arrested," I said dryly.

"I would never suggest anything illegal," Alexander assured me.

He opened a desk drawer and pulled out a small flat black leather case about the size of the calculator I carry around with my checkbook in case I ever get the urge to balance it. With his thumbnail he unzipped the case. Inside, nested in a black foam cocoon, was what looked a camera no larger than a cigarette lighter.

"Cute," I said. "Is this for me?"

"It's a video camera. Barry found it at a place called Spy Supplies," Alexander said, playing with the ends of his mustache. "You ever been out there?"

"Hate to disappoint you, but I rarely do spy stuff," I told him. "I don't have a body bug or a shoe phone either. It's just me and my Rolodex most of the time. Still think I can handle the job?"

He opened another drawer and brought out what looked like a miniature tape recorder. "This is the VCR it hooks up to," he said. "You're supposed to use it with a briefcase. But I guess for a woman, a pocketbook would do. It's got a tape and nine-volt battery. All ready to go. We need shots of the apartment interior, of Dobbs and the girlfriend together at the very least. Later on, if you can catch somebody coming or going from the Windward town house who might have a connection to Dobbs, that would be excellent. In short, we need anything that'll prove to the judge that Carson Dobbs is not hitchhiking to the poorhouse."

"The girlfriend's name and everything is in the file?" I asked.

"It's Suzanne Shaddeau," Alexander said.

"And we've got listings of all Dobbs's bank accounts and charge cards and that kind of stuff?"

"The ones we know of."

"How often do you want a report?" I asked, hoping it wouldn't be often. I hate paperwork.

"As soon as you come up with anything at all give me a call," Alexander said. "His people have asked for a court date in two weeks. Given Whitney's reputation, the judge is likely to grant it."

I smelled coffee brewing as I walked to the back door. Baked goods too.

"Who called a summit meeting?" I asked.

Neva Jean, Ruby, Baby, Sister, and Jackie were all crowded around the kitchen table. They were sipping coffee and buttering what looked like apple cranberry muffins.

"I did," Edna said, setting a jar of jam on the table beside the butter dish. "This is a big case, Jules. Lots of stuff to track down. And for once, there's nothing dangerous involved. Just a nice clean swindler. Not a reason in the world the girls can't all help out."

"That's right, Callahan," Neva Jean said, taking a big bite of muffin. "Edna says you're gonna let her help. So we want in too."

"Don't forget that last case," Miss Sister screeched. "Didn't I take care of that little old Chinese gal? Didn't I fix her little red wagon?"

The woman in question was actually Korean, but Sister and Baby had done a masterful job of searching her home and "borrowing" a tape from her answering machine. I poured myself a mug of coffee and leaned against the counter, since there was no room at the table.

"Okay," I said, trying to sound reluctant. I'd already reached the conclusion that I'd need help. I filled them in briefly on what needed doing.

"By the way," I said. "This is a rush job. The other side is asking for a hearing in two weeks. We'll really have to put the pedal to the metal to get everything done. But it'll mean more money for everybody."

"We can do it," Neva Jean said. "That's right," Ruby chimed in.

For a moment their enthusiasm was puzzling. The girls have always loved to poke their noses into my private investigation cases. But this case? This client?

"Did Edna tell you I'm working for Whitney Dobbs?"

"Whitney Dobbs?" Jackie said, doing a double take. "*The* Whitney Dobbs?"

"Why should that make a difference?" Edna said defiantly. "Her money's as good as anybody else's. And she's got plenty of it."

Jackie put her coffee mug down with a bang. "You all hear that? Callahan wants us to help a baby killer. Help that rich bitch that ran that little girl down and left her dead, like she wasn't any better than a squirrel or a frog that ran out in the road." She looked around for support from the other girls.

Ruby folded her hands in her lap. "Oh my," she said dully. "I didn't know that's who it was. Is that right, Callahan?"

"That's right," I said simply. "I don't like what she did any better than you do, Jackie, but I've met her, and she's not like they made her out to be in the paper. She's quit drinking, and she's trying to straighten her life out. She needs help and we could use the money. It's as simple as that."

"Tell that to Faneeta Mayes's mama and daddy," Jackie said. She stood up and grabbed her purse off the back of her chair. "Y'all can do what you want. That bitch should have gotten the chair. She can rot in hell as far as I'm concerned."

Jackie stalked off and let the screen door slam behind her.

"Who she talkin' about?" Baby said loudly. "Who we workin' for?"

"That rich white lady done killed the child in the park," Sister said, cupping her hand to Baby's ear. "Terrible thing, terrible thing." She clacked her tongue loudly against her dentures.

"Whitney Dobbs is no saint," I told them. "But her husband's left her for another woman and he's trying to get away with kicking her out of their house and not paying their daughter's child support or college tuition. We think he's been hiding all his money, crying poormouth."

"Bet he's a doctor," Neva Jean said. "Doctor or a lawyer."

"Doctor," I told her. "A cardiologist. Anybody else object to working for Whitney Dobbs? I won't blame you if you don't want to. Ruby?"

Ruby closed her eyes for a moment, then opened them again. "All right," she said simply. "I prayed about it. And I believe the Bible has a lot to say about forgiveness. This poor lady needs that."

"Miss Baby," I said loudly, "would you be up to working tonight? You'd get paid of course."

"Yes ma'am," she said, quickly. "I'll do it. Can I get ten dollars? We got a senior social at church and I been thinking I'd like me a new winter pocketbook. They got brown leatherette, looks just like suede, at Kessler's for eighteen ninety-nine."

"You can get twenty-five dollars," I assured her.

"And how come Miss Smarty Pants get all the good jobs?" Sister asked, her arms crossed over her bony chest. "Ain't I good enough to be a detective no more?"

"We need you too," I said quickly. "We need everybody."

7

WE WERE FINISHING AN EARLY DINNER when the doorbell rang.

It was Whitney Dobbs, looking small and terrified, like a kindergartner who'd peed in her pants on the first day of school.

"How did you know where I live?" I asked.

She glanced over her shoulder into the quiet dusk. "Could I come in? Please?"

I stepped out of her way and she scurried inside.

"Could you lock that door?"

I raised my eyebrows. "I know this isn't Ansley Park, but it isn't that bad a neighborhood. You're perfectly safe here."

"Somebody has been following me," she blurted. "All day. Every place I go, the same car shows up. I didn't know what else to do."

"Jules?" Edna's voice called from the back of the house. "If

it's one of those schoolkids selling those goddamn candy bars again, you tell them I don't . . . "

"It's a client, Edna," I shouted back.

I heard the scrape of a chair leg against the floor, and a minute later she walked into the living room, patting her hair into place as though this unknown client were somebody needing an audience with her. She knew exactly who it was, of course.

"This is my mother, Edna Garrity," I said. "Edna, this is Whitney Dobbs."

"Albright," she corrected me.

"She thinks she's being followed."

"I *am*," Whitney insisted, her voice echoing in the high-ceilinged room. The slant of the afternoon sun on the big picture windows in our living room keeps the room uncomfortably warm long after sundown most days, but Whitney rubbed her arms with her hands and shuddered.

She was a mess. Big dark circles under her eyes, her short blonde hair uncombed and unwashed. I noticed she was wearing the same shirt she'd worn two nights earlier. It was wrinkled now, and she'd safety-pinned it together where a button had fallen off.

"Why don't you sit down," Edna said, ignoring my bad manners and motioning toward an armchair. "Or you could come in the kitchen and have some coffee. We were just finishing supper, so it's messy."

Whitney picked at a thread on her shirt. She had the grace to blush. "You were eating. I'm sorry. I didn't realize what time it was." She smiled wanly. "It smells wonderful."

"Just a little old pork roast and some fried apples and a broccoli casserole," Edna said apologetically. "I'd be happy to fix you a plate. There's plenty."

"She cooks enough for Pharaoh's army and then poor-

mouths it all night long until you tell her how wonderful it was," I said.

Whitney swallowed. "I couldn't." Her eyes darted from Edna's look of concern to my flinty-eyed stare. I didn't care for her showing up here unannounced and uninvited like this.

"Well, come have some coffee," Edna said, touching her arm. "You look cold."

Whitney bit her lip. "There's a white car. A Ford, I think. It followed me all the way here. I was going to go to a meeting. Then I was so frightened, I couldn't think. I had your business card. I recognized the address. Carson and I rented a garage apartment over here on Clifton when he was a resident at Grady."

She kept on talking. "I pulled right up into your driveway and he stopped at the curb. "For a minute, I thought he was going to come after me. Then he drove by, slowly. That's when I got up the nerve to get out of the car and come to your door."

I went to the window and looked out. There's a streetlight at the foot of our driveway. Warm yellow light spilled onto the pavement like a pool of buttermilk. The street was empty.

"Nobody out there now," I told her, letting the curtains fall back into place.

"He was there a minute ago," she said.

"Never mind," Edna said. "Come into the kitchen and get some coffee. You can tell us all about it."

"Maybe just some tea," Whitney said.

"The car was parked across the street from my house when I left this morning," she said, stirring the tea, then lifting the spoon out of it and letting the amber liquid drip back down into the cup. "It was sort of an odd car for our neighborhood," she said. "Everybody mostly drives Volvos or BMWs. I just figured somebody had a new cleaning person.

"But then the car started up and followed me to the post office. And when I came out of my aerobics class it was there, and then at the A&P, I noticed it again."

"You keep saying he," I said. "Do you know who this person is?"

"No," she admitted. "The car has those dark tinted windows."

"All right," I said. "What else can you tell me about the car? Year? Model? License plate?"

She shrugged. "I don't know cars. It's sort of stubby, like a compact. White, with some rust on the hood. I tried to get a look at the license plate, but he was always a couple cars behind me."

"Did you consider calling the police?" I asked, growing more annoyed. I'd agreed to help Whitney Albright Dobbs find her husband's hidden assets, not guard her against the boogeyman.

"The police?" She set the spoon down in the cup abruptly, slopping tea over the side and onto the saucer. "All the police would do is haul me in for a Breathalyzer test. I told you, I'm not very popular in this town."

"What about your lawyer? Tell him. If it's your husband who's following you, he can get a restraining order."

"I'll call Zack when I get home," she said, her lips set in a grim line. She picked up a napkin and blotted the spilled tea with it. "It's not just the guy in the car," she said. "There have been phone calls too."

"Does Zack know about this?" I was already regretting getting myself involved in this mess.

"No. It seemed so piddling. At first I thought it was one of Alison's friends. Maybe somebody who wanted to talk to her but not to me. But I had a new line installed last Friday. It's an unlisted number. Sunday morning, the calls started coming. They call and call. I've quit picking it up now."

"What do they say?" Edna asked, leaning forward.

Whitney hesitated.

"Don't worry about her," I told Whitney. "Believe me, there's nothing you could say that could shock my mother."

"The first few times he didn't say anything," Whitney said. "After that, he got braver. He whispers, so I can barely hear. Ugly things."

"Like what?"

"Bitch. Drunk. Slut. Baby killer. Like that."

"Nobody's voice you recognize?"

"It's a whisper. I can't even tell if it's a man or a woman."

"It couldn't be one of Alison's friends?"

She shook her head emphatically. "No. She's at school. She knows the number but she wouldn't give it out."

"Does your husband have the new number?"

"No. Just Zack and a few close friends. And Dr. Cook."

My eyes strayed to the kitchen clock. I'd promised to pick Baby and Sister up at seven P.M. It was six-thirty now.

"Look," I said, "I've got to leave. My associates and I are going to try to fast-talk our way into your husband's apartment. You've got to tell the police about those phone calls and the car. If someone is harassing you, they can handle it."

"Why can't you handle it?"

"I don't have the time or the legal authority," I said. "The police can put a trap on your line, to catch the person making those calls. They can question your husband, see if he's behind it, maybe even assign someone to watch your house if you're really being stalked."

She shook her head again and mumbled something under her breath that I didn't catch.

"Call your lawyer when you get home tonight," I told her. "He'll call the police for you, and talk to them."

She got up from the table, looking doubtful.

I got my purse and car keys and followed her to the front door. "Will you be okay driving home?"

"I was going to go to my meeting," she said, sounding undecided. "At the Unitarian Church. I try to go to a meeting every day. The Unitarians have the only one inside the Perimeter tonight."

"A.A.?"

She nodded. "You think I'm being silly. That I'm a big old scaredy-cat. I guess I am. Ever since Carson left, it's different. I wasn't like this before. It never bothered me when he was late, or out of town. It's different, him being gone. Not having a man. That's why I started drinking, I guess. Because I was scared."

I didn't know what to tell her. I like men, miss having one around since Mac and I broke up last year, but it never occurred to me that a man would protect me from anything.

"Do you want me to follow you home?"

She squared her shoulders. "No. The car's gone. I'll be fine. And I'll call Zack. He'll know what to do."

"Good." Edna had followed us onto the front steps. "Call me when you get home," she told Whitney. "So I know you got there with no problems."

Whitney looked up and down the street. A black pickup truck blaring loud country music rattled by, and she jumped slightly.

She had her keys in her hand as she walked to her Volvo.

"I don't think Carson is doing this," she said, unlocking the car door. "It's not like him."

"Who else would do this to you?" I asked.

Her smile was sad. "I lost count."

"Yeah, yeah," she said, walking around the kitchen, aiming the purse out the windows. "You really think somebody's following that poor woman? Making threatening phone calls?"

"I don't know," I sighed. "I'm already sorry I took her on."

"She's pathetic, Jules," Edna said. "What if there is somebody out there? How would you feel if you just told her to take a leap?"

"Stop playing on my Catholic guilt, Ma," I said.

"Some Catholic," she muttered. "How long does this tape run?"

"This one runs for four hours," I said. "Plenty enough. And Whitney's lawyer says it runs best if you can sit the purse down somewhere and move it slightly, so it pans the room. But I don't know if Baby can pull that off. I don't even know if they'll let her in."

"Who would turn her away?" Edna demanded. "A harmless senile old lady like that. Baby Easterbrooks has the sweetest, purest face I've ever seen."

"That's what I'm counting on," I said.

Baby and Sister were inside the lobby of the apartment building when I pulled up. Before I could honk the horn they were making their way determinedly toward the van.

Baby looked perfect for the part. She was wearing a faded housedress that hung down to her bony ankles, with a moth-eaten colorless sweater thrown over it, and a pair of run-down house shoes. She'd added a flowered plastic shower cap to the ensemble, and Sister's contribution was a pair of dangly Day-Glo orange earrings.

"You look wonderful," I said, helping the two old ladies into the van. Baby got to sit up front, mostly because she got there first.

Sister appraised Baby through her thick glasses, pursed her

8

EDNA WAS ENTHRALLED with my new toy. She hung over my shoulder and watched while I took an ice pick and gouged a hole in the clasp of one of her old leather pocketbooks, then used duct tape to attach the pinhole video camera to the purse lining. I hooked the cable to the tiny eight-millimeter VCR and sat it gently in the bottom of the purse, then hit the on button and watched as the cable silently spooled.

"We've got to get one of these things," Edna said, picking the purse up and aiming it at me. "It's great. I can think of all kinds of things I could do with something like this."

"Like what?"

"Find out whose dog is crapping in my azaleas every morning, for one thing. The damned animal must be the size of an elephant. If I knew who it was I'd get your brother's old BB gun and give that hound a taste of birdshot some morning."

"Well, forget it," I told her. "This thing costs twelve hundred dollars. You'll just have to run your own surveillance."

lips, and made an unflattering sound. "You look like hell, sure do. Like somebody just come out of that state nuthouse down in Milledgeville. You come to my door lookin' like that, Missy, I'd call 911."

Baby put her hand up to the dangly earrings. "Where you get these fancy earrings from—huh? Miss Suzie Deeters, the pastor's wife, didn't she have a pair of earrings just like these at missionary circle last week?"

"Might be," Sister said, cutting her eyes slyly. "Might be she give 'em to me cuz I told her I like 'em so much."

"Might be you stole 'em right offa that woman's head," Baby shrieked. "Lord, I'm wearing jewelry stolen from a woman of God. Sister Easterbrooks, you goin' to hell in a handcart and takin' me with you."

"Hush, you two," I said, heading toward the interstate. "I want to tell you the plan again."

"We done talked the plan backward and forward," Baby complained. "Now lemme hold that pocketbook so I can practice making movies."

She snatched the purse out of my hand and clutched it against her bosom, pointing it this way and that out the window. "That's fine," I told her. "Just remember to show as much of each room as you can. Try to aim it at furniture and stuff."

"How's she going to get in the rest of the apartment?" Sister asked anxiously. "They're not gonna just let some crazy old colored lady wander around anyplace she wants."

"That's where you come in. Give Baby five or ten minutes to convince them she really is lost and disoriented, but not enough time for them to call the cops. Then you go in and explain what happened. That she wandered away and got lost while you were visiting somebody who lives here. It's a ground-floor apartment. If I point you there, will you be all right?"

"I'll be fine," Sister declared. "It's that deaf old fool in the front seat you want to worry about."

I turned into the Clarenden Park apartment complex right at eight P.M. Carson Dobbs lived in the last building on Shropshire Way, the second apartment from the end. I could see lights burning from inside. The doctor was in.

"Showtime," I said.

Baby shuffled toward the apartment at an agonizingly slow pace, clutching her pocketbook under her right arm. Normally she's positively spry, moving at the speed of a waterbug. That night, she was playing it for effect. Finally, she was at the door, knocking loudly. We could hear her voice echoing in the concrete hallway.

"Letha Mae? It's me, Baby. Let me in. You hear?"

I'd parked in a visitor slot close enough to the apartment that I could get there quickly if they needed me, but far enough away that I hoped I would be inconspicuous. Not an easy thing to be when you drive a bubblegum-pink Chevy van.

Sister and I slouched down in the seats as soon we saw the outside light flicker on. I edged my head up over the steering wheel and peeped out. A woman opened the door and was silhouetted in the light, hands on her hips, trying to make some sense out of Baby's jabbering.

"Letha Mae!" she hollered. "I know this be Letha Mae's house. Y'all let me in and take me to Letha Mae. My legs done cramped up doin' all that walkin'. Oh Lord, I think I might fall out . . . "

I saw Baby's wispy figure sway and then start to crumple. The woman sprang forward and caught Baby in her arms.

"Carson," she called sharply. "There's an old lady out here. She's sick. I think she's fainted."

The man appeared then, and gathered Baby's limp body

into his arms. The woman stepped out onto the breezeway, looked in both directions, and out into the parking lot. I ducked down. I heard rather than saw the door shut.

"I never told her to faint," I whispered, annoyed. "The man's a doctor. A cardiologist. He'll figure out she's faking any second now."

"Huh," Sister said. "She been fallin' out like that since she was a little girl tryin' to get out of hoeing weeds in Mama's garden. She can fool Mama, she can fool that doctor man."

We waited another ten minutes before I anxiously slipped out of the van and guided Sister toward the door.

"It's right here," I said, pointing her to the doorway just a few feet away. "Can you see it all right?"

"See just as good as anything," Sister said, waving me away. "Lemme be now. I take care of me and Baby."

As soon as I was back in the van, Sister launched into her act. She had no intention of letting Baby upstage her.

"Baby," she called loudly. "Baby Easterbrooks. You round here, Baby?"

She knocked on the door next to Dobbs's, and called her sister's name again, but there was no answer. Now she moved over to door number two. "Excuse me, mister and lady," Sister called. "My fool sister done got lost. Baby, where you at?"

Sister was pounding on the door now. "Baby Easterbrooks! You hear me? Come out of there now. That ain't Letha Mae's house. You come on home with me right now!"

The door opened. This time I could see Carson Dobbs in the doorway. He was tall and slender. Without preamble, Sister pushed him aside and stepped into the apartment. "Baby!" I heard her call.

Carson Dobbs shrugged and pulled the door shut behind.

"Okay," I thought. "Take it easy, but get it done."

I kept my eyes on the apartment. This part of the job was

the part I was used to. It was the hidden-camera work that bothered me. Something about it felt off. Carson Dobbs was slick, I knew that much. To catch him would take some slick detective work. But this, I thought, was slimy.

I'd brought along the file folder Zack Alexander had given me. I opened the glove box and let the light flicker on. It was enough to read by, but I knew better. I glanced at my watch. It was eight-thirty. Baby had been in the apartment fifteen minutes. Sister had been there for about five. In another five they should be out. That's the way we'd planned it, but that was before Baby had decided to pull her dying swan routine. I sighed and glanced at the file folder again. Maybe just a peek. To help pass the time. I leafed through the papers. The financial reports made my eyes swim. But there was a newspaper clipping I hadn't remembered seeing before.

"Victim's Family Holds Vigil Outside Accused Killer's Home," was the headline. The photograph showed a woman, in shorts and a T-shirt, standing in the street with a stately home in the background. She held a placard aloft. KILLER, it said.

I glanced back up at the apartment window. No change. I'd give the girls three more minutes, then I'd have to think of a pretext to go in there and get them all out. In the meantime, I scanned the article. The woman in the photo was Janie Mayes, the mother of Faneeta. And the house Mrs. Mayes was holding a vigil in front of was Whitney's. Shit. Why hadn't somebody mentioned this complication to me? This job was getting messier by the minute.

The story said that Janie Mayes, who worked as a secretary for a Southside hotel, had been standing outside Whitney Dobbs's house every Sunday since the trial. Neighbors had complained and Zack Alexander had sought a restraining order, but the judge had turned him down, ruling that the

Mayes woman was standing on public property, exercising her First Amendment right to freedom of speech.

I heard a door open then, and I stashed the clipping back in the file folder and shut the glove box.

Carson Dobbs stood in the doorway with his arm around the woman who'd answered the door. Suzanne something. Her name was in the file somewhere. She was tall and willowy, with the body of a dancer, and shoulder-length hair that gleamed the color of copper in the lamplight. Baby and Sister held on to each other and moved away from the door.

"Bye now," Sister called loudly. She pointed toward the parking lot and my van. "That's my niece right there. Come on, Baby, we got to get home now."

I held my breath as they inched away from Carson Dobbs and Suzanne, moving slowly and carefully, the purse clutched tightly in Baby's hand. "Come on. Come on," I coached silently. "Just a few steps more."

A movement from the doorway caught my eye. Carson Dobbs had closed his door, satisfied, I supposed, that the sisters were off his property and that he was no longer legally liable for any injuries the two old ladies might sustain.

I didn't dare get out of the car to help them, for fear that Dobbs might be looking out the window. It seemed like years before Baby wrenched the back door open and shoved her protesting sister into the seat. She got in, fastened her seat belt, and held the purse up like she'd just scored the winning touchdown in the big weekend game.

"How'd it go?" I asked, pulling out of the parking space with my lights off. I wanted to put some distance between me and the doctor.

"Ooh, that's a nice apartment," Baby said with a sigh. "Got pretty green carpet and a big soft sofa. That lady she real sweet."

"They had her lying down on that sofa, and the doctor was taking her blood pressure when I went in," Sister said.

"I put the pocketbook right up on my chest like you tole me," Baby said proudly. "Didn't let nobody mess with it."

"Were you able to get in all the rooms?"

"Sure did," Sister said, leaning into the space between the two front seats. "She tol' those white people, big as anything, that she needed to pee," Sister said disapprovingly.

"Well I *did*," Baby said. "Had me a beer before I come out tonight, on account of I was scared."

"It was two beers. Two tall ones," Sister reported.

"Then she wandered into the bedroom, even though the lady told her it was the one on the right, not the one on the left."

"I don't hear too good," Baby said. "But I showed my purse all around that bedroom before the lady come in and shooed me out. Those folks don't have much clothes, do they?"

"And when she come out of there, I took my turn," Sister said.

"I told them my sugar was acting up and did they have some orange juice I could borrow. Then I borrowed Missy here's camera-purse and followed that white lady right into the kitchen. You know what they got in that icebox?"

"What?"

"Nothin' but a couple bottles of something I couldn't see too good and look like a box of Arm & Hammer baking soda," Sister said smugly. "They living on mighty short rations if you ask me."

"Tell me you got it on film," I said.

"Just like you showed Baby," Sister said. "That's good, ain't it, showing that empty icebox?"

"Very good," I told her.

"I know that's right," I heard them say to each other.

"That place is sure enough pretty," Sister said.

"Too clean," Baby pronounced. "Ain't nobody lives that neat. Unless they got the preacher coming over."

I handed each of the girls their money.

They spent the rest of the ride back to their senior citizen high-rise discussing how they would spend their loot and planning a bus trip downtown to shop at Kessler's.

"I'll take the videotape over to the lawyer's office tomorrow to look at it," I told them when I stopped at the high-rise. "It's too small to run on a regular VCR. You girls did real good tonight. Go home and get some sleep."

9

"COULDN'T SLEEP LAST NIGHT?"

I tried to keep my voice casual. Edna hates to be coddled or fussed over, and she seemed to regard her recent illness as an embarrassment. But I'd been awake myself. I'd heard her get up in the middle of the night, heard the creaking of the chair springs as she tried to settle into her armchair, and the dull drone of the television. Now Edna had dark circles under her eyes, and her hand shook as she poured her coffee.

"I'm all right," she said, grimacing and running her fingers through her hair. "That perm Frank gave me burnt my hair to a cinder. It's nothing but frizz."

Her hair looked to me like it always does, blue-white, teased and pouffed in whorls and scallops and waves. Besides, she was being deliberately evasive. "You're not sleeping," I said flat-out. "And you're short of breath. I noticed it yesterday. I want you to call Jeanne Payne and talk to her about it."

"Mind your own business," Edna said, stirring half-and-

half into her coffee. "Tired from the hospital, that's all. They wake you up and baste you every fifteen minutes in that place. I'd sleep a lot better if I had a cigarette."

I got up and sniffed her. She smelled like Aqua Net hair spray, Ban aerosol, Jergens hand lotion, and Doublemint chewing gum. No cigarette smoke, though. I narrowed my eyes. "You're not sneaking cigs on the side and chewing gum to hide the smell, are you?" Once a cop, always a cop.

She tried out a wounded look.

"Are you?"

"No, dammit," she snapped. "Let's drop the interrogation. Okay? When can I see the tape from last night?"

"You can't," I said. "It won't fit our VCR. I'll take it over to the lawyer's office this afternoon. Whitney's supposed to meet me there."

"Did you get a good look at the girlfriend? What's she look like?"

I took her nosiness as a healthy sign.

"Suzanne? It was dark, and I was in the van, but she's sort of tall, very slender, but with big boobs and long wavy auburn hair."

"And fifteen years younger than the doctor, I'll bet," Edna said.

"Probably," I agreed. I picked up the briefcase I'd already packed with the video camera and my files and notebook. "I'm late. I'll tell you everything when I get back."

I spent most of the morning at the Fulton County Courthouse, wading through deed books and real estate indices. Barry, the summer intern, had provided me with a copy of the deed to the Windward town house Dobbs had bought a little over a year ago. From the tax stamps I could tell he'd paid $300,000, with the second debt deed listing a $250,000 mortgage with

Peach State Realco. With taxes and insurance the monthly payment on Carson Dobbs's bachelor pad had been around $3,000. And the whole time he'd been keeping up with Whitney's expenses too. Cardiology had been very, very good to Carson Dobbs.

I found the documents listing the recent resale of the town house to Paradox Properties too. Paradox had paid $88,000. Odd that a penny-pincher like Carson Dobbs would take such a loss.

I tried the alphabetical index, to see if Dr. Dobbs had made any other real estate transactions in the past two years. None were listed. Paradox Properties had no other transactions either. I looked Paradox up in the phone book. No listing.

Back down in the lobby of the courthouse building, I checked the building directory for the business license department.

Behind the frosted glass door, I waited for five minutes while the only clerk on duty fidgeted with a malfunctioning photocopy machine.

He was white, with thinning brown hair, a greasy gray cardigan sweater, and a build that said he lived for lunch hour. The nameplate on the desk facing the counter said Scott Eastman. I cleared my throat.

He looked up at me with mild disinterest. "Just a minute," he said. With a flourish he mashed a button on the top of the machine. It made a strangled gurgle, and all the panel buttons flashed red.

"This copier hates me," he said, giving it a swift kick.

"I know how that is," I said sympathetically. "I've got a fax machine the same way." The truth of the matter is that I don't own a fax. But he didn't have to know that.

He bustled over to the counter then, Mr. Helpfulness. He showed me how to use the microfiche to check for a Paradox

Properties listing. And when we didn't find one, he was disapproving, but unsurprised.

"It's this telecommuting trend," he said. "Everybody with a phone and a modem is in business. And nobody wants to buy a business license. Fulton County gets cheated out of millions. *Multimillions.* And that's tax dollars we don't spend on *your* services."

"Scandalous," I agreed. "These people are on file in the secretary of state's office, but their registered address is one of those law firms that does that for anybody."

"Could they maybe be in business in another metro county?" Scott asked. "DeKalb, Cobb, Gwinnett, Henry, Cherokee, Rockdale?"

"Who knows?" I said. "All I know is they bought some property up at Windward. That's Fulton County, so I figured they'd be in Fulton County."

"Hmm." He was taking Paradox Properties' lack of a business license very personally. "Could they be listed under any other names? Like the names of one of the principals of the company?"

I dug out the names of the three principals from the file folder. "Johnnye B. Adams, V. R. White, and J. F. Farmer," he read aloud.

"Adams and White are so common, I'll get two or three hundred hits when I try to cross-reference it," he said. "Let me try Farmer. It's not so bad."

He typed rapidly into the computer, his pudgy fingers a blur.

"Forty-four Farmers with business licenses," he said a moment later. "It doesn't list the initials on the search. You have to scroll the list. You want to pull them up and we'll take a look?"

I checked the time. I was supposed to meet Whitney at

Zack Alexander's office at four. It was nearly three now, and his building was at Interstate 75 and Powers Ferry Road. Traffic this time of day would be murder. Still. I'd have loved to have something to offer them beyond Baby and Sister's unproven videotaping skills. "Sure," I said.

He flipped open a gate and invited me over to his computer. I stood behind him as he scrolled down the list. There were Farmers who were locksmiths, taxidermists, manufacturers' representatives, Realtors, barbers, and insurance agents. There were eight different Farmers with the first initial J, but no J. F.'s.

We scrolled to the bottom of the list. "Again?" he asked, looking up at me.

I nodded. This time he took it slower, letting me look at each listing. And when we got to the Fs, we hit. Felicia Farmer had taken out a business license for a firm called Cardiovascular Associates of Atlanta, P.C. The address was on Peachtree Road. I knew without looking that it was the same address as Carson Dobbs's main office, but I checked the file to make sure. Same address.

"Bingo," I said.

I picked up the phone beside the computer. "May I?"

"Go ahead," he said. "I'll print this out."

When the receptionist answered the phone "Cardiovascular Associates of Atlanta," I had to talk fast to keep her from putting me on hold.

"Wait," I said. "I'd like to speak to J. F. Farmer."

"Who? J.F?" She sounded genuinely puzzled for a minute there. "Oh," she said, laughing. "You must want Felicia Farmer. Dr. Klein's wife. She doesn't work in the office. You'll have to call their residence."

"I'll do that," I said, and I hung up.

"Scott," I said, grinning and clapping him on the shoulder,

"You have made me a very happy person. I hope you get a big fat raise."

He squirmed a little and blushed. "Here's your printout," he said, handing it to me. "I've enjoyed working with you too."

Even the snail's pace of traffic couldn't dim the buzz I'd gotten from uncovering Carson Dobbs's little real estate scam. I felt smug, clever, in control. If there had been a pair of goalposts outside the county courthouse, I would have done one of those funky touchdown dances the football players like to do. Maybe Whitney Dobbs wasn't the ideal client, but by God, Callahan Garrity was on the case.

I zipped in and out of slowed cars on the interstate like an Indy car racer and when I got to the green glass tower at Powers Ferry, there was a visitor's parking slot right near the door. No doubt about it, it was my day.

"I got him," I announced, as the secretary showed me into Zack Alexander's office. He was on the phone, talking to somebody, and he frowned at me, but got off the phone a second later.

"Who? Dobbs? You got him on the videotape?"

I'd almost forgotten about the camera and the tape. I unzipped my briefcase and laid the camera and the tape on his desk. Then I brought out the computer printout and waved it with a flourish.

"We got Dobbs and his girlfriend last night on tape. And today, just now, I went one better. Carson Dobbs sold his three-hundred-thousand-dollar town house right back to himself. Paradox Properties. Get it? Pair of Docs? The J. F. Farmer who is a Paradox Properties corporate officer is Felicia Farmer, wife of Dr. David J. Klein, who practices medicine with Dobbs."

"Very nice," Alexander said, reading the printout. "You got this from the business license office?"

"Yeah," I said. "I didn't have time to look up the other two corporate officers, but you can bet they're tied into Dobbs somehow."

"I'm impressed," Alexander said. "And the judge should be too. If he's hidden his interest in the town house like this, he'll probably use the same dumb scam to hide his other assets. These guys never get wildly creative. Now tell me about the apartment last night."

He tapped his fingers on the tape as I briefed him on what the girls had told me about Carson Dobbs's apartment, and he nodded his head in approval as he made notes.

"Excellent," he said. "No food in the refrigerator, no personal effects lying around. If it shows up on your videotape, we might really have something."

As we talked I noticed him glancing surreptitiously at his watch, a black diver's model with more dials and gauges than a new BMW.

"Whitney's late," he said, frowning. "I promised her we'd wait and watch the tape together."

"Can we go ahead without her?" There was still a ton of legwork to be done, and I was feeling uneasy about Edna's health.

He picked up the telephone and punched in a number. He waited a moment, then listened. He'd gotten an answering machine. "Whitney, it's Zack. It's four o'clock, and we're waiting on you. Pick up if you're there."

But she didn't pick up. He twirled the cards on his Rolodex, found the number he wanted and punched in another number. He waited, then hung up again. "She doesn't answer her car phone," he said, tugging at the end of his mustache.

"Is she usually like this?' I imagined her somewhere, having her tennis racket restrung, or her cuticles buffed, or maybe she was back at the Driving Club, tanked up on Tanqueray and tonic again, oblivious to the fact that she was taking up other people's time.

Alexander tapped his watch, as though prompting it to make his client appear. "Never," he said. "She's usually five minutes early."

He buzzed his secretary in the next room on the speaker-phone.

"Myra, have we heard from Whitney Dobbs today?"

"Not a word," Myra said. "But isn't this Wednesday?"

"That's right," Alexander said, frowning. "Trash detail. But she's always done by two o'clock."

"Trash detail?"

"Her community service hours," Zack said. "The judge made sure she got the dirtiest, most humiliating detail you can get. Picking up roadside trash with all the other wife beaters and shoplifters and drunk drivers. Right out there in public, dressed in a neon orange vest so all her former friends can drive by and see her."

He pressed the button for Myra again. "Myra, see if you can raise Dr. Dobbs. Find out if he's heard from Whitney today. Then try that neighbor of hers, Audrey Newsome. Let me know what you hear."

"She's only a half hour late," I commented. "Maybe she had something better to do."

He shook his head. "You don't know Whitney. She's been obsessed with trying to prove Carson is hiding assets. She calls me two, three times a day to make suggestions or ask questions. This is one meeting she wouldn't miss."

We both sat there, thinking about the possibilities. "Have you considered calling the police?"

"I could," he said reluctantly. "But not until I check with Carson, or we talk to one of her neighbors."

"You're worried she's drinking again," I guessed.

He thought about that. "Not really. She goes to A.A. meetings nearly every day. No, I guess I'm worried something's happened to her."

His phone buzzed and he punched the speakerphone button.

"Zack? Dr. Dobbs is in surgery, and can't be reached. I did talk to that neighbor, Mrs. Newsome. She said she saw Whitney leaving the house shortly after nine this morning, and hasn't seen her since."

"Thanks, Myra," he said. "Could you get Whitney's parole officer for me? Look in the trial folder, the name should be in there."

He wrote something down on a piece of paper. "This is Whitney's address. You're sort of going that way anyway, back to town. Could you run by the house, see if anything looks amiss? I want to stay here in case she calls, or we hear from someone else."

"I can do that," I said.

"There's a key to the back door under the eave of the toolshed," he said. "There's an alarm system, but she usually doesn't keep it set during the day."

"She doesn't set the alarm, after the phone calls and threats?" I asked.

Alexander's face froze. "Threats?"

"She didn't tell you she was getting calls, and that she thought someone was following her? Last night, she showed up at my door, nearly in hysterics because she thought someone was following her. She promised me she'd call you and let you know about it."

"I was out last night," Alexander said softly.

"I thought she was imagining things," I admitted. "She said it was a small white Ford. And that whoever was calling had gotten her new, unlisted number."

"Jesus," Alexander said. "She never said a thing to me about being afraid."

"I'll call you from the house," I told him, "or you can reach me on my car phone if something comes up before I get there."

By the time I got to the van, I'd forgotten about doing a victory dance.

10

WHITNEY DOBBS LIVED IN ANSLEY PARK, in midtown. A long time ago, Ansley was considered suburban. That was before the developers decided midtown would be a nice place to stack their high-rise office towers. Somehow, though, the neighborhood has managed to retain an aura of green tranquillity. The roads there are wide and pleasantly curving, with houses set back away from the street, their wide lawns blanketed with ivy beneath towering oak trees.

Whitney's house was on The Prado, the most prestigious street in the neighborhood. It was a gray clapboard Dutch Colonial, with cute little eyebrow windows up near the roofline, giving the house a look of bemused surprise.

I pulled the pink van up into the driveway and parked in front of a two-car garage covered in the same gray clapboards. The parking spaces were empty. The key was where Alexander had said it would be.

Autumn had decided to linger this year. Leaves from a big

oak tree fluttered silently down around me. The grass and shrubbery were covered with little brown oak leaves, splashy red maple leaves, and the brilliant yellow slash of ginkgo leaves. My footsteps made a scrunching sound as I walked up a short granite stairway to a covered side porch. There was a black iron mailbox screwed to the wall. I could see the day's mail still inside. "Whitney?" I called loudly, and tried to peer through the glass of the side door. If she was home I didn't want to walk in on her uninvited.

Behind me, a loud metallic pinging noise made me jump. I whirled around to see who was there. A fat gray squirrel scampered across a branch that stretched across the driveway. Acorns. Shit. I was getting jittery.

I unlocked the door and stepped into the hallway. "Whitney?" I called again. I made a quick search of the house. It was two stories high, a comfortable family house with that effortless shabby chic decor that old money adores: big saggy sofas, tons of family photos in silver frames, every available surface covered with books and magazines. In the corner of the living room a quartet of tennis rackets leaned against a baby grand piano.

The kitchen told me how Whitney had started her day. A cereal bowl, a juice glass, and a single coffee cup were set in the drainer. The morning paper was folded in half on a big marble-topped farmhouse table, still in its plastic wrapper. There was a stack of mail on the counter. I had my hand on the stack when a shrill ring cut the silence. I looked wildly around for the phone. It was on a built-in desk in the corner of the kitchen.

"Dobbs residence," I said.

"Callahan?"

It was Zack.

"She's not here. I don't think she's been home since this morning. Today's mail is still in the mailbox."

"I finally reached Whitney's parole officer. Whitney signed in at their office at eight-thirty A.M. and was picked up, along with the other people, by a van from the sheriff's office. They were assigned to pick up trash on a stretch of Brown's Mill Road. That's South Atlanta. The sheriff's van was supposed to bring everybody back to the parole office at three o'clock."

"Did it?" I asked.

"Nobody seems to know," Alexander said, sounding frustrated. "I can't raise anybody at the sheriff's office who can tell me anything. And her parole officer says she never actually saw Whitney, just the sign-in sheet."

"Well, that's helpful," I said sarcastically. "Anything from the doctor?"

"Still in surgery, or else he just doesn't want to return my calls," Alexander said. "Understandable, under the circumstances. Look. I'm really concerned now. Are you still willing to help out with this thing?"

My stomach did a guilty little flip. "What do you want me to do?"

"Myra and I are going down to the parole office, to see if we can spot her car anywhere, or find someone who saw her today. There are a dozen or more lots down around the county complex downtown, so it'll take some time. Would you mind going out to Brown's Mill Road? The sheriff's van is supposed to be beige and brown. And her car is a dark gray Volvo."

"I've seen her car," I reminded him. "Any idea where on Brown's Mill? That's a pretty long stretch of road as I recall."

"The damned parole officer didn't know," Alexander said. "And to tell you the truth, I'm not real familiar with that part of town."

"I used to be an Atlanta cop," I said. "It's been a few years, but I can at least find the road."

"Call me if you find anything," he said.

* * *

"Whitney—Zack was worried after you missed your appointment today. Please call him ASAP. Callahan Garrity."

I left the note on the kitchen counter, faking optimism. Then I locked the side door, crunched my way back through the leaves, and got in the van.

Ansley Park and Brown's Mill Road were worlds apart.

For a while the street passed mostly warehouse and industrial-type buildings, interspersed with down-at-the-heels Pentecostal churches and small, hopeless-looking strip shopping centers.

Eventually, the commercial buildings petered out. Oaks and pines and sweetgums crowded close to the road now, with occasional fields swallowed whole by kudzu. The dark green vines draped from trees, power lines, and the remnants of old buildings.

Up ahead I saw something on the side of the road and I slowed down to get a better look. It was a cluster of bright orange plastic trash bags, half a dozen of them, neatly tied and stacked. I looked down the road and saw that more clusters of the bags dotted the roadside at what looked like quarter-mile increments. So the trash crew had been this way. Maybe Whitney had left me a trail of bags, like Hansel and Gretel with the breadcrumbs.

It was nearing six o'clock now. Dusk was rapidly approaching, and with it a definite chill. I rolled up the van window and peered out the windshield, following the trail of orange bags. I passed the Brown's Mill Golf Course, a city of Atlanta facility, with its good-enough-for-government shagginess.

I pulled over to the right when I spotted what looked like a driveway into the park. But wooden barricades blocked the road, and now I could see a handful of trucks and pieces of heavy machinery. Five men stood around the equipment,

drinking water from a big orange cooler on the tailgate of a pickup truck. I parked the van and walked over to the men. Their faces under their caps were dirty and sweat-streaked, their work boots caked with red mud.

"Excuse me."

The man nearest the cooler put his cup down and turned to face me. "Yes, ma'am?" He was black and the red bandanna he wore tied around his head made him look like a buccaneer.

"Did you see a county work crew down this way earlier today, picking up trash?"

He nodded vigorously. "I seen 'em. Got a sheriff's deputy standing over 'em hollering at 'em like a old-time chain gang." He smiled broadly. "Only this time they got some white folks breaking up rocks."

"Did you see a white woman on the crew, very petite, with short blonde hair, in her early forties?"

He looked at the other men. "There was a whole gang of 'em. Any of y'all notice a woman with that trash crew?"

"There was mostly men, and a couple of big old mean-lookin' black mamas, but I woulda noticed somebody like you talkin' about," an older man said.

"Did you notice when they left?"

"No," the foreman answered. "But it's been a couple hours since I saw that van. You look around by the entrance to the golf course?"

"Isn't this the entrance?"

He laughed and pointed at the wooden barricades. "This here's the maintenance entrance. You want to go down here to the stop sign and turn onto Cleveland Avenue. You'll see it."

I followed his directions and cruised slowly into the deepening dusk for any sign of the work crew or the trash bags.

The golf greens were fading into their winter colors of sage and gold. The course rolled along on my right, the fairways lit-

tered with fallen leaves. I saw a couple of golf carts bumping along the paved cart paths and I saw one hearty foursome actually walking, pulling their bags along behind them on wheeled dollies.

The sky overhead was that queer purplish color you get at dusk in autumn, and the leaves were raining down on the roof and windshield of the van. Ahead, I saw what looked like another cluster of trash bags. The crews must have worked their way around the perimeter of the course. Maybe I'd find the van and Whitney up ahead in the public parking lot. Maybe they were taking a water break too.

I slowed as I approached the bags. There was a big pile of them, more than a dozen, and what looked like a big tree limb thrown across the top of the stack. As I passed, something about the bags caught my eye. I pulled onto the grassy shoulder and got out to investigate. I was two steps away from the van when I went back, reached under the seat, and got my Smith & Wesson, tucking it in the waistband of my skirt.

I'd parked the van a dozen yards away from the trash bags. As I walked closer my stomach started doing those little flips again. I walked unsteadily, the heels of my dress shoes sinking into the soft soil. My right hand crept under my jacket and I let it rest on the grip of the pistol. To somebody walking or driving by, it would look like I was giving my tummy a scratching.

I was five yards away from the stack of trash bags when I realized that the tree limb was actually a pair of legs, clad in tight black pants. On the feet were a pair of new white Nikes. I sucked in my breath and ran over to the bags. I kicked one of the bags aside, revealing the rest of the body. He was young and black, maybe twenty years old, wearing a gray sweatshirt with cutoff sleeves and one of the orange reflective vests I'd seen roadside construction workers wearing. A sweat-stained red Falcons cap lay on top of one of the bags, which was spat-

tered with blood. Beer cans and McDonald's wrappers and soiled disposable diapers spilled out of one of the bags, which had been ripped open by a powerful blast—shotgun probably. One side of the man's face was nothing but a pulpy bloody mass. "Jesus." I could feel my heart thumping in my chest.

I backed slowly away from the body, swallowing hard to keep from throwing up. The man was past dead, but I had my pistol out now, my index finger trailing along the barrel. I stood there a moment before I realized the shooter could still be around, taking target practice as he pleased. I kicked off the heels and began to jog back to the van. The car phone. I'd call the cops from the car phone. Something made me stop, turn around. I was still in my stocking feet, walking back toward that headstone of orange bags. It was twice as big as any of the other piles I'd seen. Maybe someone had combined two or three piles to conceal something. My chest hurt. I realized I wasn't breathing right. I trudged back. In through the nose. Out through the mouth. The sun was gone now, the air chilly. My skin prickled under the thin twill suit jacket, and my feet were cold.

I stood over the stack of bags and took a long look at the scene, deliberately averting my eyes from the man's face. Over to his right, half-hidden by another exploded trash bag, I saw something. I had to kick aside three or four bags to get a good look. And then I found what I hadn't wanted to.

Another body. Dressed in Ralph Lauren designer jeans, the hair swept under a matching denim baseball cap, she could have passed for an adolescent boy. But the bullet had ripped a hole in the protecive orange vest, baring bits of the delicate white lace of a bra, tinged with blood. For some reason, I pushed the bags away and knelt down beside her. Funny the things you notice. Whitney's Timberland boots were barely worn. And unlike the man, she wore a pair of white cotton gloves on her hands. For protection.

11

THE HAT SQUAD WAS OUT IN FORCE. Two bodies, and one of them was Whitney Albright Dobbs.

I should explain about the hats. A couple of years ago, somebody on the Atlanta homicide squad decided he'd look more detectivelike in a fedora and a suit that didn't come from Sears. Now all the detectives dress to the nines: three-piece suits, flashy silk ties, and the aforementioned hats. They all look like they've turned out to audition for the road show of *Guys and Dolls*.

Bucky Deavers wore the most outrageous outfits of all. That night's selection was a green tweed suit the color of cheese mold, a yellow silk shirt, brown and black spectators, and a dark green superbad Borsalino. The man he brought over to the van to talk to me was somebody I'd seen a lot on the eleven o'clock news.

"Callahan, this is Captain Mackey," Bucky said.

Lloyd Mackey's hat was a conservative snap-brim; the suit

was taupe, expensively cut, and worn with a black shirt and a geometric-print beige-and-black tie.

I'd given a statement to the first uniformed officer to arrive after I'd called in the shooting from my car phone. Then I'd given another statement to the first detective on the scene. Now it looked like I was expected to spill my guts again.

Bucky squeezed my shoulder. "We sent somebody out to get food. I ordered you a cheeseburger and some coffee."

"Thanks," I said. Hot coffee might stabilize my nerves, but I didn't know if I could stomach a greasy burger.

"Any idea who the man was?" I asked Mackey.

"You won't be talking to the press? We haven't released names yet."

"Somebody released Whitney's," I pointed out. The place was crawling with reporters.

Mackey ignored that. He flipped open a small notebook. "Sheriff's office ID's the guy as Shawan Taylor. Age is iffy. Say twenty. No known next of kin. He got locked up for urinating in a Burger King downtown. The manager pressed charges and the judge decided Shawan could use a little work ethic to straighten him out."

"So he got shot to death for taking a leak in public," I said.

The temperature had dropped a good twenty degrees since nightfall. I'd found an old blanket in the back of the van and wrapped it around myself, but I was still barefoot; the shoes I'd kicked off in haste were out there somewhere, lost in the inky darkness. It took effort to keep my teeth from chattering.

Mackey shrugged. "He was a Grady rooter. Still had on the hospital ID bracelet. Deavers called over there. He was in last week for an infected cut on his foot."

Rooter was the cop word for the homeless regulars who spent more time in Grady's emergency room than the docs and nurses. According to my sister Maureen, who works in the

E.R. there, half the time rooters came in by ambulance just to get a bath or a hot meal.

"What was a rooter doing with Whitney?" I wondered aloud. "Where was the rest of the trash crew?"

"We're working on that," Mackey said. He put his notebook back in his inside jacket pocket and pushed up the brim of his hat. He had high cheekbones, deep-set brown eyes, and sideburns worn a little long, like they were wearing them lately.

"Deavers tells me you were working for Whitney Dobbs. Private investigating. You got a license?"

"I got a license," I said evenly.

"You want to tell me what kind of work you were doing for her?"

"Just some domestic-type stuff. She and her lawyer felt her soon-to-be-ex-husband wasn't being straight on the financial distribution."

"Was he?"

I thought about how much I wanted to divulge of my investigation. Not much, until I'd had a chance to discuss things with Zack Alexander.

"The ex is a doctor. Cardiologist. And he was claiming to be suddenly broke. We were just starting the investigation."

"Carson Dobbs. I know the name. Did the doctor know his wife had hired somebody to check up on him?"

I felt my face fluch at the memory of our videotaping expedition.

"I don't know," I told him. "I'd just been hired. I only met Mrs. Dobbs a few days ago."

"But you came out here tonight, looking for her?"

"She missed an important meeting with her attorney. He got worried. It wasn't like her. So he called Mrs. Dobbs's probation officer and found out she'd been assigned to a trash detail down here. I came out here to look for her."

"And found her."

"Yes."

"And you didn't see anybody in the area before you found the body?"

I took a deep breath. "Not really. I passed some golfers trying to get in a last hole before dark, but they were walking away from the area. I told Bucky, I stopped and talked to some workmen on Brown's Mill, at the maintenance area. They said they'd seen the trash crew working earlier, but hadn't noticed a white woman. She's very slender. From a distance you wouldn't know she was a female.

"Somebody did though," I added.

He looked surprised. "You think so?"

Was he joking or deliberately playing stupid?

"Come on, Captain," I said. "The Faneeta Mayes hit and run? Whitney Dobbs couldn't walk down the street without somebody hocking a loogey at her. And I know for a fact that she'd been getting harassing phone calls. She told me last night that someone had been following her too."

"Told you."

"That's right. She was terrified. It wasn't an act." I didn't add that I had only recently come to that conclusion.

"Did she make a police report about any of these alleged phone calls or an alleged stalker?" Mackey asked.

"No," I admitted. "She knew how people felt about her. She thought the cops would say she'd been drinking."

"What makes you think she hadn't?"

He had me there. Just the night before I'd been willing to write Whitney Dobbs off as a self-pitying hysteric, seeing boogeymen in every shadow. Twenty-four hours later I had a new perspective on things. Seeing your client's body with a gunshot hole through her chest will make a believer of you.

"She was in recovery," I told Mackey. "She went to A.A. meetings almost every night."

"According to whom?"

"Her lawyer," I said. It sounded lame even to me.

"Okay," Mackey said, not bothering to hide his skepticism. He turned away from me to check on his investigators' progress. Crime scene technicians, uniformed officers, hat guys, and sheriff's deputies scurried about in the glare of a high-beam portable lamp that had been brought in and hooked up to a generator. They'd strung yellow plastic crime scene tape around the trees along the road and back about fifty yards onto the edge of the golf course.

Fluttering about the edges of the tape, like so many moths, were the media. All the local television stations had sent their satellite trucks and another dozen or so radio and print types were there too. The reporters weren't there because of Shawan Taylor. A dead Grady rooter was everyday stuff.

I followed Mackey's gaze to the knot of reporters who were shoving microphones and cameras into the face of the tall guy wearing the ugly green pimp hat.

"Deavers," Mackey said, shaking his head in resignation. "Somebody oughtta burn that outfit he's got on."

He shifted his attention back to me. "You've obviously got some theories about who killed your client. How about names?"

I bit my lip. I knew talking to Mackey was a mistake. I should shut up and mind my own business. I was cold and barefoot and I had a sick mother at home to tend to.

"Her husband certainly comes to mind," I said instead. "Whitney's lawyer tried all afternoon to reach him. He never called. I'd certainly want to know where Carson Dobbs was."

Mackey looked amused. "One of our people talked to Dr. Dobbs right after we identified her. He is next of kin, you know. He said he was in surgery. We'll check on it."

"Oh no." A sickening thought occurred to me.

"What?"

"Her daughter. Alison. She's away at college. Somewhere up north. Has anybody notified the daughter?"

"Wouldn't that be up to Dr. Dobbs? He is her father."

I shook my head emphatically. "She won't speak to him or see him." I grabbed Mackey's sleeve. "I've got to call Whitney's lawyer. Zack Alexander. He'll have somebody call Alison. Or do it himself."

I should have called Zack earlier. But things had happened so fast. The cops had been interrogating me for nearly two hours.

"Mr. Alexander's been notified," Mackey said. He nodded in the direction of the roped-off crime scene. I hadn't seen him arrive. But he stood there, hands shoved in his pockets, listening intently to what one of the detectives was saying.

"You done for now?" I asked Mackey.

"For now."

I limped over to Alexander. He saw me coming and met me halfway. His face looked drawn; the mustache seemed to tug downward even more than before. He put an arm around my shoulder. "Poor kid."

I didn't know if he meant me or Whitney.

"Have you called her daughter?"

"She's flying out in the morning."

We heard a commotion then, coming from the area where the reporters had been interviewing Deavers.

A tall, heavyset black man dressed in jeans and a down vest charged into the circle of cameras. "The bitch," he shouted, flailing his arms. "She got what she had coming to her. Goddamn bitch. She was garbage. You see where she ended up? Garbage!"

He pushed through the crime scene tape, headed for the area where the technicians were still examining the bodies. A woman clung to the man's sleeve, trying to pull him back. "No," we heard her cry. "Don't do this. Don't."

"I want to see her," he hollered, striking out at the woman and sending her sprawling onto the golf course. Three uniformed officers lunged at him, dragging him away from the crime scene tape. The reporters surged forward, cameras rolling.

"Who the hell is that?" I asked Zack.

"Who else?" he said. "Bryant Mayes. He's a firefighter with the city. Must have heard about it on the police scanner. Or else one of his cop buddies called and tipped him. The woman is his wife, Janie." Faneeta Mayes's parents. Come to witness Whitney Dobbs's final justice.

"Is he drunk?"

Bryant Mayes was still hollering, trying to shake off the cops who were attempting to stuff him into a patrol car. He leaned backward in the backseat of the car, kicking out at the officers, who struck back at his flailing legs with nightsticks.

"Probably," Zack said, watching the show. "I hear he hasn't had many sober moments since the accident. He was supposed to be on leave. To get his act together."

Janie Mayes stood numbly beside the cruiser, staring off into the dark. She wore a pink sweater tossed over a gray sweatsuit and her feet were stuffed into sneakers with no socks.

Alexander was watching her too. "Wonder if she's happy now?" he said quietly. "She got what she wanted. All those days standing out in front of Whitney's house with that sign. Tormenting her. She can stay home now."

I sighed. "You think the cops will let me leave? I'm beat."

He straightened his shoulders. "I'll talk to Lloyd Mackey. Tell him you're my client and you're done for the night. That all right?"

"I'd be grateful."

He walked quickly over to Mackey and was back a minute later.

"Let's go."

He walked me to my van and stood by the open door.

"It's not over, you know," he said.

"What? Whitney's dead. You don't have a client anymore."

"Sure I do," he said. "I'm Whitney's lawyer. Alison's too. I represent the estate. And I'll be goddamned if I'll let Carson Dobbs get away with cheating his daughter out of her inheritance."

"Whatever," I said. I was exhausted. Drained. I dreaded the drive home.

"I'll call you tomorrow," Zack said.

I had to leave the windows open on the drive home; the cold air rushing past my face was the only thing that kept me awake. When I got home, Maureen's car was in the driveway, parked in my space.

"Shit." I parked in the street. And then I remembered. Edna. Maybe she'd gotten worse and called Maureen for help. I jogged up the driveway, heavy-footed and full of dread. But when I let myself in the back door, the house was quiet. The only sound was the ticking of the big kitchen clock.

I tiptoed to Edna's bedroom door and looked in on her. She was asleep, propped up on her pillows, a chiffon scarf wrapped around her hair, a paperback romance novel turned facedown on her chest. I crept in, took her glasses off her face, put them on her bedside table, and stood listening to her breathing. There was a slight wheeze, but otherwise her breath was steady and she wasn't coughing. I turned off the light and went out.

By the time I got to my bedroom door, I'd unzipped my skirt and had my blouse halfway off. But my bedroom door was locked. What the hell?

I jiggled the door handle.

"Just a minute," Maureen's voice came, muffled.

I saw a light come on under the door and then my sister opened it a crack and peered out at me, annoyed. "What?"

"What yourself? This is my bedroom."

I took a closer look. Maureen had a terry cloth robe clutched to her bony chest, but otherwise she was naked as a jaybird. "And that's my robe. I'm beat. Get the hell out."

"Didn't Mom tell you? She said it was okay for Steve and me to stay here. The contractor started work on our bathroom today. You know, so we can rent the house out for the Olympics. We can't stay there without a bathroom. It'll only be a week."

Edna hadn't mentioned any houseguests to me, but if she had, I never would have agreed to give up my bedroom, especially to Maureen and her half-wit husband.

"Sleep in the den," I said, yanking at the door.

She jerked it back toward her. She was surprisingly strong for someone so skinny.

"We can't," she said fiercely. "Mom made up the sleeper sofa for you already."

"Fine," I said. "You two can sleep out there. I want my bed."

"Dammit. You know we're trying to get pregnant." She paused for a bit of drama. "Listen, Callahan. I'm ovulating."

"I don't hear anything."

"Bitch." Before I could stop her she slammed the door shut and locked it again.

I rattled the door some more, and tried knocking, but lightly, because I didn't want to wake up my mother. The only sound from inside was some giggling, and then the creaking of my bedsprings. She knew how to torment me all right.

I put my lips to the door frame. "I want those sheets burned in the morning," I whispered. Then I stomped off to the sofa bed.

12

LIKE EVERY SOFA BED I'VE EVER EXPERIENCED, ours hid an evil secret. It was cute, charming even, with a curved back and chubby rolled arms and a faded floral slipcover. But the mattress was thin and lumpy and smelled musty. Worse, the metal bar that ran horizontally across the middle hit me at the base of the spine with the accuracy of an ice pick.

Edna had made up the bed with a pile of pillows and a quilt, and she'd even set out my flannel nightie. I tried burrowing into the pillows like a hedgehog, but every time I closed my eyes I saw those black-clad legs and the white sneakers, then the suede boots and the wisp of bloodstained lace.

I found the television's remote control and flipped through the channels. I can never remember any of the numbers for the cable channels. Late-night talk shows with twerpy yuppie hosts gave way to the Home Shopping Channel, where they were modeling the latest in cruisewear. I switched to arena football, then to a Spanish-language soap opera. Finally I

found what I was looking for, the old-movie channel. I was hoping for screwball comedy, something with Cary Grant or Myrna Loy. Instead I got *The Three Stooges Meet Hercules*. I could have wept.

After that I watched a thirty-minute infomercial about how much weight you can lose if you live on a juice diet. When I found myself looking for my credit card to order an $89.95 Mister Juicey I realized it was time for drastic measures. It was two-fifteen A.M., to be exact.

Edna's new prescriptions took up a whole shelf in the bathroom medicine cabinet. Antibiotics, steroids, decongestants, stuff I couldn't pronounce. My hand settled on a bottle with a large orange warning label on the side and a cartoon of a droopy eye.

"May Cause Drowsiness," the label said. Good. That's what I intended. "Do Not Operate Heavy Equipment," it added. Darn. I'd have to park the backhoe.

The tablets were tiny so I gulped down two with a handful of water. The last thing I remember was staggering back to the sofa bed.

"Jules? Jules! Wake up!"

Edna shook me again and again. Finally she snatched the quilt off and took the pillows too. I struggled to sit up. My bones had all liquefied overnight. Shades of Mister Juicey. Sun streamed through the windows. I covered my eyes with my hands. Somewhere in the house someone was frying onions. Onions for breakfast?

"The phone is for you," Edna said, poking my leg with her finger. "Get up now. What's wrong with you? Do you know it's after noon?"

"Sleeping pills," I said, my words swallowed in a huge yawn.

I followed her unsteadily into the kitchen. The phone was off the hook.

"Callahan?" It was Zack Alexander. "We need a strategy session."

"What for?" I asked. Wasn't our client dead? "You've got the videotape. The business license is proof of the shenanigans Carson Dobbs was trying to pull."

"It's not enough," Zack said. "We need more. I've already tried to have the hearing postponed. His lawyer won't go for it. And have you seen the paper today?"

I hadn't seen today, period. "No. What?"

"Unbelievable," Zack said. "Mackey made a statement to the press last night. He's saying it could be just a random shooting. He says there have been all kinds of scattershot shootings down there in the Promised Land for the past year. Dogs, street signs, cars. They've even had golf carts full of people under fire."

"The Promised Land?" Were we talking about the same thing? Had Zack gotten hold of Edna's sleeping pills too?

"It's what the locals call the area out there," Zack said. "Freed slaves settled there after the Civil War. Anyway. Random. Do you believe that? As though Whitney Dobbs and this derelict just happened to be in the wrong place at the wrong time."

"Maybe it's just a bullshit story," I said. "Sometimes cops release statements like that just to keep the press off their backs." But Edna was holding up the *Constitution* for me to see, pointing to the story stripped across the top of the front page.

"Socialite Slaying Accidental?" the headline asked.

I took the paper from her and started to read.

"Can you get over here by two?" Alexander wanted to know.

"Yeah," I said, distracted. "I'll be there."

I hung up and sniffed the oregano-scented air. "Spaghetti? For breakfast?"

Edna poured me a cup of coffee and left it black. "Drink that. Breakfast was hours ago. You're smelling the marinara sauce. For dinner." She looked pointedly at the kitchen clock, which showed it to be twelve-thirty P.M.

"I got the girls all straightened away. Baby and Sister showed up wanting to work, so I sent them over to old Mrs. Schall's. Neva Jean's still sneezing her head off from the damned ostriches."

"Emus," I said, still reading. The *Constitution* reporter didn't come out and say it in so many words, but you could tell she wasn't buying any bullshit story about somebody accidentally killing Whitney Dobbs while they were out shooting up street signs.

I finished reading and put the paper down.

"How come you didn't tell me you were turning my bedroom over to Romeo and Juliet?"

"Oh. Didn't I mention that I said they could stay here a couple days? Just until the bathroom is working again?"

"No," I said pointedly. "You didn't mention it because you knew I'd never stand for it. And I don't appreciate coming home late after two hours of police interrogation to find my sister and brother-in-law rutting in my bed like a couple of hogs in a mudhole."

"The newspaper spelled Garrity wrong," she said, pointing at the paper. "That poor woman. Was it awful, finding her like that?"

"Don't try to change the subject," I warned. "Look, Mom. They both make decent money. They're just cheap. Maureen told me herself that Steve bought a piece of that ambulance company he works for. So as far as I'm concerned, tonight they

can check into the Motel Six. I'm officially switching on the No Vacancy sign at Chez Callahan."

"Hmph." She flounced out of the kitchen. When she came back she had her arms full of bed linens. She opened the door to the laundry room and began stuffing them into the washer.

"And I told Maureen. She can buy me a new set of sheets," I called. "I'm not sleeping on Steve's sperm. I don't care how much hot water and bleach you use."

"Fine." Edna slammed the lid of the washer shut. She went to the stove and lifted the lid of the big cast-iron kettle. The room filled with the warm perfume of tomatoes and garlic and oregano. She picked up a wooden spoon and gently stirred the bubbling sauce.

"It's your house, I reckon," she said to nobody in particular. "If you want to turn away family and send them to some sleazy motel, I guess it's no concern of mine."

We both knew Maureen and Steve had been plotting their Olympics strategy for months now.

"Five hundred dollars a night, a bedroom," Steve had announced at Sunday dinner at our house. "We've got four bedrooms. The agency says you've got to have two bathrooms though. Then we can get two thousand dollars a night—for three weeks."

"Our share is fourteen thousand dollars," Maureen said smugly. "And we end up with the new bathroom I've been wanting."

"But where do you plan to stay while the house is being rented out?" I'd asked. "Can two people really sleep comfortably in one of those ambulances of Steve's? Won't it get crowded with all those heart monitors and stuff?"

Steve and Maureen exchanged worried looks.

"You could stay here," Edna began . . .

"Except that I'm sure you'd want your privacy," I said

hastily. "Besides, with all that money you're making, why stay here in town? Why not go on vacation? Someplace exotic. Beirut? Bosnia?"

"We'll think of something, Mom," Maureen said, patting Edna's hand. "Don't you worry about us. You know how Steve feels about imposing."

My mother had a blind spot when it came to my sister's conniving.

"It wouldn't hurt you to be nice to your sister," Edna said now. "This is a bad time for her, trying to get pregnant and not having any luck. You could be a little more understanding, you know."

I took a big swig of the coffee and let it scald my throat. Better that than say what I really thought about a blending of those two particular gene pools.

The phone rang and I grabbed for it gratefully.

"Garrity?"

It was Bucky Deavers.

"Can you get down here pretty quick?"

No joking, no vulgar comments about my appearance the night before. Something must be wrong.

"Mackey wants to ask you some more questions," Bucky said.

"What's this really about?" I demanded. "I told you, I told Mackey, I told everybody on the force last night, exactly what I saw. Which was two bodies. Dead. End of story."

Deavers sighed. "This is all a big fuck-up. Big fuck-up."

"Tell me exactly what's going on. Or I won't come."

"Shit," he mumbled. "You know we took Bryant Mayes into custody last night, right? The dead kid's father?"

"I saw the guy making a scene," I said cautiously. "Drunk as Cooter Brown."

"You left before it really got good," Bucky said. "The guys

were just gonna take him downtown. Get him calmed down away from all the press, then let him go. Then the drunk sumbitch kicks out the window of the cruiser and bites Randy Barnes on the hand, with all the cameras rolling. Barnes had to go to Grady and get stitches."

"Uh-oh," I said.

"Yeah," Bucky said. "So we had no choice then. Had to charge him with drunk and disorderly and assault on a police officer. Mayes's wife was crying, all upset. So I tell Mackey, don't call the tow trucks. It'll just make things worse. I'll drive Mayes's truck downtown, and she can bail him out and take his sorry ass home. I'm getting in the truck, I glance in the back, what do I see?"

"A case of Pabst Blue Ribbon?"

"Probably two dozen empty Heineken bottles," he admitted. "And a ratty old piece of carpet. And sticking out from under the carpet, the barrel of a rifle."

"Oh shit."

"That's what I said. We've got the weapon from Mayes's truck over at the crime lab. And Mayes is still in custody. So you and me and Mackey need to have a serious talk about what you saw out on that golf course."

"But I thought Mackey was saying it was just a random shooting," I protested.

"That was before," Bucky said. "The shit's really hit the fan now. And Garrity?"

"Yeah?"

"You might want to powder your nose before you come down here. Every reporter in the free world is standing outside with their cameras aimed right at us."

"Goody," I said.

13

THE ALL-NEWS RADIO STATION had a live bulletin about Bryant Mayes's being questioned in the Whitney Dobbs murder, so I wasn't surprised to pull up to the Atlanta Police Department on Decatur Street downtown and see the sideshow that had gathered.

Television and radio station vans had pulled up onto the sidewalk, and a knot of camera- and microphone-wielding reporters had gathered around a woman who was standing on the top step, facing the crowd: Janie Mayes. Her face was agitated; she gestured wildly. I could see her jaw working, but her words were inaudible. An older black man stood beside her, holding up the same framed portrait of Faneeta I'd seen so many times in the newspaper.

I pulled into the parking lot. Every space was full. After I'd circled the tiny lot twice waiting for a slot to open, Bucky Deavers appeared. "Park next to my unit," he called, waving me over to a spot marked RESERVED FOR DETECTIVES.

He hustled me in a side door, and we went up to the homicide office. Lloyd Mackey pointed me toward a chair. Bucky came in and sat down too. Mackey got up and closed the door. He was minus the hat this morning, wearing a rust-colored shirt, dark gray slacks, and a rust-and-gray sport coat. He had on bifocals too.

Bucky was dressed in jeans and a Falcons sweatshirt. He must have been off the clock.

"We need to talk to you again," Mackey said bluntly. "I know Deavers told you we found a weapon in Bryant Mayes's car last night. So let's go over what you saw."

I shut my eyes to try to envision the details better. I told him about the two guys in the golf cart and the foursome I'd seen on foot. I even told him about the city maintenance workers I'd stopped to talk to on the other side of the golf course.

"We know about them," Mackey said, waving a dismissive hand. "They saw even less than you."

"What about vehicles?" Bucky asked, leaning close. "What vehicles did you notice around the area?"

I shook my head. "I only remember not seeing the car I was looking for—Whitney's gray Volvo."

"You didn't notice a truck?" Mackey asked.

"Sorry."

"You saw Bryant Mayes last night?" he asked.

"Yeah, of course. I was standing there talking to Zack Alexander, Whitney's lawyer, when he started the ruckus."

"You'd seen him before?"

"I guess. During Whitney's trial. On television. Yeah. I have the impression I'd seen him then."

"But not at the golf course. Or around there, yesterday?" Bucky asked.

I'd thought about that as soon as Bucky called today. Could Mayes have been on the golf course? All I could remem-

ber of the golfers was that they wore bright-colored sweaters, and it seemed as though they wore caps, too.

"No," I said.

I had questions for the cops too. "What happened to the other people on that trash crew? Where were they yesterday afternoon?"

Deavers looked for guidance to Mackey, who nodded slightly.

"Gone," Bucky said. "The deputy in charge said he had six people in his crew on that part of the golf course. The driver, another deputy, and six more crew members were up Brown's Mill about a mile. The plan was for everybody to meet back in the middle and the van would pick them up at two o'clock."

"And?" I said expectantly.

"Screw-ups," Bucky said. "They were late leaving the parole office because some of the crew members reported late, and there was some problem with the van, so they didn't even get out there until around eleven."

"Whitney was due at her lawyer's office at four," I pointed out.

"Well, since it's part of their sentence, workers don't get to decide when it's quitting time," Bucky said. "Like I said, it was four o'clock before they picked everybody up."

"And nobody missed Whitney and the other guy—what was his name?"

"Shawan Taylor," Mackey said. "Like Deavers said, it was one giant fuck-up out there."

"They'd had an incident," Bucky said. "One of the crew members found a half-empty bottle of rotgut wine in a ditch, picked it up, and took a big swig. The glass was chipped, it cut his mouth, and he was bleeding all over the place. He saw his own blood and went nuts, and when the others saw it, they went nuts too, and then the deputy fell apart."

"Fuckin' sheriff's office," Bucky said bitterly. "The deputy wouldn't touch him. Afraid of AIDS. At the end of the afternoon, they just loaded everybody on the van. The hell with procedure, counting heads, any of that."

"Maybe one of the other crew members saw a pickup truck," I offered.

"They'll make great witnesses," Mackey said dryly. "Bad check artists, public drunks, shoplifters. We're talking to them."

"You guys are really going to charge Bryant Mayes with murder?" I asked. "You lookin' for a riot?"

"The rifle looks good," Deavers insisted.

I saw Mackey give him a warning look.

"Bryant Mayes could have taken a potshot at Whitney any time he wanted to," I pointed out. "What's he get out of this now? Vengeance? And how'd he know where Whitney would be working yesterday? Has he got an alibi?"

"Says he was over at Piedmont Park, riding around in the truck," Bucky said. "The wife said he does that all the time, like he's looking for his little girl."

Mackey got up and went to the door. He held it open for me.

"What about Carson Dobbs?" I asked. "Where was he?"

"With a patient," Deavers said.

"We'll call you," Mackey said, practically closing the door in my face.

The crowd had swelled by the time I got back out front. It was an odd mix: a group of elderly and middle-aged black ladies who were obviously there with Janie Mayes, firefighters, and a ragged assortment of college students from the nearby Georgia State University campus and street people who'd wandered up to check out the action.

I stopped on the sidewalk to watch. An earnest-faced

young "community affairs" officer was trying to speak calmly to the reporters, but the crowd was restless.

"Persecution!" an elderly lady in a flowered hat yelled. "Persecution, persecution. They goin' after Bryant Mayes 'cause he's black and he's poor!" she hollered.

"Uh-huh," a group of church ladies echoed in unison. "That's right."

"Police conspiracy!" somebody yelled. I could have sworn it was one of the street guys. "White conspiracy!"

That was enough for me. I hurried to my car and got in.

Zack Alexander and Alison Dobbs hadn't waited for me. They were staring intently at a tape running in the VCR. The picture was grainy, but the images were identifiable if you knew what you were looking at. Right now it was Carson Dobbs, shirttail out, no tie, in his stocking feet. He sat in a recliner, talking to someone out of the camera's range. He had receding sandy-colored hair, dark eyes, and a big hole in his left sock.

The living room looked like one of those settings they have in furniture stores: nondescript sofa, two armchairs, a big framed landscape behind the sofa, two end tables, and a coffee table. The furniture was centered around a small television that sat on a card table. Suzanne Shaddeau walked past the camera and sat down beside Dobbs. Alison sucked in her breath.

The daughter was attractive, like her mother, but like a lot of college girls, she'd decided that makeup and hair spray were passé. Her face was pale, she had dark circles beneath her eyes, and her mouse-colored hair hung uncombed, below her shoulders. She wore an ankle-length flowered dress and heavy black lace-up shoes.

"She's pretty, huh?" Alison said, gesturing toward her father's girlfriend.

"Not as pretty as your mother," Zack said.

They watched the tape for another minute, while the camera inexpertly panned around the room, showing the furniture, the blank walls, the happy couple. Then the wobbly camera moved down a narrow hallway and into a bedroom. There was a dresser, an unmade bed, and two nightstands. The closet door was ajar, showing a half dozen garments on hangers, two pairs of shoes. There was more footage of the hallway, then we were in a bathroom. An age-spotted hand opened a medicine cabinet, showing empty shelves inside. Two towels were folded neatly over a metal bar.

Zack Alexander held up the remote control and clicked the tape off. "We've already watched it once," he explained.

"It's not too bad," I offered.

"It's fine."

Alison Dobbs stood up and shook my hand. She must have been right at five feet tall. "Hello," she said.

"I'm Callahan," I said. "I'm sorry about your mother."

"Zack told me about you," she said, sitting back down, crossing her feet at her ankles. She cocked her head to one side and looked at me. "You're going to help us?"

"Alison believes her father had something to do with Whitney's death," Zack said.

"He hated Mom," Alison said bitterly. Her hands clutched the arms of her chair. "After he left, he didn't want us to have anything. They fought all the time about money. It was like, all of a sudden, Mom and I were the enemy, trying to steal from him."

"Carson told Alison she'd have to leave school," Zack added. "In the middle of her semester."

"Public school was good enough for him, it would have to be good enough for me," Alison said. "He told me that!"

I looked down at my hands. My cuticles were a mess. I picked at a thread of skin by my thumbnail. "The police are

probably going to arrest Bryant Mayes," I told them. "He had a gun in his truck, like the one Whitney was killed with."

"Who told you that?" Zack asked, clearly taken off guard.

"I was with the police. That's why I was late," I explained. "Lloyd Mackey wanted to talk to me again, go over my statement. They're running tests on the rifle. If they arrest Bryant Mayes, it'll be a hell of a mess. It's already on the news. His family's already claiming it's a white conspiracy."

"Bryant Mayes?" Alison said, puzzled. "The little girl's father?"

"Yes," Zack said. "Both the parents had been harassing your mother since the trial. She didn't tell you?"

"Nothing," Alison said. "Mom didn't want to worry me while I was at school. I think she felt guilty about everything that had happened. She said everything was great."

"Have you spoken at all with your father?" I asked.

Her faced flushed. "He asked me to come by his new apartment, right before I left for school in September. To pick up my tuition check. It was a trick, to get me to meet *her*."

"Suzanne?"

"She walked in the room and started to say something. I turned around and left," Alison said. "He yelled at me. Said he wouldn't give me a dime if I couldn't accept the most important person in his life."

Tactful guy, Carson Dobbs.

"If Bryant Mayes did it, my dad put him up to it," Alison blurted out. "My dad did it."

"The police have just started their investigation," I said. "Why don't we just sit back and see what they find? I know the lead investigator. Bucky Deavers. He's good. Smart. Very thorough. He wouldn't talk much in front of his captain today, but if they're planning to arrest Mayes, they must have some real evidence to link him to Whitney."

Alison bounced up out of her chair. "That means my dad will get away with it," she cried. "He's rich, and he's white, and he's a doctor. He's smart too. If we leave it up to the police, they'll never catch him."

Zack hurried over to her and put an arm around her. She buried her face in his swell sport coat and sobbed. Zack's eyes drooped at the corners and the ends of his mustache seemed to reach clear to his chin.

"Never mind, honey," he soothed. "Never mind."

With one hand he rifled his pants pockets for something. He came up with a set of car keys. He looked at me over his client's head.

"I'm going to have Myra take Alison back to the house. There's a memorial service tomorrow, and Alison wants to call some people."

As she walked toward the door, hanging on to Zack's arm, Alison stopped and turned around. Her face was tear-streaked and swollen. She started to say something, shook her head, and walked out.

Five minutes later he was back.

"Was that show for real?" I wanted to know.

He raised an eyebrow. "The first thing she said when I called her last night? Told her her Mama had been killed? 'My dad did this,' that's what she told me."

"I don't know," I said, shaking my head. "It was a divorce, for Christ's sake. And he's a doctor. You really think he engineered all this? Put Bryant Mayes up to killing Whitney? Over a divorce settlement?

He sat down, not behind his desk, but in an armchair close to mine. "When you do divorce work, Garrity, you see people at their very worst."

He stroked the mustache. "I had a client once, when I first went into solo practice. The divorce was over and done with.

Substantial assets to be divided because she helped him run a very successful family business. And my client's ex hated writing that alimony check every month. By God, he hated it. One day, I get a call from the FBI. They have me bring my client downtown, put us in a little room, and they show us a surveillance video. My client's ex hired a guy he met at a gas station to stab his ex-wife to death. For four hundred bucks. And the gas station guy had to supply the knife."

"Jesus."

"That's what my client said," Zack said. "The FBI agent had her climb inside the trunk of her car, they had a makeup artist put fake blood all over her, the knife stuck in her ribs, so the hired killer could take a picture to prove what he'd done."

I made a mental note to myself not to piss anybody off so bad they'd have me killed for four hundred bucks. I'd been inside the trunk of a car not so long ago. It's not an experience I'd recommend.

"I meant what I told Alison about letting the police handle this," I told Zack. "It's pointless to have me trying to investigate Whitney's death. I don't have the experience or the resources the cops have."

"You already proved Dobbs was hiding assets," Zack said. "Just keep doing what you were doing."

"What's the point?" I argued. "As far as Carson Dobbs knew, he'd gotten away with screwing Whitney. The hearing was coming up, he thought he had his ducks all in a row. Why go to all that trouble to kill her? Why put himself at risk?"

Alexander shook his head. "Carson knew Whitney. She could be stubborn. He knew she wouldn't give up if she thought he was hiding something. And there's something else you don't understand, because you haven't met the man."

"What's that?"

"The trial? The press coverage, all that? If Dobbs was

pissed before Faneeta Mayes was run down, he was enraged afterward. He took it personally. Thought Whitney had done it to get attention. To make him look bad. That's how this guy's mind works."

"I'm not going to be able to prove Carson Dobbs did this," I insisted. "I'm not a cop, Zack. And if I do find anything, I'll have to hand it over to the cops, and get out of the way."

"Fine," Zack said. "What's the plan?"

"And I'm still charging you double."

14

THE PLAN WAS, I had no plan.

We turned on the television to catch the news of Bryant Mayes's non-arrest. It was like a replay of the publicity surrounding Whitney's trial, only now Whitney was dead too. The television cameras showed the crowd milling around outside the police station, and then Bryant Mayes, emerging through the front doors, head ducked. Cheers arose.

Mayes's attorney thrust an arm around Mayes, and gave some rambling speech about his client being innocent of everything and anything. The attorney was white, tall, and gangly, with strawberry blonde hair parted severely down the middle and a lantern jaw.

"Fred Grossbart?" Zack leaned forward to get a better look.

I'd never heard the name before. "Who's he?"

"Grossbart?" Zack snorted. "He's a well-known ticket fixer. What the hell is he doing representing somebody looking at a homicide rap?"

After Grossbart hustled Bryant Mayes off in a white stretch limo, Lloyd Mackey came out. Mackey stood on the steps tight-lipped, his gray felt hat tipped low over his eyes. Bucky stood beside him, staring down at his shoes.

"Mr. Mayes was charged with assault on an officer, public drunkenness, and resisting arrest," Mackey said. "He was booked and released pending a court date."

"What about the Whitney Dobbs murder?" one of the reporters called, shoving another microphone in Mackey's face. "Will Mayes be charged with murder?"

"The police gonna lock up another innocent black man?" someone in the back called out.

"Our investigation into the slayings of Whitney Dobbs and Shawan Taylor are continuing," Mackey said. "We're looking for any witnesses who might have seen something unusual at the Brown's Mill Golf Course yesterday afternoon. All information will be kept confidential." He gave a police department hot-line number, then turned on his heel and went back inside the police headquarters building.

The news did a recap of Whitney's killing, showing footage of her taken after the Faneeta Mayes trial and a live shot taken at the golf course. They even showed tape of work crews picking up roadside trash.

Zack Alexander was scribbling notes in a leather-bound booklet.

"Can you get me a list of the other people who were working on that trash crew?" I asked.

He nodded without looking up. "Whitney's parole officer called today, to offer condolences. Name's Colleen Danaher. Young. She's a decent type. If I ask, I think she'll get it for me."

The combination of Shawan Taylor and Whitney Dobbs was nagging at me. "It'd be interesting to know how they pick people for which work crews," I said.

"Probably random," Zack said. "I'll see if Colleen knows."

"Can I see the rest of the video the girls shot?" I asked.

He popped the tape back in the VCR and this time we watched it together, all the way to the last shaky shot of an empty refrigerator.

"They're definitely not staying there full-time," I said when the screen went gray again.

"No."

I walked over to Alexander's desk, picked up the remote control, backed the tape up again to the first clear shot of Suzanne Shaddeau, and froze it.

Her face was half turned away from the camera, but her left hand was extended, offering a drink. Grainy or not, I could see she was wearing a handsome diamond solitaire on her ring finger.

"Nice engagement present," I said.

Zack squinted. "I didn't notice."

"You're not a woman," I said. "That thing looks like a couple carats at least."

He went back to writing in his notebook. "We'll check on it. See whose assets were used to buy that little bauble." I kept staring at the ring, thinking back to Alison's expression when she got a look at Suzanne.

"We need to find somebody who works in that medical office," I said. "Somebody who liked Whitney maybe, or even better, dislikes Suzanne. If she's working in a doctor's office, flashing that ring around, chances are she's stirred up some jealousy."

He nodded. "Whitney talked to one of the nurses occasionally. That's how she found out Suzanne was pregnant." He rubbed his forehead, as though the doing would bring forth a name.

"Carol maybe," he said. "I remember the woman had been with Carson for years."

"Maybe Alison would know," I suggested. "You mentioned a memorial service. Is it a big deal?"

He shrugged. "It's at the Botanical Garden. Whitney wasn't religious. Old friends, neighbors. Alison made the list and Myra made most of the calls this morning."

"Much family?"

"Almost none. Whitney was an only child. Her mother died when Alison was just a baby. There's a father and step-mother, but they live out in Arizona, and they're not well enough to travel."

"Dobbs won't come?"

"We didn't invite him," Zack said. "Alison is supposed to meet him for coffee in the morning."

"Would she mind if I showed up at the memorial service?"

He seemed surprised at the idea. "You're serious?"

"I'd be the soul of discretion," I assured him. "I'll stand with you, you can tell me which people I should talk to. I'll even wear a dress."

He looked me up and down, noncommittally, like Exhibit A in a boring civil trial. "You should wear a dress," he said evenly. "You've got great legs."

15

THE OLD GRAY PONTIAC parked out front of the house had a stuffed dog sitting in the rear window. I went in through the front door. A glance into the den confirmed my fears. Two brown paper sacks full of clothes were sitting on the sofa bed, along with a bright pink train case.

Neva Jean was in the kitchen, rattling dishes. Edna was setting the table and coughing.

"Mom?"

She looked up at me and frowned.

"When did the coughing start again? Have you taken your medicine?"

She coughed and nodded her head.

"I'm fine," she gasped. "Neva Jean put red pepper all over the salad, that's all. I got a big snootful."

"I thought it was paprika," Neva Jean said, shamefaced. "I'm awful sorry."

I waited until we'd finished the salad to ask the obvious.

"You spending the night tonight?" I asked her.

Neva Jean rubbed at her eyes and gave an exaggerated sniffle. "Edna said it would be all right. Until Swannelle comes to his senses and gets rid of them emus. I'm awful allergic to 'em, Callahan. And he says they're expensive. He can't sell 'em until they've laid some eggs and he can get his investment back."

I sighed. "How long will that be?"

"They're supposed to be in season right now. Swannelle, he runs home from the shop every few hours to see if anything's happened. But so far, no eggs. It's kind of cute, really."

"Except that you can't live in your own home," I pointed out.

"Just until they lay some eggs," Neva Jean said. "We can sell 'em for five hundred dollars apiece. Ain't that something?"

The old cliché about not counting your chickens before they were hatched occurred to me. But if the truth were to be told, I'd much rather have Neva Jean in the house than Maureen and Steve. She would never have dared to try to appropriate my bed. Besides, I knew Swannelle was a creature of habit, and his habits mostly revolved around having Neva Jean wait on him hand and foot. It wouldn't take him long before he found a way to talk his bride into moving back home.

"How'd your meeting go with that lawyer?" Edna asked. "Did he like the girls' tape?"

"He liked it fine," I said. "I guess you saw the news?"

She started to sputter. "Police conspiracy! I never heard such a load of bull in my life. Where do these people get these ideas?"

I speared a mushroom with the end of my fork. "Haven't we already been over all this before?"

"Well, Jackie's sure enough got a bee in her bonnet about the whole thing," Neva Jean reported. "She's still pissed off at you 'cause you were working for Whitney Dobbs."

I put my fork down.

"Is she serious? Jackie's mad at me? For agreeing to help Whitney prove her husband was trying to cheat her in a divorce settlement?"

"She told Baby and Sister they oughtta be ashamed of themselves, working for Whitney Dobbs," Neva Jean said, still chewing on a bite of the lasagna.

"She did what?" I could hear my voice getting shrill.

"Jackie says Whitney Dobbs was a racist bitch, and now the police have a conspiracy to get back at that little dead girl's family by framing the daddy for killing Whitney," Neva Jean said.

"Black, white, who cares?" Edna said, scowling. "All this rioting and ranting. Why aren't those preachers I saw on television today out feeding the poor or preaching the gospel instead of standing on the police station steps shooting their mouths off about a white conspiracy and getting everybody all stirred up?" she demanded. "Whatever happened to love thy neighbor? Doesn't anybody believe in that anymore?"

"This is the nineties, Ma," I said, dipping a hunk of garlic bread in the tomato sauce on my plate. "It's called paranoia. And it cuts both ways."

"Jackie says the police and the white power structure won't be happy until they lock up every black man in Atlanta under the age of thirty," Neva Jean said.

"What white power structure?" I asked. "Atlanta has a black mayor, a majority black city council. Fulton County has the first black woman sheriff in the country. And the Atlanta Police Department has a black female chief of police. Are all of them working together to frame poor old Bryant Mayes?"

"Don't be yelling at me," Neva Jean said, reaching for the lasagna pan. "I'm just telling you what Jackie said, that's all."

I took a deep breath. "I've got nothing to do with Bryant

Mayes's arrest. And if Jackie's got a problem with how I run my business, she needs to discuss that with me. Race has never been an issue around here. She knows that. Hell, I didn't even want to work for Whitney Dobbs. I only took the job because we need some extra income."

The more I thought about Jackie's criticism, the more it stung. She was the youngest of the girls, in her early thirties, single, hardworking, smart, and ambitious. She'd taken night-school classes to be a paralegal, but she'd readily admitted that she'd never make as much working at a law office as she could as a House Mouse.

"Jackie'll be all right," Edna said, trying to calm me down. "She's young. Got a lot of pride. That's good. It sticks in her craw that people think of her as a cleaning lady. You know, a domestic."

"Well, shoot," Neva Jean said. "That's what we are. All of us. Don't bother me none. Just give me my paycheck at the end of the week and don't expect me to empty no cat boxes. That's what I say."

I pushed away from the table, took my half-full plate, and scraped it into the trash.

"Now what?" Edna asked. "We're not through with dinner here, Miss Julia Callahan Garrity."

"Sorry, Ma," I said. "The lasagna was great. I've got a lot on my mind. I've got this huge folder to read, financial stuff. You guys have dessert without me."

16

WHITNEY DOBBS'S MEMORIAL SERVICE was memorable. You could say that. Sunlight teased the shadows on the small brick-paved courtyard at the Botanical Garden. A string quartet—three women and a man, all dressed in black turtleneck sweaters and trousers—played something sedate and classical. A skirted table was set up off to one side. There was a silver urn of coffee, trays of dried-out-looking cookies and little sandwiches, and a platter of fruit and cheese. Waiters in white shirts and black bow ties and cummerbunds passed silently among us, offering white and red wine. Two large electric heaters stood tastefully in opposite corners, warming the courtyard quietly and efficiently.

There were maybe fifty or so people, mostly women, with a few business-suited men sprinkled around for variety. People milled about, chatting in hushed tones among the potted palms and chrysanthemums.

Alison Dobbs drifted around the courtyard, a butterfly,

resting only long enough to be air-kissed or hugged lightly but fondly.

"I had to pay admission to get in here," I told Zack. "I never had to pay admission to a funeral before."

"It's a memorial service, not a funeral," he pointed out. "You'll be reimbursed."

"Six bucks. Plus four fifty for the panty hose."

He gave me a quick, appraising glance.

I'd dressed for the occasion: a simple burgundy velour dress with gold buttons and tiny gold earrings. And I had new shoes too, heels. I'd paid full price, 140 dollars, and still they pinched my toes.

"Not bad," he said grudgingly.

"I should charge you for the shoes too," I said, sniffling. "I lost my good pair the night I found Whitney."

"We'll need a receipt for the shoes," he said, handing me a handkerchief. "You catching a cold?"

The handkerchief was real linen, monogrammed. I dabbed at my runny nose with it. "Maybe just a tiny one. I made some phone calls last night," I told Zack. "My friend Bucky is being unusually closemouthed. I did get him to admit they've been checking up on Bryant Mayes. So far, Dr. Dobbs is in the clear."

Zack thought it over. "Not for long. I know divorce work, Callahan. This is a domestic murder. The stakes are higher than what the cops are used to, but believe me, Dobbs is behind it."

I wasn't persuaded yet. "Bucky says Mayes was pretty much living at the firehouse, even though it's against the regulations. In between times, I think his buddies took turns looking after him. He and the wife have been unofficially separated since the kid was killed."

"She's leading a march on City Hall, screaming about police conspiracy," Zack said. "Some estrangement."

"Bucky says that's for the benefit of the media," I told him. "When they brought her down for questioning the night Whitney was killed, she admitted she didn't know where Bryant had been sleeping the last couple of months. He'd come home every few days, give her his paycheck, pick up some clean clothes, and leave."

"She was with him the night of Whitney's murder," Zack said. "We both saw them there."

"Janie Mayes heard about it on the news. Bryant called right after that. One of his buddies got it off the scanner. So he came by the house and picked her up before they headed down to the Southside to gloat over Whitney Dobbs's corpse."

I glanced around at Whitney's friends. People were somber, but dry-eyed.

"When does the memorializing start?" I asked. My feet really did hurt.

"This is it," Zack said. "Alison wanted something, uh, unstructured."

"Like a cocktail party for the dead," I observed. "Only not so much fun. You see anybody I should talk to?"

"Let me ask Alison," he said, gliding away.

I sipped my wine and lifted one foot discreetly out of my shoe. I swear, I could hear my toes thanking me.

That's what I was doing, wiggling my toes, sipping my chardonnay, minding my own business, when the pâté hit the humidifier.

"What's *she* doing here?" I heard a woman hiss.

Conversation stopped. Heads turned, a choreography of shock and disbelief.

Carson Dobbs and Suzanne Shaddeau stood beside a large topiary swan, holding hands. Carson was dressed in protective coloration: dove-gray suit, off-white shirt, forgettable necktie. Suzanne, on the other hand, was dressed to kill. Her dress was

black, short, and tight, modestly high-necked, but the fabric clung to her lithe dancer's body like a glove. Her black suede heels left her towering two inches taller than Carson. It looked like what a high-class hooker wears to her pimp's funeral.

After everybody got a good look at the brazen hussy they naturally started searching for Alison Dobbs, the wronged woman's daughter.

It didn't take long. She was having a heart-to-heart with a tiny white-haired dowager type when Zack slid up and whispered something in her ear.

Alison looked up and spotted Carson and Suzanne.

Suzanne gave a small wiggly-fingered wave.

I put my foot back in my shoe and downed the rest of my wine. Now maybe things would get interesting.

Alison steamed toward the newcomers, towing Zack in her wake.

Carson smiled tenderly at his daughter and leaned down to give her a kiss on the cheek.

"What are you doing here?" Alison said shrilly. "What's *she* doing here?"

"It's a memorial service, Alison," Suzanne said. "We both cared very deeply for your mother. You're not the only one to grieve, you know."

"I want you out!" Alison said, her face flushing.

Suzanne's full lips twisted in a half smile. "That's not for you to decide."

"Ali," Carson said, putting a protective arm around Suzanne. "We've come to pay our respects to Whitney." He lowered his voice. "You're making a scene. It would embarrass your mother."

"You killed her!" Alison said. "Don't you stand there and talk about embarrassing her. You killed her. The two of you."

"Alison!" Carson said sharply. "Stop that right now. Do you hear me, young lady? I won't have you talking that way. I'm your father. You're just upset. Now. I want you to walk over here, and we'll talk quietly and calmly. There are a lot of things we need to take care of."

Alison backed away a little. "I'm not talking to you," I heard her say. "Murderer."

Suzanne's hand whipped out so quickly, the slap was so lightning fast, it was a blur. Maybe we all imagined it. But no, I didn't imagine the sick sound of the palm of Suzanne's hand meeting the soft flesh of Alison's cheek.

Zack Alexander caught Alison as she instinctively raised her hand to strike back.

"Enough," he said calmly. "That's enough."

Suzanne turned and stalked out of the courtyard. Carson Dobbs seemed rooted to the spot, his backbone ramrod straight, a muscle in his forehead twitching in rage.

"You've poisoned her against me," he said to Zack. "My own daughter."

"You'd better go, Dr. Dobbs," Zack said. "People are staring."

They were staring, too. All those well-bred country-club types were gawking and gaping at Carson Dobbs like a two-headed calf in a carnival sideshow.

He walked off slowly and deliberately, nodding stiffly in acknowledgment to an older man's greeting, but not bothering to meet the outstretched hand with his own.

"Cripes!" The woman next to me picked up a glass of red wine from a tray abandoned by a waiter. She took a long slug and smacked her lips in enjoyment. "I'll say one thing for Suzanne. She knows how to make an entrance and an exit."

"You know her?"

The woman was wearing a nicely cut black suit. She was

short and slender, with graying brown hair that she wore clipped behind her ears with a black velvet bow.

"We work together," the woman said. "At Carson's office. Or we did work together. I've quit my job there."

"Were you friends with Whitney?" I asked. Zack and Alison had headed off toward the conservatory, Alison sobbing her heart out. It was too late for polite introductions. I'd have to make my own.

I stuck my hand out. "I'm Callahan Garrity. I'm a private detective. I'm working on behalf of Alison. Would it bother you if I asked you some questions? About Suzanne and Carson?"

"I'm Carol Steiner. I'm a nurse. And no, I'd be delighted to answer your questions."

Just the lady I'd been looking for.

"What do you want to know?" Carol asked. "I've already given Carson my notice, so it's not like I owe him anything. He knows how I felt about Whitney, he didn't even try to talk me out of leaving."

"Uh, well." I glanced around to be sure we wouldn't be overheard. I needn't have bothered. Half the guests had hurried away after the catfight, the others were gossiping their hearts out about what they'd just witnessed.

"The divorce was never finalized. Were you aware that Whitney thought Dr. Dobbs was hiding assets? That's still an issue. We need to know how he and Suzanne Shaddeau were living. Did it appear that they were strapped for cash? And I'd also like to know more about the financial manager, the one Dr. Dobbs claims bilked him and skipped town."

"Ben Dwyer," Carol said. "It's always the quiet ones, isn't it?"

"Did you know him well?" I asked. "How believable is it to you that he could rip off Carson?"

She chewed her lip until only pink grains of lipstick were left.

"I didn't know him well. He kept to himself, shut up in that office with his file folders and his printouts. He was bright enough to pull it off. You know the kind—so smart they're scary?"

I nodded. "Did it surprise you when Dr. Dobbs fired him and announced the practice was practically broke?"

She shrugged. "It surprised us Ben got fired. But Carson never did announce it. Suzanne just told one of the clerks one day to clean out Ben's office. That's how we found out he was gone. As for finances, who knows? I'm an R.N., not an accountant. I know I got paid. There was a problem with the insurance billings, I can tell you that."

"What kind of problem?"

"The insurance billings were definitely messed up. All the patients complained about it, and Ben was constantly tagging after Carson, telling him there was a problem. Carson kept blaming it on the new computer system.

"Which," she said mockingly, "was Suzanne's little baby. That was her job, programming that computer. Big deal."

"Did anybody in the office socialize with Dwyer?" I asked. "Anybody have any contact with him since he left?"

She shook her head no to both questions.

"Any idea where he lived?" According to the files Zack had given me, Carson Dobbs claimed a post office box was the only address he had for Dwyer in the office personnel records.

"He lived in one of those furnished executive suites," Carol said. "It was someplace in midtown, I think. Oaks something."

"Cumberland Oaks?" I asked hopefully.

"Maybe. But nobody has heard from him. Whitney asked me to ask around, and I did. One minute his stuff was in that

office, the next minute the place was empty." She laughed. "Suzanne waited about five minutes before she commandeered it for herself. I guess that's one of the perks of being the boss's fiancée. A private office."

"So you're not exactly a fan of Suzanne's," I ventured.

"Sneaky, conniving bitch. Suzanne doesn't have a lot of fans at the office. Unless you count Carson, the big doofus."

"Tell me about Suzanne. What's she like?"

"She's a schemer," Carol said. "Whatever she says, there's always an agenda behind it. She knew Carson and Whitney were having a rough time. And she moved in on him like a shark to a minnow. He never had a chance."

"So she's ruthless and she likes other women's husbands," I said. "Tell me something new. Lifestyle, hobbies, friends, whatever."

"Three things she cares about," Carol continued. "Herself, her animals, and Carson. In that order. I never heard her talk about friends, or family, for that matter."

"What kind of animals?" I asked.

"Horses and dogs. She raises some kind of fancy show horses. She talked about them constantly."

"Really?" There hadn't been any dogs at the condo when Baby and Sister had visited. "Where'd she keep the horses?" I asked.

"I never paid any attention to that stuff," Carol said. "I never really liked her even before she and Carson hooked up. I remember, though, one of her horses got really sick this fall. Suzanne was in a state about it. She took off a whole week from work. The horse had surgery, I remember. Suzanne went on and on about how worried she was about it."

Horses were an expensive hobby. My old boyfriend Mac rented a house on a horse farm in North Fulton, and he used to marvel at the money and attention his landlord lavished on his animals.

"Did Suzanne ever talk about where she and Carson were living?" I asked hopefully.

"Some condo, is all I know," Carol said. "Alison went there once."

"But nobody from the office has ever been invited over there?"

She laughed. "To socialize with Dr. Warmth? Maybe the doctors have, but I doubt it. The only socializing Carson ever did was when he was still with Whitney. She was the people person, not him."

Another woman, in her late fifties, with white hair worn in a tight French twist, walked up. "Carol?" She stood a little way from us, not wanting to interrupt.

"Oh, that's my ride," Carol said. "I'd better go."

I gave her my business card, and she and her friend drifted away down the garden path, away from me and all my questions.

17

WHEN I GOT BACK TO THE FESTIVITIES, Zack and Alison were huddled together on a bench in the conservatory. Probably plotting an assault and battery charge against Suzanne. The place had thinned out considerably. The string quartet was packing up and the only food left was the carrot curls and radish roses. I gulped down another glass of white wine and glanced over at Alison and Zack. They were oblivious to everything.

I could stand around here and get pie-eyed on cheap white wine—or go home and take off the tight shoes and dress and get comfortable.

At home, Edna was sitting at the kitchen table, scribbling notes in the schedule book. She had an unreasonably smug look on her face.

"You seem pleased with yourself," I said, after changing into my real working attire of jeans and a sweatshirt.

"I am," she said. "I've got a doctor's appointment tomorrow. And I can't wait."

"Good," I said, opening the refrigerator to look for some sustenance. "Jeanne should be pleased with your progress on the no smoking thing."

"I'm not seeing Jeanne."

I'd found the pan of leftover lasagna. I considered heating it up, putting it on a plate, and sitting down to eat properly. But it wasn't that kind of a day. So I got a fork and ate it out of the pan, by the light of the refrigerator.

"Who are you seeing?" I asked.

"Carson Dobbs. What do you think about that?"

I paused in midbite. "Really? Who set that up?"

She took the pan out of my hands, cut a slice of the casserole and put it on a plate. Then she re-covered the dish and put it away.

"Jeanne. She called a little while ago. She said you'd asked her to do it. And you know Jeanne." Edna was so pleased with herself she was humming. "I can't wait. Where's that pocketbook with the video camera? I want to start practicing."

"Whoa." I put the fork down. "No, no, no. No video camera. That's not what I need from you."

"Well, it's what I want to do," she said, as though that settled it.

"Too bad," I said. "We just need you to look around the office. See how it's set up. And make sure you pay with a check. Tell them you don't have any insurance."

"A check?" Her eyes bugged. "Do you know how much it'll cost? Five hundred bucks, minimum."

"Tell the clerk you don't have insurance," I repeated. "You just want the doctor to listen to your chest. Maybe take your blood pressure. Like a second opinion. And don't worry about the cost. Zack is going to reimburse us. Just make sure you write a check. Got it?"

"That's it?"

"It's really important, Ma," I assured her. "We want to see where he deposits that check of yours."

She raised an eyebrow. "You think he's keeping two sets of books? Hell, you should have said something. I know lots of those tricks."

"What?" I said, horrified. "Don't tell me that. You know how I feel about screwing around with the IRS, Ma."

"Relax," she said. "I never cooked any of our House Mouse books. But when I first went to work for Frank at the beauty shop, his old receptionist had been doing it for years. I told Frank, 'No way. I'm not going to prison for you.'"

"You never told me that," I said. "What kinds of things was he doing?"

"Nothing too fancy," she said, opening up one of our own account books. "The majority of our customers liked to pay in cash. Most of that never went on the books. And of course, the girls only paid taxes on maybe ten percent of their tips. Then, Frank had certain vendors, they were only too happy to supply monthly invoices for supplies and services we never got."

She had me thinking now. "Zack believes Carson Dobbs has been siphoning money out of the practice for at least a couple of years. Planning this, ever since he left Whitney. Zack had another P.I. doing some preliminary work on it, but Whitney never liked the guy. That's why she insisted on bringing me in. And one of Dobbs's nurses says there was something wrong with the insurance billings. Which are handled by the new girlfriend, Suzanne."

I opened the file folder Zack had given me, leafing through the pages, looking to see if there were any reports or documents I'd missed on my initial read-through. All I found was a business card, stapled on the back of the folder. Doyle Bollinger was the guy's name.

I dialed the number. A machine picked up on the first ring. "This is Bollinger. Leave a number."

I left a message saying that I was working for Whitney Dobbs's family and wanted to talk to him about his work on the case.

Edna had our schedule book out, erasing and marking through entries, trying to balance our clients' demands with our supply of mice. She looked up at me.

"Oh," she said suddenly. "I forgot."

She pulled a long white business envelope out of the schedule book. "This came for you this morning. A courier service delivered it."

The envelope was unopened. I looked over at Edna. "You feeling all right?"

"I was busy," she said tartly. "Besides, you make it sound like I go around opening your mail all the time."

"Only the good stuff," I said, slitting the envelope. There was a single piece of paper inside. It was a computer print-out of six names. All had addresses, only three had phone numbers. Somebody had made handwritten notes by each of the names.

"What is it?" Edna asked, leaning across the table to get a look.

"There's no note, but I'm pretty sure it's a list of the other people who were on that public works crew with Whitney the day she was shot," I said. "Zack asked Whitney's parole officer, a woman named Colleen Danaher, to get it for me."

The list reminded me of something else. "Ma? Can you make a call for me?"

She put her pencil down. "What?"

"Call Reg Vaughn. He's the manager over at Cumberland Oaks. Ask him if he remembers a tenant named Ben Dwyer. He would have left town recently. Dwyer was Carson Dobbs's

financial manager. If Dwyer did live there, I'm going to want to talk to Vaughn. Holler at me, okay? I'm gonna use the phone in my room to try and track down the people on this list."

I put the phone on my bed, got out my yellow legal pad, and took a look at the list again.

The first name was Annie Lou Axley. The address was in Decatur. The handwritten note said Annie Lou had drawn a sentence for driving under the influence. "Chronic offender," the note said.

"Who's this?" The kid who answered the phone was a teenager with extremely poor interpersonal skills.

"Could I speak to Ms. Axley?" I repeated politely. "This is Miss Garrity with the Miller Brewing Company. We're test-marketing a new brand of beer in Atlanta and need qualified tasters . . ."

"Mama!" the kid shouted. "This lady on the phone wants to give us free beer."

Annie Lou was interested. "You say you giving away beer?"

"I might," I said cautiously. "If you can give me some information."

"About what?" she demanded. "Who'd you say this is?"

Annie Lou's son had obviously learned his telephone skills at his mama's knee.

"I'm a private investigator. I'm interested in talking to you about Whitney Dobbs's murder. If you can give me any information at all, I'd be happy to pay for your time. Maybe we could meet?"

"Shiiit," she said, disgusted. "I didn't see nothing. Told the cops that. Free beer, my ass."

The next name on the list was Harold Eaves. The address was puzzling, Trinity Street, which was downtown, near the

state capitol. Not a typical residential neighborhood. But the note explained it all. Mr. Eaves had been convicted of petty theft. And his address was a men's shelter at the Shrine of the Immaculate Conception.

I looked the number up in the phone directory. It was after five. The phone rang, and then I got a recording giving me the time for masses, confessions, and bingo. If I wanted to talk to Harold, I realized, I'd have to go down to the shelter to do so. The trip might be worth it. Maybe he could tell me something about Shawan Taylor, the homeless man who'd been killed alongside Whitney. Tomorrow night, I promised myself.

The next two names had addresses, but no phone numbers. And I couldn't find any listings that matched in the telephone directory. I skipped down to the next-to-last name on the list. William J. Tucker's address was interesting too. It was on Tuxedo Road, an even ritzier address than Whitney's, and within spitting distance of the governor's mansion. There was, oh joy, a phone number. And the note beneath the listing said William J. had been convicted of assault and battery. "Wife beater," the note said tersely.

Yippee, I thought. But I made the call.

A woman answered the phone. There was a long cold silence when I asked for William J.

"He has a new number," she said finally. But she didn't offer to share it.

"It's important that I reach him," I said.

"With Billy, everything's important," she said wearily. Then she gave me the number. "He never answers it," she warned. "He's afraid of bill collectors and lawyers. If it's really all that important, try the hardware store."

She hung up on me too. Maybe I was the one with the telephone etiquette problem.

"What hardware store?" I asked when I called back.

"Please, don't hang up. I really need to talk to your husband."

"Who did you say this was?"

At least she was curious. I decided to try a different angle. The truth. "I'm a private investigator. I'm working for the family of Whitney Dobbs."

"Her." Mrs. Tucker's voice was flat. "I'm sorry about what happened. We didn't know each other, but we had a mutual friend."

"She and I had a mutual friend too," I said. "That's why I took this case."

"What's Billy got to do with it? Were they drinking buddies?" Her laugh was bitter and hurt-sounding.

"He was on the community service work crew, the day Whitney was killed. I need to talk to him, to see if he remembered seeing anything."

She sighed. "I didn't know he was there. Not so surprising, if you know Billy. You know the Paces Crossing Shopping Center? In Vinings? Village Hardware. Try there. He's not allowed to practice law anymore, you know. Disbarred."

"Oh."

"I've got to go," she said. And she hung up on me for the second time that day.

At least I wouldn't have to get dressed up to go looking for Billy Tucker. Jeans and a sweatshirt are the perfect outfit for a hardware store. Even one in Vinings, which is considered the "country" annex to Buckhead. I called the store. The woman who answered said they stayed open until seven P.M.

"Billy?" she said, when I asked. "Yeah, he's probably around here somewhere."

When I walked in the kitchen, Edna was sitting at the table, peeling carrots and watching the news.

"You were right about Ben Dwyer," she said. "I looked in to tell you, but you were talking to somebody. Reg Vaughn

said Dwyer was living there. He moved out in the middle of the month. Left a power bill, and the phone company's been around looking for Dwyer too. Nobody saw him leave. Just, poof, one day they noticed mail was piling up in his box in the lobby."

"No forwarding address?"

"No," Edna said. "But Mr. Vaughn said if you want, you can stop by. He still wants to talk to you about submitting a bid for their cleaning business."

"Great," I said, grabbing the van keys from the table. "I'm going out to Vinings to talk to somebody about Whitney. If I'm not too late, I'll swing by Cumberland Oaks on my way back to town."

She threw down the carrot she was peeling. "No sense in doing any more of these then. Guess I'll just heat myself up some soup."

"What happened to our boarder?" I asked, looking around.

"Swannelle called, all upset, said there's something funny about those emus. Like they're not acting right. He sweet-talked Neva Jean into going out there to take a look at 'em. Sounds like a conjugal visit, if you ask me."

"Well, you can leave the light on for me," I promised. "And don't forget to take your medicine. We don't want Carson Dobbs to decide to do emergency surgery when he sees you tomorrow."

I got to the hardware store at five minutes before seven. A middle-aged man wearing faded overalls and a sweat-stained Georgia Bulldogs cap was loading flats of pansies and ornamental cabbage plants onto a wheelbarrow.

"I'm looking for Billy Tucker," I told him, following him inside the store.

"What for?" he asked, starting to pile the flats on a rack just inside the door.

"It's, uh, personal." I took a look around the store. The shopping center was fairly new and upscale, but somebody had deliberately gone for the dilapidated country general store effect in here. There were smoke-stained exposed wooden beams overhead, galvanized bins of nails and nuts and bolts, even a big cast-iron potbellied stove in the middle of the center aisle, with half a dozen rocking chairs pulled up in a semicircle. Talk about your marketing genius.

"Does Mr. Tucker work here?" I asked the overall man.

He laughed. "Work? I never thought about it like that. Get here at eight, leave at seven. Hell, that's almost a job. Even if I don't get paid."

"Billy Tucker," I said, putting my hand out to shake his. "I'm Callahan Garrity. And I need to talk to you."

He wiped his hands on his overalls and reluctantly took my hand in his. "Looka here," he said. "I'm broke. My wife kicked me out. I don't have a checking account or any credit cards. I'm driving a junker car my oldest son gave me. Lady, there ain't nothing I got that you want."

"I think maybe there is," I told him.

An older man walked deliberately to the front of the store, opened a panel in the wall, and began switching off the lights.

"Hey, Billy," he said loudly. "Let's call it a day." He stood there with a key ring in his hand, obviously waiting to lock up.

"Okay, Ed," Billy said. He walked in a slow loping gait out the door. I followed right behind him. "I'm not a bill collector or a lawyer," I said, grabbing the sleeve of his flannel shirt to get him to stop walking. "I'm trying to find out who killed Whitney Dobbs. You were there. How about I buy you some dinner?"

He shook his head. "I'm not getting mixed up in that mess. Sorry."

I shook his shirtsleeve again. "Come on, Billy," I said, try-
ing not to sound as desperate as I felt. "Dinner, okay? What
could a little dinner hurt? You're broke. I'm buying. Anywhere
you say."

"Aw hell," he muttered. He gestured down at his work
clothes. "My three-piece suits are all at the cleaners."

"Fine," I told him. "I'm not dressed for the Ritz-Carlton
either. I noticed a barbecue place down the road. You like bar-
becue?"

"Toady's," Billy Tucker said. "That'd be all right. They got
a bar. I like to drink. You got a problem with that?"

"Not as long as you let me drive," I said, gesturing toward
my van.

18

IT HAD STARTED RAINING by the time we were on the road. "Take this curve slow," Billy Tucker said, leaning forward in his seat, as though to guide me through it. "Cars coming the other way can't see you until it's too late." It was the first thing he'd said since we left the hardware store.

I kept my eyes on the narrow two-lane road. The barbecue place was on the right in a fake stucco building that looked like it had been a Mexican restaurant in a past life.

We walked into the entryway and Tucker headed immediately to the bar. When he came back, he had a highball glass in one hand and a glass of wine in the other.

He handed me the wine. "They're running a tab at the bar for us. You like wine—right? I never met a woman your age who doesn't."

I nodded and sipped. It was cheap white zinfandel, cloyingly sweet.

The hostess, who wore tight blue jeans and a brass-studded

cowboy shirt, showed us to a table in the dimly lit dining room. The old owners had apparently tossed in some of their decor along with the real estate. The walls were covered in velvet bullfighter pictures and tattered sombreros and serapes, and ancient piñatas swung overhead from exposed pipes.

As soon as we were seated, a waitress appeared. She handed us each a large laminated menu. "The special's all-you-can-eat ribs with baked potato and salad bar for eight ninety-nine. Coffee and tea extra."

Billy jiggled the ice in his now-empty glass. "Bring me another one of these, will you, darlin'? Dewar's and water. And just bring us a couple of ribeyes and some onion rings and the house salad."

"What the hell was that?" I asked, when she was gone. "It's a barbecue place. I wanted barbecue. I'm buying—remember?"

He chewed on a piece of ice, unfazed by my objection.

"Nah, you don't want the barbecue here. Toady's brother bought the place this summer. He can't cook barbecue worth shit. Meat's as dry as sawdust. They do a good steak, though. You'll like it. What did you say your name was again?"

"Callahan. Garrity." I took a sip of the Kool-Aid wine while I deliberated about how to get Tucker to talk to me.

The waitress brought our salads then, and another double scotch and water for Tucker. I waited while he took a couple of good-size belts of his drink, and nibbled at the greens, which were crisp romaine, with a surprisingly decent vinaigrette dressing. Maybe Toady's brother didn't know barbecue, but he'd at least figured out how to make a salad.

"My wife tell you where to find me?" he asked suddenly.

"Yeah," I said. "She did."

"Huh," he said. "Usually she tells people I'm dead or in jail."

"She didn't know you were at the golf course when Whitney Dobbs was killed," I said.

"There's a lot she doesn't know," Tucker said.

"According to the cops, you were part of the same crew Whitney was assigned to."

"I was," he said. "But then the van left. I didn't hear or see nothing." He took another gulp of scotch and speared a lettuce leaf with his fork.

"You saw Whitney earlier, though—and Shawan Taylor too—right?"

"Taylor. That's the black guy?"

"Yes," I said. "Nobody can figure out how the two of them got separated and then left behind."

"Some big screw-up," Tucker said. "Those sheriff's deputies couldn't guard a dime-store gum machine. Half those sons of bitches on the crew never did any work anyway. Malingerers, all of 'em."

He fixed me with a look. "You're not drinking your wine. What's the matter—you don't drink?"

The wine was so sweet it made my teeth hurt. "It's a long way home in this rain," I told him. "I think I'm just going to stick to iced tea."

"Whatever." He polished off his own drink. "My wife tell you what happened?"

"When?"

"You know." He toyed with his salad, poking through the lettuce in search of something more substantial. Finally he found a crouton, which he popped in his mouth.

"Your wife hung up on me," I told Tucker. "Twice. I think she's kind of mad at you."

"Mad. That's a good one. You want to know what happened?" He was slurring his words now. Ready to talk, but not about my favored topic.

"I want to know what happened at the golf course. The day Whitney Dobbs and Shawan Taylor were shot to death.

The murder weapon was a rifle. Somebody must have seen or heard something. The police have a suspect. Did you see a truck that day . . . ?"

"Mayes," Tucker said. "Brian, or something like that. I read the papers, you know. You think the natives will riot if he gets arrested?"

"People are stirred up," I said. "First Faneeta Mayes is killed, then Whitney gets off, then this. It looks like a setup to some people. What about it, Billy? Quit screwing around with me. Did you see anything that afternoon?"

The waitress brought our food before he could answer. The steaks were sizzling on oval metal platters, a small hill of onion rings mounded on the side. The aroma of the meat and the onions nearly made me swoon.

"Could I have some iced tea?" I asked the waitress. Billy jiggled the ice cubes in his empty glass and nodded at her. "Another Dewar's, sugar."

I wanted to stop her and tell her to bring him tea too. He'd had enough scotch to anesthetize a bull elephant. But I didn't.

Tucker attacked his steak, sawing away at the meat as though it were his first meal of the day.

"The golf course, Billy," I reminded him. "Tell me what happened."

"Not much to tell," he said, chewing with gusto. "Hell of a lot of trash down there. Those people have no pride. Just throw shit out the windows. You wouldn't believe the stuff I picked up. That's all that happened. Pick up, bag, stack. The others were a bunch of derelicts. Me and your friend and that big redheaded woman, Annie, I think her name was, we were the only whites out there. Kind of degrading, you know?"

Personally, I thought having wife beating on your permanent personal record was a hell of a lot more degrading than having to pick up trash with petty thieves and public drunks.

"Annie Lou Axley—was she with you?"

He ate some more steak, picked up an onion ring, and sucked it down in one swift motion. "Nah. She was up farther with the other black guys and some big black mama."

"So you were with Whitney and Shawan?"

"I didn't say that. I could see them, but they were down the road, maybe two hundred yards away. That dude stuck to her. From the minute we got on that van downtown. I think he kind of liked the way she looked in those tight little jeans. Cute, like a boy, but sexy, you know?"

The Whitney I was remembering had a hole blown in her chest, the blood mingled with dead leaves and roadside trash. I swallowed hard and took a bite of steak. Maybe I should have felt queasy, but I didn't. The steak was divine. Vegetarianism will never be a way of life for Callahan Garrity, I am sorry to say.

"No one could see Whitney then? Not even the guards? When was the last time you saw the two of them?"

"Wasn't wearing a watch."

A thought occurred to him. "My watch is at the house. A Rolex. If my wife didn't throw it away. She hit me first, you know."

I tried to concentrate on my steak. The last thing I wanted tonight was to hear the gory details of Billy Tucker's combat-packed marriage.

"Diane's a little bitty gal," he said, scarfing down another onion ring. "Ninety pounds soaking wet. You believe she blacked my eye?"

"What did you do to her?" Bad question. Why wasn't I making him stick to business?

He put his fork down, still agitated at the unfairness of life. "We'd both had a couple drinks, okay? She got on me about some business decisions. I've had a really bad, bad year. I told

her to shut the hell up, maybe pushed her, just slightly. Not even a real push. Just put my hand on her chest to get her out of my face. She hauled off and walloped me. So I gave as good as I got. We were out on the deck. One of the busybody neighbors called the cops, the next thing I know I'm standing in front of a judge, probably got his law degree through the mail. And he gives me two hundred hours of picking up trash."

He shook his head. "You believe that mess?"

Billy Tucker was a good-sized good old boy. Maybe six two, 240 pounds, narrow through the hips, big through the gut. He had a permanent slump to his shoulders and his face had the florid enlarged-vein topography of the career drinker. A long-term diet of scotch and red meat and fried foods, I told myself, could do this to a person. I laid off the onion rings.

"Billy," I said, losing patience with his game-playing, "we're not here to talk about your fight with your wife and you know it. Quit fucking around. You were two hundred yards away from Whitney and Taylor. Why would the van pick them up and not you?"

He chewed silently. "I didn't see the van leave. Maybe they passed by when I was off in those woods. I came out, looked around, everybody was gone. The redhead and the black dudes, everybody. So I walked over the golf course to the pro shop. There's a pay phone. I called Ed, he's sort of a cousin. He came out and picked me up."

"What time was that?" I urged. "Think."

"Let's see. It took Ed at least thirty, forty minutes to get there. It was coming onto dark when he pulled up."

It had been dusk when I'd gotten to the golf course, so Tucker couldn't have been gone long. There was no way he didn't see those bodies.

"You said you were in the woods. Doing what?"

"Taking a leak. No law against that."

I took a bite of steak. It had gotten cold. I could see the white grease congealing in the pools of juice on the platter. Suddenly steak didn't seem so attractive.

"Billy, I got out there at dusk," I told him. "There were two bodies piled up in those orange trash bags. If you left when you say you did, you'd have to have seen them. Tell me what you saw. Please."

"I need a drink," he said stubbornly. "I've had a hell of a day. Hell of a week."

"Compromise," I said finally. "Tell me the truth, and I'll buy you one more drink. Just one. Afterwards, you let me drive you home. You're in no shape to be on the road."

He scowled. "Damn nag. Like Diane. Always on me about drinking."

"I'm not your wife," I said coldly. "What about the truth?"

He shut his eyes and rubbed them with short, work-callused fingers. No wedding band.

"Goddamn. I don't need this. Get my drink."

When his hand had closed around a full glass again, Tucker took a deep breath.

"I didn't see it happen, okay? I swear to you. If I'd seen what happened, I'd have told the cops. The way it was, I had to pee, something fierce. So I walked across the street, to those woods. I don't think anybody saw me go.

"There was an old fence separating the shoulder from the woods. But in back of that burnt-out store, the fence had been pulled down. I walked until I couldn't be seen from the street. And I took a leak. Just about the time I was zipping up, I hear it. *Pop. Pop.* Two pops, I think. At the time, I thought it was a car backfiring. But a few seconds later, I hear somebody come crashing through the bushes. Running. Knocking aside branches, really ripping it up. It was all tangly and viny back in there. A regular jungle. But he was running like a spooked deer."

"Did you see who it was?"

Tucker took a tentative sip of his drink, then a long gulp. "No. He was moving too fast, and it was dark in there. Hardly any sunlight coming through all that brush. I think maybe he had on a jacket, dark green, maybe, with some kind of hood."

"Did you see where he went?"

"I wondered where those woods let out onto. I wasn't in a hurry to get back to picking up trash, so I walked a little ways, and came out onto an old dirt road. A dead end, turned into a dump. Mattresses and tires and cans and bottles. And right there, right in the middle of this junk pile, there's an old shack. And I mean a shack. Made out of pieces of rusted tin and baling wire. And this old black fella, he was standing on this falling-down porch. I looked at him, he looked at me, then he turned around and walked inside and shut the door. Damn spooky, I tell you."

"So you didn't see where the shooter went?"

"I didn't see anything," Billy repeated. "It's like I've been telling you. Nothing. A piece of a green jacket. That's all."

"What did you do after that?"

"Walked back across the road and called Ed to come get me," Tucker said. "It was damn cold out there."

"And you didn't see the bodies?" I pressed. "You'd heard gunshots and seen a man running away. You're telling me you didn't look around, see what had happened? You didn't wonder where Whitney Dobbs and Shawan Taylor had gotten to? Come on, Billy, do I look that stupid? Or am I supposed to believe you're that stupid? You're a lawyer, for God's sake."

"Was." He was shredding the bar napkin under his drink, rolling the damp paper into little bullets, lining them up side by side on the tabletop.

"She was dead," he said, looking up at me. "There was nothing I could do for her. I didn't even see the other guy until I leaned over to feel for a pulse. They were both dead. Nobody was around. What was I supposed to do?"

"Ever think of calling the cops?"

"I just wanted to get out of there. After I called my cousin, I walked down to the corner. I had to get away."

"You put the trash bags on top of them?" That had bothered me, the bags covering the bodies. Not hidden, really, just covered.

"Seemed like the thing to do."

He had funny ideas about decency, this guy.

"Was there anybody else around at all?" I asked. "Did you see anybody on the golf course? Anybody at the pro shop when you went to use the phone?"

"It was getting dark. I didn't pay attention. I'd just seen two people with holes blown in them. You understand?"

He was getting testy now, tired of talking to pesky, nagging women like his wife. Maybe he'd reach out and pop me one. Maybe he'd draw back a bloody stub, too.

"Why didn't you tell any of this to the police, Billy?" I asked.

"I got enough problems," he said, and he drained his glass.

"Now you've got one more," I told him, motioning for the waitress to bring the check. "The cops will be back to talk to you. They'll figure out you weren't on that sheriff's van as soon as they talk to the others. You need to tell the police what you saw, Billy, before they arrest the wrong guy and things get really, really ugly in this town."

Tucker pulled himself up from his chair and hitched his jeans up off his hips.

"From where I stand, they're already ugly," he said. "Meet you outside. I gotta visit the men's room."

I put the money on the table with the check and watched Billy Tucker weave unsteadily through the collision course of tables and chairs toward the rest rooms. He was wrecked. On scotch I'd paid for. I just hoped he could remember his own address.

19

I'D FORGOTTEN THAT WE HAD CALLED a meeting of all the girls for nine that morning. At eight-thirty, I wobbled into the kitchen, my hair still damp from the shower.

"You baked biscuits," I said, sniffing. "What's the occasion?"

"The meeting. Remember? Besides, I felt like it," she said, opening the oven door to take a peek. "The girls love my biscuits."

I loved them too, but she didn't feel like fixing them for me every morning. I sat at the table and sipped my coffee and pondered the injustices of life.

Edna bustled back and forth, setting out cups and saucers, plates, knives, the butter dish, and assorted bowls of preserves and jams.

"You came in pretty late last night," she said, getting the cream out of the refrigerator. "Did you find that fella you went looking for?"

"I found him," I said grimly. "I took him out to dinner and plied him with scotch until he felt like talking. As soon as he got in the van so I could take him home, he fell dead asleep. I thought I was going to have to fire my pistol to get him awake and unloaded."

"You're carrying your pistol in the van now—aren't you?"

"Yeah. I'm carrying it. I don't like it, but I'm doing it."

"Good," she said. "Times are bad out there, Jules. I've never seen Atlanta like this. So much hate."

Edna opened the oven again and pulled out two sheets of biscuits. They were puffed up tall, with straight, snowy white sides and golden-brown tops. She dumped the biscuits into a basket lined with linen tea towels, then covered them lovingly, like a baby in a crib. She put the basket on the table, then stepped back and did a slow pirouette. Or something like a pirouette. "How do I look?"

Now that she mentioned it, she looked pretty good. She was dressed up in a navy blue wool pantsuit with a crisp striped blouse under the jacket and tiny gold hoop earrings. Her blue-white hair was teased and puffed, and she'd added a smidgen of blue eye shadow to her usual lipstick and powder. She'd even forsworn her favorite rubber-soled waitress shoes for black suede flats.

"You look like Mrs. Gotrocks," I said admiringly. "All this just for a meeting with the girls?"

"I've got an appointment with Carson Dobbs. Remember? At eleven."

"I'd forgotten. Do you want me to drive you?"

"What for? I'm not sick. Besides, if he sees you, it might blow my cover."

"Right. But remember, no real snooping. The important thing is the check. And if he starts talking surgery . . . "

"I'll run like hell," Edna said. "I still think you should let

me use that camera. I bet I could get a look at some papers and stuff."

Before we could start arguing, we heard a car pull up in the driveway. As we watched out the window, Ruby got out and opened the door for Baby and Sister, who sat regally in the backseat, like Queen Elizabeth and Princess Margaret. Ruby got each one by an arm and escorted them slowly toward the back door.

"Oh now Edna," Ruby exclaimed when she came in. "You been cooking and baking for us, and here I come empty-handed. And you sick with the heart trouble."

"Y'all sit down and get something to eat," Edna said. "And anyway, I'm not sick."

"Yeah, Ruby," Baby said. "Edna, she feeling good. She gone do some spying for Callahan today. Spying on that doctor man we tricked the other night." She rocked and tee-heed at the memory of it.

Sister took a biscuit from the basket and pulled it apart with long quivering fingers. I moved the strawberry preserves in front of her plate. "Here's your favorite, Miss Sister," I said.

"Callahan," she said, dipping a spoon into the preserves. "When you gonna let us do some more secret agent stuff? Me and Baby want to take some more movies with that purse camera. We could go with Edna right this morning, be her backup."

"Sorry," I said. "The doctor knows you two now. But I'll let you know if something comes up."

"Isn't there anything I could do?" Ruby asked wistfully.

Baby and Sister were a good twenty-five years older than Ruby, but because of her high blood pressure and circulation problems, I'd always tried not to get her involved in my investigations. And the one time she had helped me out, we'd been the victims of a drive-by shooting in which a baby had been killed.

"We'll find something for you to do, Ruby, don't you worry about that," Edna said, patting her shoulder.

"We?" I asked.

The back door opened then and Neva Jean came rushing in, along with a gust of cold damp wind.

"I knew it," she exclaimed. "I got out of the car and smelled 'em in the driveway. Edna's biscuits. I could eat a half a dozen in one bite."

She was buttering a warm biscuit before she'd taken off her coat.

"How are the emus?" I asked. "Any signs of eggs yet?"

She looked pained. "No. And Swannelle's been feeding them this expensive breeder ration too. He stays out in that pen, watching those damn birds hour after hour, waiting for Sluggo, that's the boy, to get the jump on Nancy, the hen. All they do is a lot of squawking and pecking and running up and down. You believe he ain't seen no sex yet?"

"Not from those birds anyway," Edna said meaningfully. "I notice you spent the night out last night."

"Oh. Oh my." Ruby was blushing and fanning herself. She was deeply religious. "Oh my goodness."

"Swannelle's breeding emus to sell," Neva Jean explained. "If he hatches them and raises them, a pair sells for about sixteen thousand dollars. That's why he's interested in their sex life. It's nothing kinky."

I wasn't so sure about the nature of Swannelle's interest in the emus, but there wasn't time to go into it if we were going to get the meeting out of the way. It was already nine-fifteen. Everybody but Jackie was present and accounted for.

"Let's get started," Edna said. "We'll catch Jackie up when she gets here." We laid out our problem for the girls. Money was tight. We had more work than we could handle and we were having to turn away lucrative new business.

"To stay in business we've got to grow," I told the girls. "But Edna and I need more help."

The back door opened and Jackie stepped inside. "Sorry," she said briefly. Instead of sitting down with the others, she got a cup of coffee and stayed standing, leaning up against the kitchen counter.

"Two things could happen," I continued. "We could ask everybody to work more hours, which will mean more money. Everybody includes me, but not Edna, not until her health is better. You girls will have to let me know if you're willing to take on extra clients. It's up to you. The second thing is, we could hire some new people. Right now, we could use two new girls."

Ruby raised a timid hand. "Callahan, do you have anybody in mind?"

"Somebody good," Edna said. "Hardworking. Dependable. No drinkers or druggers."

They all laughed together at the last requirement.

"We were hoping you all would put the word out that we're looking to hire," I said. "We'll run an ad if we have to, but we think word of mouth is the best way to find the kind of employees we're looking for."

Edna looked at Jackie. "We tried to hire your cousin Antoinette. She wasn't interested. Can you think of anybody else, Jackie?"

Jackie's face flushed. "What? You only want black folks coming to work here? You think because I'm African American everybody I know wants to be a housemaid?"

Edna's jaw dropped and I could see her face getting red too. The girls froze, as though someone had dropped a rattlesnake into the middle of our cozy little kaffeeklatsch.

"Hey!" Neva Jean said sharply. "I'm white. Callahan and Edna are white. What's wrong with you lately, Jackie? Why are you being so touchy?"

Jackie crossed her arms defiantly. "Somebody like you wouldn't understand, Neva Jean. Maybe I'm tired of seeing people exploited. And discriminated against. Maybe I'm just fed up with living in a racist society."

The room got very quiet.

"What'd she say?" Baby asked Sister in a loud stage whisper. "Is she fussin' at Callahan?"

"Hush up, fool," Sister said.

Stung, I searched in my mind for the right words. The girls were all watching me to see what I would do and say. Even Edna.

"We've asked all the girls for referrals," I said slowly. "Because we value you and trust your judgment. Not because of your race. I thought we'd all gotten past that around here."

"That's because you're the boss," Jackie said.

Suddenly, Ruby pushed her chair away from the table and stood up, the wooden chair legs shrieking as they scraped against the floor in the oppressive silence. "I've got to get to work now," she announced. "Come on, Miss Baby and Sister. Callahan, I'll ask my pastor if he knows somebody good who's looking for work."

The three of them left quickly and Neva Jean followed, saying that her car had Ruby blocked in the driveway.

Edna murmured something about making some phone calls and disappeared. That left the two of us, standing at opposite sides of the room like gunslingers, sizing each other up.

"Whitney Dobbs is dead," I said finally. "I'm trying to prove that her husband was hiding marital assets. My investigation has nothing to do with Faneeta Mayes or her father. It's not about race, Jackie."

"Not to you," she said bitterly. "That's what white people always say when an African American gets the shaft. Not about race?" she hooted derisively. "It's always about race. How do

you think it makes me feel, all of y'all running around, working for Whitney Dobbs? She killed a black child and got away with it because she was white. You think if I got drunk and ran over her kid some judge would pat me on the head and tell me to go home and get counseling? My black ass would be in prison. And you know it, Callahan. She's dead, but you're still working for her. Those old fools might not know it. But I do. And I don't want anything to do with any of it."

Edna bustled into the kitchen then. "Can't find my car keys," she said, pushing some papers around on the counter. Her look went from me to Jackie.

"Are you quitting us?" God bless Edna. Always to the point.

Jackie took her coffee cup over to the sink and rinsed it out, placing it carefully in the dish drainer.

"Not yet," she said. "Not this close to Christmas."

20

THE CONFRONTATION WITH JACKIE left me shaken and depressed. Edna, on the other hand, was certifiably pissed.

"Let her go if she feels that way," she groused, still scrabbling around, opening cabinet doors and drawers in search of her car keys. "I'm not going to apologize to her for being white and owning a business. The others don't feel that way."

"I don't want her to quit," I said. "We need Jackie. But I don't like her making me feel like a bigot, either."

"Here they are!" Edna said jubilantly, holding up the key chain. "Somebody put them in the junk drawer."

She pulled on her coat and headed for the back door. "Don't stew about it," she ordered me. "You heard her. She's not going to quit before Christmas. She's got a car payment to make. And you know how she is about that Mustang of hers. It's her baby."

We both knew Jackie could get another job anytime she liked.

After Edna was gone, I decided to call Bucky Deavers. Ordinarily I didn't volunteer information to the police about one of my cases, but this one time, I had a bad feeling about their case against Bryant Mayes.

When I called I got a voice mail recording telling me that Bucky was in the office, but away from his desk. I left a message.

I got out the Whitney Dobbs case file and started making notes about my conversation with Billy Tucker. I wanted to go back down to the Brown's Mill Golf Course and the Promised Land to check out the shack he'd told me about. And I wanted to follow up on some of the stuff Carol Steiner had mentioned. If Carson Dobbs was stashing money away, could he have been fooling around with the insurance billings in his office?

While I was making a list of things I needed to check on, Doyle Bollinger called.

"Yeah, how you doing?" he asked. I could hear traffic in the background. He was calling from a car phone. "I understand you're on the Whitney Dobbs investigation now."

"I'm working for her daughter," I said. "Would you have some time to talk to me about your findings?"

"Why not?" he said. "There wasn't much. I didn't even write up any paperwork. You know where my office is?"

I looked at the business card. The address was unfamiliar.

"It's an office park," Bollinger went on. "Come out 285 to Peachtree-Dunwoody and turn left. Come past the hospitals, and you'll see a little office park called Dunwoody Plaza on the right. I'm in Building G, number four. Between an oral surgeon and a physical therapist. I'm on my way. You want to meet in about twenty minutes?"

"Better make it thirty," I said.

I grabbed my jacket and the phone rang again.

It was Deavers, returning my call. "You staying out of trouble?"

"You know me better than that," I said. "How's the case coming against Bryant Mayes?"

"Why do you want to know?"

"This one's a hummer, Bucky."

"Not what the crime lab says."

"You got the ballistics report back?"

"You know I can't talk about that."

"Look," I said. "I talked to a witness. Somebody who got left behind when the deputies loaded those people up. He was there. Heard the gunshots, then heard somebody come running through the woods. He saw a glimpse of a green jacket. And he saw another witness, an old man sitting on the porch of a shack out there in the middle of a junkyard. The old man probably saw our shooter run past."

"Let me guess who the witness is," Bucky said. "Billy Tucker. Am I right?"

"Yeah," I said cautiously. "He admitted to you guys that he wasn't on the van?"

"He hasn't admitted anything to anybody that I know of," Bucky said. "We took his statement the night of the shooting. He said he didn't see nothing. You know anything about this guy Tucker?"

"I know he's not Santa Claus. That still doesn't change the fact that he was out there. And he saw something, and it doesn't sound to me like what he saw was Bryant Mayes."

"Tucker tell you he saw the shooter's face?"

"No," I admitted.

"Could he tell whether the person was black or white? Male or female?"

"Just a glimpse of a jacket, maybe with a hood."

"Any reason that couldn't be Bryant Mayes?"

"Why would he run through the woods?" I asked. "Why wouldn't he just do a drive-by in that truck of his?"

"Why indeed?" Bucky said. "Mayes and his firehouse buddies played golf down there, all the time, on their off shifts. Did you know about that?"

"No."

"Just a minute." I could hear Bucky talking in a low voice to someone in the same room. "I gotta go, Garrity. One more thing, though. Did Tucker mention to you what kind of trouble he's in?"

"You mean the wife beating? Yeah, he's a scumbag."

"I'm not talking about wife beating," Bucky said. "Ask around. The guy's a career liar."

"Are you going to arrest Mayes?"

"I can't comment on that," Bucky said rather grandly. Probably for the benefit of Lloyd Mackey.

Dunwoody Plaza was a regular rabbit's warren of look-alike red brick Georgian buildings. Each facade had white columns, two Palladian windows, and double front doors.

After ten minutes of cruising, I finally found the smallish brass "G" affixed to the front door of Bollinger's building. Number four was on the first floor. BOLLINGER & ASSOCIATES was the name on the small brass door plate.

The outer office was empty and tiny, nothing more than a desk with a swivel chair, a phone, and a navy blue leather armchair. The door to the inner office was directly behind the absent secretary's chair. From behind the door, I could hear a radio.

It was tuned to an all-news station. Even from where I stood I could clearly hear the booming voice of Ellis McIntyre, the station's noontime talk show host, a right-wing Rush Limbaugh wannabe. He was immersed in one of his famous "McInTirades."

"I tell you, friends, the time has come for decent citizens to tell these Third World, crack-smoking, welfare-cheating, shot-gun-toting thugs that we've had enough. We're living in a city of fear, a place where City Hall politicians handcuff the police to keep these nervous nellies from carrying out the law because they're afraid these hooligans will loot and sack if one of their own is arrested. You know what I say, friends? I say let them riot. And let the governor call out the Georgia State Patrol, the National Guard, the Georgia Bureau of Investigation. Call 'em all out!"

I'd had enough. If I had to wait, I would do it without Ellis McIntyre's company. I knocked briefly, then opened the door and peeked inside.

The office was empty. It wasn't much larger than the outer room, an oversized closet, with a huge wooden desk covered with stacks of file folders, a stand holding an electric type-writer, and an open laptop computer set up on top of a teeter-ing stack of papers and magazines. The radio was sitting on the top of a bookshelf crammed with telephone and crisscross directories. I stepped inside to shut it off.

As soon as I did, the outer door opened. I turned around and smiled brightly, hoping I hadn't been caught. The man standing in the doorway dropped some file folders on the sec-retary's desk. He was a little taller than me, maybe five nine, stocky, but solid, like a weightlifter. He had thick brown wavy hair, heavily streaked with silver and moussed like a television weatherman's, and tinted aviator-style glasses. He was dressed in blue jeans, a sweater, and a windbreaker.

"Sorry I'm late," he said, putting down a bulky briefcase to shake my hand. "I'm Bollinger."

"Callahan Garrity," I said, shaking. "You left your radio on. I thought maybe somebody was here."

"I never turn it off," Bollinger said, gesturing for me to fol-low him into the office. "Sort of keeps me company." He sat

down in a chair, swiveled around, and turned the radio down, but not off.

"So," he said, turning back to face me. "I hear you used to be on the job. Me too, East Point Police. I took early retirement about eight years ago. Maybe you know some of my old running buddies. Earl Parker? Sonny Ferguson?"

The names rang a bell, but the faces I connected with them were those of old-timer street cops from the Southside precinct, where I had never worked.

"I know who they are," I said. "I've been gone six years myself. Seems like a lot longer."

"Still, you've probably still got some connections down there."

"A couple," I said. "Maybe you knew C. W. Hunsecker?"

"I knew him from around," Bollinger said. "Good guy."

"Yeah," I said. "The best."

"Look at me," Bollinger said suddenly. "Dressed like this. I've been working a case, that's why no coat and tie. You'll have to excuse me."

"Sure," I said. "I prefer casual myself. What kind of cases do you usually handle?"

"Different stuff," Bollinger said. "Some worker's comp cases, some skip tracing. I do a little domestic work. Got quite a few attorneys who keep me busy."

"That's how you came to work for Whitney Dobbs?"

He laughed ruefully. "Yeah, well. That didn't really work out. I did a little sniffing around, like Zack asked me to, even met with Mrs. Dobbs one time, but then Zack called and said the client preferred to work with a woman. Next thing I hear, Whitney's dead. Seems like the case is snakebit—huh?"

"How far did you get with your investigation?" I asked.

"Not very. I followed the doctor and his girlfriend to a restaurant two or three times."

"Suzanne Shaddeau."

"Yes," he said. "Tall redhead, great body."

"That's her."

"Anyway, it was always to the same restaurant, an Italian place out in Sandy Springs. Seems like they went there two or three times a week. I thought, don't these people ever cook?"

"If you look like Suzanne Shaddeau, cooking is probably beside the point," I said.

"True. I even tried to scam them. The last time, I followed them inside, sat down at the bar with them, and tried to strike up a conversation. Suzanne, she's pretty friendly, but not him. Very shut-mouthed. We got to talking about houses, that kind of thing. When their table was ready, she even invited me to join them. I thought we were getting someplace then."

"You had dinner with them?"

"Yeah. And the food is not that good. Which is why I can't understand how they can eat there all the time. But he's a very cautious individual. Every time the conversation turned personal, which I kept trying to do, he'd give her the high sign and she'd shut up again."

"So you didn't find out anything about where they're really living."

"You know what I found out?" Bollinger said. "I found out he's a cheap son of a bitch. He had a buy-one get-one coupon."

"Where was the restaurant? I never saw anything in the case file about that."

"Out on Spalding Drive. Off Holcombe Bridge Road. Nothing ever got written up. Zack called the next day and sent me a check for my time. That was it. Zack's a decent type. I know he'll give me more work down the line. So I didn't pursue it. Some clients just don't click. You probably found that out yourself."

"Sure. I didn't click with Whitney at first myself," I said.

"What did Suzanne talk about at dinner, if Carson wouldn't let her talk about personal stuff?"

He shrugged. "I don't know. The usual. How bad traffic was. We talked about the Braves winning the Series. I don't get the feeling the doc is a big baseball fan, but she sure was."

"What was the name of the restaurant?"

"An Italian name. I forget exactly. Rubinos, Salinos, something ends with an O like that."

"And it's out on Spalding?" I tried to picture where it might be. "That's at least eight or ten miles from their condo. Not exactly the corner diner. I'm surprised they go all that way for dinner that often."

"Maybe it was a phase they were going through," Bollinger offered.

"Maybe," I agreed. "Or maybe there's a reason they're in that neighborhood that often."

"You're still working the case then? Even though Whitney got killed?"

"Zack represents Whitney's daughter, Alison," I explained. "Alison has some questions about her mother's death. And there are still some financial things to be settled. Alison and her father are estranged."

Bollinger shook his head. "Doctors, huh? They've got more money than God and they still want to nickel-and-dime you to death. I think it's a control issue."

Control. I thought about some of the doctors I'd seen over the last five years during my bout with breast cancer. How many of them wanted to pat me on the head and have me do as they said like a good little girl—no questions asked.

"You got that right," I said. "And from what I hear, Carson Dobbs is an expert at controlling people."

We talked shop a little more. Bollinger wasn't what I'd been expecting. Not nearly as bad as Whitney had described

him. Certainly not a horrible man with a tattoo. But then he had on long sleeves, so I couldn't tell whether the tattoo part was true.

He walked me out to the front of the building. "What do you think of this big stink over this Bryant Mayes guy?" Bollinger asked. "Your buddies down at Atlanta homicide going to arrest him or not?"

"If you're asking me, I think it looks like a setup," I said. "Everything's just too convenient. I don't know about the arrest part. I've got a friend working the case, but he won't tell me much."

"A setup," Bollinger said thoughtfully. "Could be."

I called Reg Vaughn, the manager at Cumberland Oaks, from my car phone. "Come on by," he told me. "I can't talk right now. I'm putting out forest fires."

A teenage kid was vacuuming the lobby when I walked in. It was an impressive lobby, if you didn't look too close. Big brass chandelier, nice wallpaper, thick carpets. A massive field-stone fireplace took up one corner of the room; around it nestled a conversation grouping of overstuffed sofas and armchairs.

If you were in the cleaning business, the room would make you cringe. The nice carpet was dingy and spotted, with a gray footpath that marked the trail from the front door to the elevators to the reception desk. The chandelier was caked with cobwebs, the painted woodwork and baseboards were filmed with dust, and the brass trim on the front doors and the elevators was dull with tarnish.

I could hear Edna tsk-tsking in my mind. Vaughn wasn't kidding when he said he had housekeeping problems. And this was the lobby, probably the cleanest space in the building, since it was the first thing a prospective tenant would see.

Reg Vaughn looked up hopefully when I walked into his office. He had thinning brown hair and a long homely face.

"I'm Callahan. Did you take care of your crisis?"

"What?" He laughed. "For now. Come on in. I don't suppose you've changed your mind about working for us?"

I gestured toward the lobby. "It looks to me like you've found some help."

"Strictly temporary," Vaughn said. "I need somebody like The House Mouse."

It was tempting. A big job, ours for the taking. But now that I'd seen the place, I was convinced. We just didn't have the mouse power to handle it. "I'm sorry," I told him. "We're looking for help, but until we can make some hires, we can't take on any new business."

"That's what your mother said too," Vaughn said. "Guess we'll have to keep looking."

"In the meantime," I said, "Edna tells me you had quite an experience with Ben Dwyer."

Vaughn's friendly face turned sour.

"It was a surprise," he said. "Our company has been managing this building for three years. In this neighborhood, with these kinds of rents, you don't expect your tenants to skip out like this. I've turned it over to an agency, but I'm not holding out much hope that they'll find anything. This man was not your typical deadbeat."

"Did you know Dwyer?"

"I met him when he signed his lease and paid his deposit, and I saw him coming and going a few times," Vaughn said. "But most of our tenants are here on a transient basis. Dwyer was like any other tenant." He frowned. "Or so I thought."

"Have you got his lease?" I asked.

Vaughn got up and went to a file cabinet. He extracted a piece of paper and handed it to me. It was a standard rental

form. Name, five years' worth of previous addresses, employer's address, bank account numbers, credit card references. Before he'd moved into Cumberland Oaks, Dwyer had lived at an address in Marietta for two years. Before that, there were two different addresses in Fort Lauderdale.

I looked up at Vaughn. "Did you check out the previous addresses?"

"The last one was an apartment complex near Cumberland Mall, four hundred units," Vaughn said. "New management, nobody remembers him, but their records show he paid his rent on time."

"How about the Florida addresses?"

"Nothing," Vaughn said. "Two different houses, two different landlords. They wouldn't give me the time of day."

"And the bank accounts have been closed, right?"

"That's right," Vaughn said.

"What have you done with his mail?" I asked.

"We had to send the first class stuff on to the post office," Vaughn said. "But the junk mail, stuff they won't forward, is right here."

He went to a closet in the office and brought out a cardboard box, which he put on my lap. "Care to take a look?"

The box was nearly full. Catalogs, newsletters on flimsy newsprint, bulk mail flyers advertising everything from office supplies to lawn services to car alarms.

"You know what you're looking for?" Vaughn asked hopefully.

"Not a clue," I admitted. "Can I take this stuff with me? Maybe I'll find some kind of pattern."

"Help yourself," he said, picking up the box for me. "I took the Victoria's Secret catalogs," he said, blushing slightly. "My, uh, wife likes to shop mail order."

"Not a problem," I said. I propped the box on one hip and

headed for the door. "You're sure none of the other tenants got to know Dwyer? Not even his nearest neighbors?"

"Afraid not," Vaughn said. "You can talk to them again if you like, but our tenants are busy people. The woman who lived across the hall, Petria May, is a fashion designer. She's down here setting up some kind of agreement with some manufacturers. Very beautiful, exotic-looking. Not Dwyer's type, I wouldn't think. Besides, she flies to New York almost every weekend. She said she'd even never talked to him. Mr. Fujiko, the tenant who lived beside him, speaks almost no English. And he left last week to go back to Tokyo."

"That figures," I said. "Is there any way I could get into Dwyer's old apartment to take a look around?"

"Sorry. It's rented. With the Olympics coming, nothing in this area stays vacant. I looked around pretty carefully after we figured out Dwyer had skipped. Clean as a whistle. We didn't even need to paint or have the carpets cleaned."

"Good for you, bad for clues," I said, stepping out into the lobby. "Thanks for the mail. I'll let you know if Mr. Dwyer turns up."

"There's a finder's fee," Vaughn volunteered. "My company's authorized five hundred dollars. They don't like being ripped off."

21

NOVEMBER'S EARLY PROMISE of mild blue skies was a big fat lie. Overhead the cloud banks were dark and ominous, and a frigid wind was gusting crazily as I got in the van outside Cumberland Oaks. I thought about home, a hot lunch, a long nap, the phone off the hook.

Instead I decided to go back to the scene of the crime. This time it was daylight, and I had my loaded pistol and Billy Tucker's description of what he had seen.

There were only two other cars in the parking lot at the Brown's Mill Golf Course. The greens were littered with leaves and small fallen branches, and the trees that lined the entryway crowded close together and swayed back and forth in a way that reminded me of the talking trees in *The Wizard of Oz* that warn Dorothy and friends to get out before it's too late.

I pulled the hood of my jacket up over my head and ran to the pro shop.

The shop was as deserted as the course. A young white guy, early twenties, stood behind a counter littered with golf towels and golf tees and golf shirts, sipping a cup of steaming coffee. He was immersed in a paperback book with submarines on the jacket. A nameplate on the counter said he was Mike Hooker, club pro.

He looked up at me with surprise. I guess I don't look like the sporting kind. I introduced myself and told him what I was working on.

"I didn't see anything myself," he said. "Everything was quiet when I locked up. I told the police that."

I looked around the shop. Linoleum floors, cheap wood-paneled walls, vending machines instead of a real grill or coffee shop. A large picture window in back of the counter looked out over the course. In the distance, I could see someone riding on a giant lawn mower hooked up to a vacuum hose to suck up the fallen leaves.

"Who plays golf out here?" I asked Hooker.

"We get all kinds. Retired people who play every day for the exercise, blue collar types, folks who live on the Northside but play down here because they can't get tee times at Bobby Jones or Chastain. We even get a fair number of pro athletes, they come out here weekdays to play because nobody bothers 'em. It's cheap, and pretty playable. Not too difficult, but enjoyable, you know?"

I didn't, but I acted like I did.

"Do you know most of the regulars by name?"

"Nah," he said. "You're going to ask me about Bryant Mayes, the fireman, aren't you? We get a lot of those guys down here. They even have a departmental tournament in the spring. But I don't know them all. The cops showed me his picture. I couldn't say yes or no."

"Did you hear any shots that day?"

He pointed at a wall-mounted television in back of him. It was tuned to ESPN, of course, and a commentator was discussing college bowl prospects. "I was either watching TV, or talking on the phone. And there's the planes overhead. The airport's maybe five miles away. We're not exactly Augusta National."

"You get any doctors who play down here?"

"Sure," he said. "All the time."

"What about a doctor named Carson Dobbs?"

"Name doesn't sound familiar, but if he played with a foursome of other guys, I wouldn't know him anyway."

The steam coming off Mike Hooker's coffee looked inviting. But I had more to do. No time for a coffee break. I stopped by the van and changed out of my leather flats and into a pair of hiking boots. They were fairly new, barely scuffed. I'd bought them back when Mac and I were still together, for when we took his black Lab Rufus out for runs through the woods. A heavier coat would have been nice, as would some gloves. I tried not to dwell on it.

I walked across the street to the abandoned gas station. The broken concrete was littered with beer cans and shattered wine bottles. I tucked my hands deep into my jacket pockets, curled the fingers of my right hand around the pistol. The weight of the nine-millimeter made the jacket sag. I wished I knew where my ankle holster was from my cop days.

Gingerly, I stepped over the broken barbed wire fence that ran along the back of the property. It was bent right where Billy Tucker had said it was. My boots squished in the soft mud. At least now I'd look like an experienced hiker. The underbrush was dense here. Vines clung to my clothes and branches obscured my vision. The farther I walked into the woods, the darker it got. No visible paths, really, but from the trash, I could tell people had passed this way.

Since I didn't know where I was going, I tried to walk in a straight direction. A tiny narrow creek trickled crookedly along in front of me, and I had to jump across its two-foot width and scramble up an embankment on the other side. After I'd walked for another two or three minutes, I could see the woods starting to thin out a little. The scattered trash was now everywhere. Abruptly, the woods ended and I was in the middle of a junkyard.

The first thing I saw was a heap of burnt-out mattresses, then piles of old tires, chunks of concrete, a couple of rusted-out car bodies, and everywhere, mounds of paper and tin cans and broken glass. On the far side of the junk pile I saw the shack Billy Tucker had described. Shack was actually a grandiose term for what was to my mind a monument to imaginative recycling.

The foundation was made of stacked-up chunks of broken concrete blocks. On top of this, someone had nailed together a series of wooden pallets, the kind they use to ship and move big stacks of potting soil and fertilizer and grass seed at garden shops. Crudely sawn sapling tree trunks sprang from each of the four corners, and across these, walls had been formed from a crazy quilt of plywood scraps, sheet metal, even asphalt roofing shingles.

A bright blue plastic tarp was tacked across the makeshift plywood roof, and the wind puffed and blew it until it resembled a silly oversized shower cap.

I skirted the edge of the junk pile, scuffing my boots loudly to alert any lurking rats or snakes that I was in the vicinity.

As I came closer, I saw what Billy had described as the "porch." Another stack of pallets sat in front of the hut, right in front of a rain-warped hollow-core door. I could see the paintings too. Bold splashes of color: red, blue, pink, black, purple, yellow, and green. Across the front of the house, metal

cans had been flattened and nailed down to provide the canvas for a painting of a wicked green devil who grinned and brandished a long pink sword. In the top corner of the front wall, a purple sun radiated rays of blue, orange, and black, and red-robed angels floated in midair, with wings dwarfed by sad bulbous heads.

I stood a few yards away and gaped. The house was like nothing I had ever seen before. A series of rocks, boulders really, each painted a different color and daubed with splashes of black and white polka dots, made a crooked pathway to the porch.

I stood in front of the porch and looked around. "Anybody home?" I called. "Hello?"

When there was no answer, I hiked myself up onto the porch, which teetered ominously under my weight. More paintings decorated the porch; some kind of robed gods raced across the outer wall in vehicles that looked like carts drawn by cats.

"Hello—anybody?" The door had no handle, just a knot of wood for a latch. It swung inward when I touched it. I stepped inside and was plunged into darkness. There were no windows, only tiny pinpricks of light coming through the gaps in the siding. After my eyes adjusted to the dark I saw a stack of empty paint cans in the corner and a pile of what looked like rags in another corner. In the middle, an old barbecue grill held charred chunks of wood. Otherwise, the room was empty. It smelled of sweat and urine, mildew and wood smoke.

I kneeled down and looked at the paint cans. Through the dim light I saw a scrap of fabric at the bottom of the stack. I tugged and pulled out a grime-and-paint-encrusted plaid flannel shirt. When an inch-long cockroach scuttled off the shirt and onto my hand, I flung the shirt away, stifling a scream. I was out of the hut and off the porch in five seconds flat.

I stood at the edge of the junkyard feeling stupid about my

squeamishness, but I'd already decided that whoever lived there was not currently in residence.

The edge of the junk heap segued into broken and pock-marked asphalt. I'd stumbled onto a dead-end street. No marker told me the name, but I assumed I'd found the Promised Land.

I walked in the middle of the road for half a block before I saw any signs of life. Suddenly, though, I could see the beginnings of a neighborhood. Tiny dilapidated houses sat close together, each with its own small patch of yard. Wind-stiffened laundry blew from clotheslines, and in a thicket of bushes near the road I saw two scrawny hens pecking at the dirt.

A powder-blue cinder-block house on the right side of the road looked to be the most prosperous. There was a high chain-link fence surrounding the lot and a front porch loaded with pots and baskets of houseplants. A maroon Delta 88, one of the big 1970s gas-guzzlers, was parked in the driveway. A bullet-strafed BEWARE OF DOG sign was screwed to the fence.

The gate was unlocked and it made a loud squealing noise as I opened it. "Doggie?" I looked around cautiously. So far no signs of any snarling Dobermans. "Poochie?" I said in a louder, braver voice. Still no dog. Maybe he only worked the night shift. Or maybe he was waiting until I got all the way in the yard, so I'd be cornered with no hope of escape.

I walked smartly up the front steps and rang the doorbell. While I waited, I brushed bits of leaves and twigs out of my hair and off my jacket.

"Who's there?" It was a woman's voice at the other side of the door.

"I'm a detective," I called back. There was a small peep-hole in the door. I hoped I didn't look too frightening. "I'm working for the family of the woman who was shot over at the golf course," I said. "Can I talk to you for a minute?"

"I ain't studying no shooting."

Damn. I got out a business card and slid it under the door. "Here's my card," I said. "It won't take but a moment."

"Go ahead and ask," the woman called back. "I ain't opening the door."

So there was no dog. Just a woman who lived alone and was nervous about strangers. Not that I blamed her.

"Do you know who lives in that shack down at the end of the street? An old man?"

"That's Arliss's house," she said. "What you want with that crazy old man?"

"I need to talk to him. But it looks like he's moved out."

"He moves out all the time," she said, laughing. "Crazy as a bedbug. Makes pictures on stuff he finds in that junk. Arliss, he's just like the weather. Comes and goes."

"But was he living there last week? Does anybody know where he is now?"

"I heard he's going around saying he saw that white lady get killed over there at the golf course."

"Did he tell *you* that he'd seen the shooting?"

"Arliss talks all kind of mess," she retorted. "'Cause he's crazy, that's why. Arliss Woods is around somewhere. But I haven't seen him. Lock that gate, you hear?"

The house next door was not nearly as nice as the first house. It was wooden, any vestiges of paint long gone. The floorboards of the rotting porch had gaping holes and a front window was cracked and repaired with silver duct tape. The front door opened before I could knock. A teenage boy, dressed in a silky black warm-up suit, barefooted, toted a sleeping infant on his shoulder.

"Roseanne just went to sleep," he said. "Are you the lady about the insurance?"

"No," I said, keeping my eyes on the baby. She was

wrapped in a pink blanket and her fat little cheek was mashed against the boy's shoulder, lips clenched around a large clear plastic pacifier.

"I'm looking for Arliss Woods," I told him.

"What you want with Arliss? You want to buy a picture?"

"I want to talk to him, then I might buy a picture. Do you know where I can find him?"

The kid shifted the baby higher up on his shoulder, but her eyes stayed shut. "Arliss stays around. Could be he went to buy paint."

I dug out another card and gave it to him. The kid took it and looked at it warily.

"Detective. You a cop?"

"Sort of," I said. "If you help me find Arliss Woods, I could pay a reward."

"Arliss don't like cops," the kid said. "Me neither." He and the baby went back in the house. I hoped Roseanne had a nice nap.

I asked around some more, knocked on a few more doors. Nobody told me nothing. After I'd walked another block, I found a cross street, the first one with a road sign. Apache Street.

It was afternoon and I was hungry. I trudged back through the woods, across the street, and back to the van. I got in and locked the door and wondered what to do next.

The sky had gotten darker and grayer and the temperature had dropped another ten degrees. Mid-November was too early for snow in Atlanta, or so I promised myself. I turned on the heat and tried to organize my thoughts.

I needed to talk to Arliss Woods. But maybe Ruby or Baby or Sister would be more effective as a sleuth in the Promised Land. Jackie could do it, I thought. But Jackie was furious at me, ready to quit.

The thought was too depressing to dwell upon. Instead I called Zack Alexander. We hadn't talked since Whitney's memorial service.

"Callahan," Zack said, after his secretary put me through. It sounded like he was eating something. "What do you know?"

"Not enough," I said. "How's it going on your end?"

"Not so good," he admitted. "I didn't get a chance to talk to you after the service. Some fight, huh?"

"Alison never had a chance," I said. "That Suzanne is a piece of work."

"To say the least," Zack said. "The scene didn't do our cause any good. Now Carson's all stirred up. What a mess. Are you coming up with anything?"

"I've got some leads," I told him. "But it's going to take some more time."

"We haven't got a lot of time. Carson has listed the Ansley Park house with a real estate broker. Agents have been tromping through the house with prospective buyers all week. Poor kid. She finally went to stay with a friend."

"Can he do that? Sell the house and take the money? I thought it was Whitney's house."

"Well, that's our position," Zack said. "The fact that Whitney's dead doesn't defeat the estate's claim to her share of the marital property. I've filed a restraining order to stop the house from being shown. But in the meantime, Carson has cut Alison off. Literally."

"He doesn't have to pay child support?"

"Alison is twenty years old," Zack said wearily. "She's in college. She's an emancipated adult. Legally, he doesn't have to give her a dime. It's not as bad as Alison makes it sound, though. Carson says he'll support her, if she moves in with him and Suzanne."

"I'll bet Alison was thrilled with that offer."

"She's not really penniless," Zack pointed out. "Of course, she inherits everything Whitney owned, but once again, everything except the funds Whitney's mother left her are tied up in this damned property settlement. We're going to have to file suit against Carson. It's going to get ugly."

It all seemed hopelessly complicated and mean-spirited to me. Rich people had problems I'd never considered. Maybe it wasn't so bad, being middle-class. At least you didn't risk being disinherited.

"What kind of suit?" I asked.

"Wrongful death," Zack said briskly.

22

"CALLAHAN? You still there?"

"I'm here," I told Zack. "Just stunned. You're going to go to court and try to prove Carson Dobbs killed Whitney? Isn't that pretty extreme?"

"I'm acting in Alison's best interests," he said.

I wondered about that. I wondered if Alison had thought about what it would be like to live through a second trial of a parent accused of a killing.

"What happens if the cops arrest Bryant Mayes?" I asked. "Bucky Deavers insists they're building a solid case against Mayes."

"They'll never take it to a jury," Zack said confidently. "Have you turned on a television or radio today?"

"I heard Ellis McIntyre ranting and raving for a few minutes. Nauseating. The man is dangerous."

"Yeah, yeah," he said impatiently. "I'm not talking about him. This afternoon, the mayor announced that he's asked the

174

Justice Department to send a special investigative unit to look into violations of Bryant Mayes's civil rights."

"Holy Christ," I said. "You mean the FBI?"

"I guess," Zack said. "Now we'll get someplace."

"Where?"

The phone crackled then. The transmission on my car phone was breaking up. "I've got to go," I told him. "I've got a good lead on a witness though. An old man named Arliss Woods might have seen something. Also, I saw Bollinger today."

"Who?"

"Bollinger," I repeated. "The first P.I. you hired? He says he followed Carson and Suzanne a few times to their favorite restaurant. An Italian place. But he can't remember the name. It might be useful to figure out why they go there so often."

"The Trattoria," Zack said promptly. "I've got Carson's credit card receipts for the past six months. They eat there at least twice a week. Whitney thought it was funny, because he always refused to eat Italian food when they were married."

"Good," I said. "One more thing. I just thought about this. You know, I have all my House Mouse employees bonded. Against theft. Do you think Carson Dobbs's business manager was bonded?"

"Hell yeah," Zack said slowly. "Lovely. Fucking lovely, Callahan. I should have thought about that myself. If Ben Dwyer was bonded—and he should have been—Dobbs should have filed a claim with the company. I'll get on it right away."

The car phone rang again as soon as I put it back in its cradle. Probably Zack with yet another lead he wanted me to run down.

But it wasn't. It was Edna. And when she said my name, "Jules?" I could tell she was upset. And frightened.

"Where are you?"

"I'm at the doctor's office. Dr. Dobbs," she said for emphasis.

I looked down at my watch. It was nearly three P.M. "You're still there? What's wrong? What's going on, Mom?"

"He says I need surgery. He says I'm really sick. I don't understand any of it. Jules, could you come right away?"

On the way to Carson Dobbs's office I alternated between screaming every swear word I knew and whispering every prayer I could remember.

"Goddamn. Bless us oh Lord for these our gifts . . . Shit . . . Hail Mary, full of grace." It went like that until I'd parked the car and gone charging into the teak-paneled suite of offices occupied by Cardiovascular Associates of Atlanta. Paradox Properties, indeed.

The receptionist looked up sharply when I barged in. She got a sheet of paper, attached it to a clipboard, and started to hand it to me, assuming I was a new patient.

Four or five people were seated in the reception area. They were placidly reading magazines. One elegantly dressed woman was doing needlepoint, a magnifying glass clamped to her embroidery hoop.

Run for your lives, I wanted to shout. I wanted to shake them, shoo them out of there, away from the man inside who deceived so easily and impressively. I gave the clipboard back to the receptionist. "Edna Garrity," I said, leaning across the counter. "She's my mother. I need to see her."

The receptionist frowned. My voice was too loud. Not deferential enough. She flipped through the pages on a list.

"Mrs. Garrity. Yes. She's just resting now. Let me see if they've completed all the tests. You can have a seat over there." Before I could tell her I wanted to see my mother—right now—the girl opened a door behind her and disappeared.

I sat down in a chair next to the needlepoint lady. She

looked up, gave me a noncommittal smile, and went back to her tapestry. The image was of the famous Blue Boy portrait. I watched, mesmerized, as she worked the needle in and out of the canvas. Her stitches were neat, the motion economical. The woman's eyes did not move from her work. But her jaw was rigid and the needle never stopped moving.

"Are you one of Dr. Dobbs's patients?" I asked in a low voice.

She looked pretty healthy to me, good color, no shallow breathing or clutching of the chest. Late fifties, probably.

"My husband," she said, still not looking up. "They're saying he needs a quadruple bypass."

I winced. "Sorry."

"It's risky," the woman said. "But Dr. Dobbs seems to know what he's talking about. He's referring us to a really good surgeon. And you have to trust your doctor."

"Do you?" I asked.

The needle paused. She took a deep breath, then let it out again. "Absolutely."

I tried reading a magazine then. But I could hear the second hand ticking on my watch, hear my stomach growling. The quiet, the absolute stillness of this waiting room annoyed me. I'd been here fifteen minutes. Where the hell was that receptionist? Where was Edna? What was going on back there?

I got up and strode to the counter. The desk behind it was empty. "Hello!" I called loudly. "Attention health care providers!" I could hear the reading and the needlepointing behind me stop cold. How could she? I could hear them thinking.

When nobody appeared, I walked over to the door beside the reception counter and rapped loudly. "Hello!" I called, even louder. I tried the handle. It was locked. I could feel my panic rising. I had to get Edna out of here.

Now I was banging with both fists.

And then the door opened. And a very visibly angry receptionist stood there, a bright pink spot on each cheek.

"Miss Garrity, please!" she said. "We have sick people here."

"Just take me to my mother," I said. "No more tests. I want to see her right now."

"I was coming to get you," she said in a tight little voice. "It's not necessary to make a scene."

"You don't know what a scene is," I told her.

She flounced off down the hall and I followed her twitching behind.

When she came to a door midway down the hall she jerked a chart out of the rack on the wall beside it, gave it a quick check, and then put it back in its place.

She knocked lightly. "Mrs. Garrity? Your daughter is here."

"Come in," I heard Edna say.

"The doctor will be in to talk with you both in just a few minutes," the receptionist said. Then she walked off.

Inside, I found Edna struggling to sit upright on an examining table. A thin paper gown covered her from neck to knees, and her scrawny white legs stuck out straight in front of her, her knee-high stockings rolled down around her ankles. She'd wrapped her arms around herself and she was shivering, her teeth literally chattering together. Her face was deathly white.

"Your jacket," she said.

I shrugged it off and wrapped it around her. Then I rubbed her hands and feet to warm them up. They were like ice.

"I'm so cold," she said. "So damn cold."

"I'll be right back," I promised.

I stopped the first person I saw in the hallway. She was young and blonde and the label on her white lab coat said she was Amy Schwartz, phlebotomist.

"Can you get me a blanket?" I asked bluntly. "My mother

was left alone in an examining room. In one of those paper gowns. She's nearly frozen."

The girl looked around wildly. "A blanket. Sure. We must have blankets somewhere." She rushed off to find one and I went back to Edna.

"They're bringing a blanket," I told her. "Where are your clothes?"

She'd managed to zip my jacket up to her chin, and she had her legs drawn up under it, close to her chest, her toes peeping out under the edge.

"In the closet," she said, pointing to a cupboard on the wall.

I opened it and got out the pantsuit and the blouse.

She started to stand up to get dressed, but she sat down, suddenly, on the edge of the table. "I'm light-headed," she said apologetically. "You'll have to give me a hand."

She'd put on her underpants and bra while I was gone. We managed to slide her into her pants while she was half sitting and half standing.

"Wait a minute," she said, when I reached for her blouse. She shut her eyes, and for the first time I realized how weak she was.

The young girl in the white lab coat knocked briefly, then came bustling in with a pale green blanket in one hand and a Styrofoam cup in the other. She wrapped the blanket around Edna's shoulders. "I brought you some tea," she said. "And I spoke to Dr. Dobbs. He'll be right in."

"Thank you," I told her.

When she was gone, Edna sipped the tea noisily. Then she quickly put on her blouse and jacket.

"He says I have to have surgery," she repeated, looking down at the buttons on her blouse. "They did all these tests. Jesus. I don't even know what all those tests were. They did a

chest X ray, and then they put me on a treadmill and hooked me up to some wires. That Dr. Dobbs came in after one of the tests and started talking about operating. I told them they needed to talk to Jeanne Payne. They said they paged her, but she hasn't called back yet."

"Finish getting dressed, Mom," I said. "We're getting you out of here right now. I'm sorry. You've had an awful time and it's my fault. This has got to be the dumbest stunt I've ever pulled."

"I wanted to come," Edna said. "They haven't given me my bill yet." She managed a smile. "Maybe they're afraid I'll have a real heart attack when I see it."

"Mrs. Garrity?"

We both turned toward the door. Carson Dobbs looked shorter then I'd remembered. His mild brown eyes and warm smile were all concern. The lock of hair falling over one eye made him look boyish, even vulnerable.

He looked at me oddly, as though he thought he recognized me, but maybe not. I was hoping he didn't remember me from Whitney's memorial service.

"I'm Callahan, Mrs. Garrity's daughter," I said. "What's all this talk about operating?"

He pulled a small rolling stool out from under a table and sat down. It was the only other place in the room to sit, so I stood, with my arms folded across my chest. The defensive posture.

Dobbs looked down at some notes. Then he leaned over and patted Edna's hands. "You're going to be fine, Edna," he said. "I know that surgery can sound frightening, but really, this is a very routine procedure. I'll do the cardiac catheriza-tion procedure. We can do it right here, tomorrow, at Piedmont. And the cardiothoracic surgeon I want you to see, Dr. McBride, is top notch."

I noticed Edna clinging to Dobbs's hands, listening intently to every word.

"What exactly is wrong with my mother?" I asked.

"Mitral valve prolapse," Dobbs said. "It's a small leakage across the mitral valve."

Edna's head snapped up. "Blood? Leaking into my heart? Is that why I have the chest pains and the shortness of breath?"

He nodded, then spoke to me, as though Edna weren't capable of understanding what he was saying. "We did an electrocardiogram on your mother today. Found nonspecific variations such as inverted t-waves." He frowned.

"Not good?" Edna asked.

"The exercise EKG showed depression of the ST segments, and then, when we did the chest X ray, we found calcium deposits in the area of the mitral valve. The echocardiogram confirmed what we already suspected: that she had floppiness of the valve."

He stood up and snapped his notebook shut. "You're very fortunate you came to us today. Another day or so and both Dr. McBride and I would be swamped. Big conference coming up. It just so happens that this will dovetail nicely into our schedules."

He stood up and squeezed Edna's shoulder, giving her an understanding smile. "When you're finished dressing, Suzanne, my insurance manager, will have some papers for you to fill out. And one of the nurses will give you your instructions for tomorrow. All right?"

"She doesn't have insurance," I said.

Carson Dobbs's smile faded fast. "Dr. Payne didn't mention that in her referral. Medicaid? I'm sorry, but we're not taking Medicaid patients right now."

"What?" Edna swung her head from me to Dobbs. She'd forgotten the original purpose of this visit. Understandable.

Dobbs sighed. "You understand you'll be responsible for today's workup, right?"

Edna bit her lip. "We understand that. I'll write a check. Will that be all right?"

"Fine." He gave Edna a sympathetic look. "They have a cardiac clinic over at Grady," he said. "You can probably get seen over there. It might take a couple of months, though."

Then he slipped out the door, pulling it closed behind him.

Edna clutched my arm. "He said I have blood leaking into my heart, Jules," she said. "What if I really do need surgery?"

"We'll talk to Jeanne today," I said. "I'll have the test results from Dobbs couriered over to her office. And she'll get you in to see that woman cardiologist she recommended in the first place."

I helped my mother down off the examining table. She was lighter than I remembered. I could feel her shoulder blades through the cloth of her jacket. Frail. Never, ever had I thought of my mother as frail.

"What if they won't give us the test results?" Edna worried. "I'll have to pay for all those tests again." I felt her shudder. "Go through it all over again."

"No you won't," I assured her. "After we pay with the check, I'll submit the bill to the insurance company directly. They'll pay."

We walked past a small glass-enclosed office that said INSURANCE in big gold letters. A smaller nameplate said S. SHADDEAU.

Suzanne was sitting behind her desk, leaning back in her chair, her fingertips laced across her belly, eyes closed. From here, her stomach bulged only very slightly. It was a lot flatter than mine, but today she was wearing a black-and-white-checked maternity top.

The nurse's station was right in front of us. The billing

clerk looked up at us, then back at her computer screen. "Will we be billing your insurance company?"

"No," I said. "We'll write a check. And I'd like complete itemized copies of the bill and all of the test results we're paying for."

She looked surprised. "We usually mail that kind of thing. You'll have it in three to five days."

I smiled sweetly. "We're paying now. We want the test results and the itemized bill now. Please."

23

IT WAS DUSK BY THE TIME WE GOT HOME. Maureen's car was in the driveway and the house was ablaze with lights. "Did you give her a key?" I asked.

Edna gave me an apologetic look.

"She's your sister. I called her when I didn't get you first. She was worried to death. Wanted to come right over and start prepping me for surgery. I calmed her down, but she said she was coming over after work to take a look at me for herself."

"Goody," I said glumly. I helped Edna out of the car. "I'm really looking forward to this."

Maureen met us at the door in full emergency alert mode. I was surprised she didn't attack Edna with a set of those defibrillators you see on television.

"Are you crazy?" she shrieked at me. "You should have let them admit her to the hospital. She shouldn't be walking around like this." Maureen took Edna's arm and nearly carried her to the sofa.

Then she whirled around to face me—the bad daughter. "We need to talk," she said. "What was Dr. Dobbs's diagnosis? All Mom could tell me was that he advised immediate surgery."

Edna twisted her wedding band nervously. "It's something called mitral valve prolapse. I think that's what he said. It means I have a leaky valve."

Maureen sat beside her and grabbed her shoulders. "That is very serious. Very dangerous, Mom. It means your heart's not operating efficiently. I want you to turn right around and go back to the hospital."

"I don't think so," Edna said slowly.

"No way," I said. "Carson Dobbs is not her doctor. I don't trust him."

"Me neither," Edna piped up. "When we told him I don't have insurance, he dropped me like a bad habit. I wouldn't let him doctor nobody."

"Jeanne Payne has a doctor she wants Edna to see," I added. "We just talked to her on the car phone. She'll see Edna next week. It's the best we could do. Usually it takes months to get an appointment with these specialists. Jeanne pulled strings to get Ma in."

Maureen chewed on her bottom lip. "We don't have time to wait," she said, her voice rising. "Ma's heart could go at any time. I'm a medically trained health care provider, Callahan, unlike you. And I'm telling you that this is serious stuff." Maureen took Edna's hand and her tone softened a little. "I know you don't want to go back in the hospital, Mom, but it's for your own good."

Edna smiled. "I'm not going back in the hospital, Maureen. Not until I've talked to this doctor Jeanne recommended, and gotten a second opinion."

She stood up, a little shakily. "You go on home now, hon.

I'm going to take a nap. I'll call you tomorrow. I'll be fine. You'll see."

Maureen gave me a withering look. "Fine. Let Callahan and her stupid detective tricks kill you. Don't listen to the only person in the family with an ounce of common sense."

After she'd slammed the door leaving, Edna shrugged. "She means well."

When Neva Jean showed up two hours later at the back door with a red runny nose and an overnight bag I felt so relieved I could have kissed her.

"The emus?"

She sneezed and nodded. "I never thought a goddamned hairy-legged bird would break up me and Swannelle, but it's gotten real bad, Callahan. He's set up a cot out in that pen. Hasn't been to work at the shop in two days 'cause he says he thinks Nancy's fixing to lay an egg and he wants to be right there when it happens."

"Come on in," I said soothingly. "Edna just got up from a nap. She'll be glad of the company."

Edna turned from the stove, where she was dropping dumplings into a pot of chicken stew. "Who says I need company?" she said sharply. The nap had done her a world of good. She was full of her old piss and vinegar again. "Where are you going, Jules? And who's going to eat all this food?"

"I've got to work," I said. "I'm going down to the men's shelter to talk to a guy who was on that work crew when Whitney was killed. I'll fix myself a plate when I get home."

Edna shook her head. She got two shallow bowls from the table and started ladling stew into one. "You're not going back out to that golf course again, are you?"

"Not tonight," I promised.

* * *

The Shrine of the Immaculate Conception has everything you want for a homeless men's shelter—namely, location. Right across the street from the state capitol building in Atlanta's downtown government complex, a potent reminder to local lawmakers of how miserably they'd done by the city's underclass.

I parked the van in a no-parking spot near the basement entrance to the shelter. I'd been there before, back in my cop days. As I was locking up the van, I saw a shadowy figure fade into the dark. Probably a latecomer, hoping for a handout from the kitchen door. The shelter at the Shrine works on a ticket system. You stay a night, mind your manners, and when you leave at six A.M. the next day, you get a ticket to come back that night. There are twenty-five beds in the basement cafeteria. The Shrine is safe and warm. You get a hot dinner cooked by volunteers and a bag lunch to take with you in the morning. But no ticket, no admittance. On really bitter winter nights, I'd heard tickets to the Shrine went for as much as twenty dollars a pop on the street.

The night shelter host, a stocky gray-haired man in a bulky knit sweater, didn't want to let me in.

"Men only," he said. "Try the Atlanta Union Mission shelter on Howell Mill. They take women."

I really was going to have to spiff up my wardrobe. "I just want to talk to Harold Eaves. He's one of your guests. Then I'll leave. Okay? It's important. A murder investigation."

"Harold Eaves? Murder?" The host picked up a dog-eared legal pad and looked down at his list of guests. "Nobody informed us of anything like that. The police haven't been around."

"He's not a suspect," I said quickly. "Nothing like that. But he might have seen something."

The gray-haired man gave it some thought. "All right.

Harold's a pretty easygoing type. Maybe he'll talk to you. He's over there."

He pointed toward a dark-skinned black man in a red turtleneck sweater who sat straddle-legged at the end of a narrow cot, a plastic bucket between his legs.

"What's he doing?" I asked, hesitating.

"His laundry," the host said. "Go ahead. Lights out in fifteen minutes."

Harold Eaves was squeezing suds out of a pair of gray athletic socks when I walked up.

"Mr. Eaves?"

He looked up warily. "Yeah?"

"I'm Callahan Garrity, Mr. Eaves," I said, handing him a business card. "I understand you were friends with Shawan Taylor."

Eaves wiped his sudsy hands on his pants and took the card.

"I knew him," he said slowly. He looked at the card, then put it under his cot, on top of a greasy brown grocery sack. Then he dipped into the bucket and drew out what looked like a pair of boxer shorts. "Seen Shawan around. He dead now."

"I know," I said, looking away out of my own bizarre sense of modesty. It didn't seem right to try to interrogate a man while he washed his undies. The low-ceilinged room was full of men. They sat in a semicircle around a television, smoking and talking, their voices echoing across the tile floor. Some of them lay on their cots, reading or sleeping. Everyone seemed to know what was expected of them.

I saw a couple of older white men, bearded and bleary-eyed, but all the rest of the men were black. Some looked at me with frank curiosity, but the majority had learned a long time ago to stay out of other people's business.

"You were on that county work crew picking up trash the day Shawan was killed," I said. "Someone told me you were close by. That you might have seen something."

"Deputies put us on the van and we left," Eaves said. "That the last time I saw that boy."

"But you saw him earlier," I said. "With Whitney Dobbs. The woman who was killed."

"He kinda liked that lady," Eaves said, a slow smile revealing cracked and blackened teeth.

Eaves was the second person to mention that Shawan Taylor stuck deliberately close to Whitney.

"Do you think he knew her? Maybe from somewhere else?"

He snorted. "How'd Shawan know a rich lady like that? She dressed real nice. New boots, all like that. She was rich. I knowed that."

It was ironic. Whitney had probably deliberately tried to dress down to make herself less conspicuous. But everybody had spotted her for what she was—a wealthy suburban housewife out slumming. I thought about the boots again, and then about Shawan Taylor's. He'd worn new shoes too.

"Mr. Eaves," I said, "the day Shawan was killed, he was wearing new Nikes. Brand new. Where would he get shoes like that?"

Eaves looked down at his own shoes. They'd been white tennis shoes once, but now they were stained from the streets, ripped at the seams, run-down at the toes.

"Stole 'em maybe," he suggested.

"Maybe," I agreed. "Did you ever see him leave the group Whitney was with that day?"

"He stuck right by her when I seen him," Eaves said. "Those old redneck deputies, I don't think they liked that."

"No breaks?" I asked. "What happens when somebody has to use the bathroom?"

"Pee in the ditch," Eaves said casually. "'Less you a woman. Then they take you to a gas station, something like that."

"Did you see anybody at all take a break? Whitney or the other women?"

He stretched the boxers and the wet socks out carefully on the tile under his cot. "Maybe. People be all over the place. Maybe I seen somebody go over to that building there on the golf course." He looked up at me thoughtfully. "Yeah. Shawan. He went over there. I seen him walk over to that building."

"The pro shop? You saw him go over there?"

"Him and some others."

I wondered what Shawan Taylor was doing at the pro shop. There were bathrooms, of course. And something else. A pay phone. Outside, with a little half roof over it. Had Taylor been a plant? Had he called somebody to tip them about where to find Whitney? Had the somebody decided to get rid of Taylor too?

"Mr. Eaves, did Shawan stay here at this shelter?"

"Sometimes. Sometime, he sleep over in an empty building they fixing to tear down over there near the stadium. Sometime, him and me, we get us a bed at Grady."

Taylor was still wearing the plastic bracelet when he was killed.

"You stayed at Grady too?" I asked.

Eaves grinned. "When I could. You got to act pretty sick. Coughing and spitting up and all. Shawan, he was good. He'd get way out somewhere, decide he needed a ride. He'd call up an ambulance, and when they get there, he seizes up like. Get hisself tooken to Grady. Get a hot bath, bed, hot dinner. You ever eat there?"

I had to admit that I hadn't.

"Shawan, he cough a lot, so they give him cough medicine. You can get high off that stuff," Eaves confided.

A thought occurred to me. "When you were with Shawan, did you ever meet a firefighter named Bryant Mayes? Heavyset black man, in his midthirties?"

"Mayes?" Eaves scratched thoughtfully at his chin.

"Maybe. One time, me and Shawan and some other dudes was staying in this old wooden house on Alum Avenue. Made us a fire and went to sleep. But that fire went bad. Me and Shawan almost burned up. Firemen had to drag us out of there. Man, that was bad."

Just then the overhead lights began to flicker on and off. The gray-haired host stood in the center of the room. "Lights off, men."

"When was the fire, do you remember?" I asked urgently.

Harold Eaves looked blank. "Last year, year before last?"

I guess he hadn't had time to enter it on his Day-Timer. I dug in the pocket of my jeans and came out with a twenty-dollar bill, which I put on the rough wool blanket. "Thank you, Mr. Eaves," I said.

He took the money and put it in the same grocery bag where he'd stored my card. "That's okay," he said. "Shawan, he was all right."

It was after nine o'clock. There was still time to get in some more work. But it had gotten colder, and I was wearing just a light sweatshirt over my T-shirt. I kept thinking about Edna. Maybe it was time to take care of things at home.

She and Neva Jean were both asleep on the den sofa when I got home. I woke Edna and steered her sleepily to her own bed, then helped Neva Jean make up the sofa bed. I stumbled off to my own bed then, exhausted. I read for a while, even tried to do some paperwork. At eleven, I turned off the light and dozed off.

All night long, though, I dreamed of new sneakers and folk artists and a doctor—a faceless, voiceless doctor who peered out from behind a surgical mask and chased my mother and me around and around a two-story-high operating table, flashing a shiny stainless steel scalpel.

24

IT WAS A DIRTY TRICK, but I decided to appeal to Bucky Deavers's baser instincts.

I called from the car phone.

"I'm sitting in front of the window at the Krispy Kreme," I said in a low throaty purr. "The conveyor belt just started up. The doughnuts are passing under the glazing thing. I can see steam rising up off them, they're so warm. Warm and sugary. Ooh. Now they're putting a big tray of those cream-filled things in the display case."

He groaned. "The ones with the glaze *and* the chocolate frosting?"

"Uh-huh. And the girl just put on a fresh pot of coffee. Meet me here in ten minutes?"

He groaned again. "You're evil, Garrity."

I went inside and staked out two stools at the counter. The Krispy Kreme on Ponce de Leon is an Atlanta institution. Hot doughnuts, twenty-four hours a day. It was eight A.M. and the

place was jammed. Cars pulled past the drive-up window out-side in a steady stream, and inside I had to wait five minutes for a couple of construction workers to vacate the stools.

While I waited, I looked idly out the window. Commuters on their way into downtown trickled past, slow as sludge. Most of the hookers and hustlers who worked this part of midtown had called it a night and gone home at dawn for some honest shut-eye, but I watched with interest when a skinny, long-legged young woman in a short, ratty fur coat wandered up and stood casually by the big neon Krispy Kreme sign. A few seconds later, a black teenager in earmuffs and an Atlanta Falcons ski cap hurried up to her. She glanced around casually, reached in the coat pocket, and brought out a hand-ful of cash. He had something for her in his hand too.

Just then, Bucky came in and slid into the seat next to mine.

"What ya staring at?" he asked.

"Nothing. I just think it's a hell of a note when you can do a crack deal in the parking lot of the Krispy Kreme. Hell, every cop in Atlanta comes in here at some point in the day. Is noth-ing sacred?"

"Strange days," Bucky agreed. "You ordered yet?"

"Waiting on you," I replied.

We both ordered coffee. I ordered a cake doughnut with chocolate frosting. Bucky ordered himself three cream-filled Bismarcks, six plain glazed, and six mixed jelly doughnuts. And then, because you get another dozen for only $1.99 extra, he ordered a dozen glazed. "For the office," he said.

He scarfed down two doughnuts and half a cup of coffee as soon as the waitress set it in front of him.

When he spoke, his expression was pained. "That lawyer you're working for? He called me up. Wants to depose me for the civil suit he's filing against Carson Dobbs. What a pain in the ass."

"I'm sorry," I offered. "Look. I talked to this guy who was on the work crew with Whitney that day. His name is Harold Eaves. He's homeless, and he was buddies with Shawan Taylor."

Bucky held up one of the cream-filleds and proceeded to suck out the filling. I had to look the other way. "We talked to Eaves too," he said. "He was on the van with the others when Whitney was killed. He saw nothing."

"Not then," I agreed. "but earlier. He saw Shawan go over to the pro shop. There's a pay phone right outside there, by the bathrooms."

"Shawan Taylor was homeless. No family, no job. Nothing. Who'd he be calling?"

"The shooter?" I suggested. "Think about it, Bucky. How did the murderer know where to find Whitney?"

"He could have followed the van from the sheriff's office," Bucky said. "That's what we think Mayes did. Followed the van, then hung around, waiting for the right moment. He takes his shot, then drives off."

"But he didn't drive off right away," I insisted. "You've got a witness who says he heard the shots and then saw somebody come running through the woods. And there's this old black man, a crazy artist named Arliss Woods, who was on the porch of his house. The shooter had to run right by him."

Bucky shook his head in exasperation. "Billy Tucker again. Was he sober the night he told you this fairy tale of his?"

My face colored a little. "He was sober to begin with."

"And then he got shit-faced, right? Billy Tucker hasn't drawn a sober breath in two years, Callahan. Hey—did he mention that he was drinking that day even before he got on that van?"

"What? Who says?"

"Once they were already on the van one of the deputies noticed Billy was acting funny. He patted him down. They

found six of those little airline bottles in his pocket. Two were already empty."

"But I've been out there, Bucky. I found the shack Tucker saw, it's exactly the way he described it. And I talked to neighbors. This Arliss Woods, he's like a hermit. Nobody's seen him since the day of the murders."

"You've been out there messing around in the Promised Land?" Bucky asked. "By yourself? Are you nuts? Those people don't like outsiders messing around out there. You wanna get shot?"

"It was broad daylight," I said, waving away his concerns. "And I was carrying. Nobody bothered me. Anyway, I thought you'd be interested in hearing about Harold Eaves and Shawan Taylor. They hung out together. Last year, they were camping in an abandoned house over on Alum Street and there was a bad fire. The firemen had to drag the two of them out of there. Isn't Alum Street somewhere near the firehouse where Bryant Mayes works?"

"Mayes worked out of Station Twenty-two. The Double Deuce," Bucky said. "Maybe five miles away. But if it was a big enough fire, Twenty-two might have sent a unit too. When did you say the fire was?"

He was busy now, making notes on a paper napkin.

"Last year was all Eaves could tell me. I know the ambulance took them to Grady. They're both rooters. Shawan Taylor also had a cough medicine habit."

Bucky nodded. "We can check Grady's admission records for Taylor and Eaves, see if they were brought in and treated for smoke inhalation."

He picked up a glazed doughnut and held it between his thumb and forefinger and dunked it in his coffee. "You hear about the special investigator the Justice Department sent down here?"

"Yeah."

"Squinty-eyed little bastard," Bucky said. "He's been going through my personnel files, talking to perps on my old cases. I'm supposed to have an interview with him later today. I know what he wants. Wants to prove I'm some kind of racist pig out to nail Bryant Mayes because he's black. This whole thing pisses me off."

I made sympathetic noises. "It's a load of crap. Kind of hard to defend yourself against being a racist though, isn't it? I've been going through the same thing with one of the girls."

Bucky chewed off the edge of the coffee-sopped pastry. "Hey. Tell me the truth. We both know you don't believe Bryant Mayes did this murder. So why are we even having this conversation this morning?"

"Remember Shawan Taylor?" I asked. "I was thinking about those shoes he was wearing. Brand-new Nikes. Where does somebody whose latest mailing address is under the downtown connector get shoes that cost ninety dollars? I've got a theory. I think Shawan was paid off by somebody to tip them about where Whitney was going that day. Shawan makes the call, goes back to work, sticks close by Whitney so the shooter can find her. Only instead of walking away with the rest of his pay, Shawan got another free ride to Grady. To the morgue."

"It could have been Bryant Mayes," Bucky said. "He had motive, opportunity, and most important, the weapon."

"Or it could have been Carson Dobbs," I said doggedly. "If Whitney went ahead with her plan to fight the divorce settlement, he could have been in serious trouble. We know he was cooking the books. We just don't quite know all the details. Now Whitney's dead. Carson's problems all go away. He marries his girlfriend, has a new baby, life is good. And he makes it look like a black guy did it. Nice plan, huh?"

Bucky tapped the side of my head with his fingertip. "Only

problem is, the plan's all in there. In your little punkin head. Me, I got to work with what's there. Evidence. And evidence don't care what color somebody is. It's just evidence."

"Check out that fire," I said. "Who knows? Maybe you're right. Maybe Bryant Mayes hooked up with Shawan Taylor back then, with the idea that he'd get him to help him with his dirty work."

"If the fire didn't happen after Faneeta was killed, it's no good to us," Bucky reminded me. "Still. It's a decent lead. Now what do you want?"

"Me?" I waited for what I considered to be a decent interval. "Carson Dobbs is claiming that his business manager bilked him for millions. Only he didn't file charges against the guy. The manager's name is Ben Dwyer. He's disappeared. I want to know if he's got a past."

"You got DOB, social security number, anything useful like that?"

I handed him the copy of Dwyer's lease that I'd gotten from his apartment manager. "You can tell the bosses this is a legit search because it's connected to Whitney," I said. "Maybe he knows something."

"Right," Bucky said, unconvinced. "Anything else, while I'm doing your dirty work?"

"Now that you offered . . . Carson's girlfriend, Suzanne Shaddeau. She handles all the insurance for the medical practice. If they're pulling the scam I think they are, she's got to be involved. I'd like to know about her past. And I'd really like to know if she has a different address. We don't think the address they're using is for real."

Bucky wrote some stuff on the back of the lease agreement I'd given him. "What do you know about Shaddeau?" he asked.

"Nothing," I said. "But at least you have access to driver's

license records. That'll give you everything you need to start with."

"Thanks for the advice on how to do my job," Bucky said.

I gave him a kiss on the cheek and slid quickly from the stool I'd been sitting on. I had to get out of there. The combination of sugar and grease was getting to be too much even for me. Besides, I had my own work to do.

25

ZACK ALEXANDER WANTED THE GOODS on Carson Dobbs. We knew about the scam he'd pulled with the sale of his town house, selling it back to his own medical practice, but we also both knew there was more.

After I left the Krispy Kreme I went back over my notes on the case and I found a thread that needed pulling. Carol Steiner, Carson's nurse, had mentioned that Suzanne kept horses.

But where? She'd also mentioned that one of Suzanne's horses had been ill the past summer. So ill it had to be hospitalized. Maybe if I found where she kept her horses I'd also find her own place.

If she kept horses, she had to feed them and buy saddles. And pay vet bills. I hauled the Yellow Pages out of the back of my van and started with veterinarians.

There were nine pages of listings. A feeling of hopelessness crept over me. Some of the vets listed specialties: cats, exotic

birds, reptiles. Some were veterinary dentists, even dermatologists. There was even a vet who specialized in homeopathic treatments for animals.

I glanced around me to make sure there were no friendly neighborhood crack dealers closing in on the van. Then I read down the listings, one by one. Finally, about midway through, I found a vet in Lithonia who advertised his specialty in equine surgery.

I made up my story as I went along. "I'm new to the area," I told the receptionist who answered the phone. "I met a woman named Suzanne Shaddeau at a horse show and she told me such wonderful things about the vet who'd saved her horse's life last summer. Now my daughter's new horse is sick, and I need a vet immediately. I can't call Suzanne," I added lamely, "because she's out of town."

"Shaddeau?" I heard the clicking of a computer keyboard. "I don't see her name in our patient files. But Dr. Jenkins is really excellent. What did you say was wrong with your horse?"

"Uh, well, I'm not sure," I said, hedging. Everything I knew about horses I'd learned from watching *Fury* on television in the sixties.

"I, uh, think he ate some locoweed," I said, remembering an episode in which Fury had nearly died from eating a poisonous plant.

"Locoweed? I never heard of locoweed growing around here. Where is your horse pastured?"

"In a field," I said. This woman was wasting my time. I had more vets to call. "So, uh, do you know any other vets who might have treated my friend's horse?"

"Dr. Jenkins is the best," she said frostily.

"So you say," I retorted.

I tried two more vets with no success until I mentioned that Suzanne's horse had had to have surgery.

"If it was anything serious they probably took it to the vet school up in Athens," the vet's young assistant explained. "There or Auburn. Do you want me to have Dr. Oglesby call you back?"

"Never mind," I said, tired of the game.

Of course, as soon as I called the first tack shop, I hit pay dirt. I'd made up some story about needing a saddle, and having met Suzanne at a horse show.

"Oh yes," the girl on the phone gushed. "Dr. Dobbs just bought the most beautiful hand-tooled saddle for her birthday. He has the most exquisite taste. We hated to have it leave the shop."

"I can't wait to see it," I gushed back. "You know, Christmas is coming up, and I was telling my husband I need a new saddle. I'd love to see Suzanne's."

"We delivered it to her barn last week," the girl said. "Otherwise you could come out and see it here. Why don't you ask her to let you take a peek at it?"

"I would, but she's out of town," I said, sounding disappointed.

"What a shame," the girl said. "Maybe you can catch the girl who comes in and grooms her horses during the day. She'd be happy to show you Suzanne's tack room."

"I'd love it," I squealed. "Can you give me directions to the barn? I just get lost every time I go out there."

"No problem," the girl said. And she proceeded to give me detailed directions to El Rancho Dobbs.

The house was in North Fulton, as we'd suspected, in the rolling hills outside of Alpharetta. Once the land had been cotton farms. Now it was too expensive to farm, but just right for five- and ten-acre "estate homes" where the BMWs and the Mercedeses roamed alongside expensive show horses.

I found a newly paved street off the state road, and off that a narrow, tree-lined dirt lane that matched the description given to me by the girl at the tack shop. It had rained off and on all week, and the road was slick with mud and rutted from other car tracks.

After about a quarter mile, I drove through an open fence and onto a paved driveway, and in another quarter mile I drove into a clearing dominated by a spanking new three-story white Greek Revival mansion.

It had columns across the front, leaded fanlights at the front door, and six matching new rockers lined up on the porch so that the gentry could survey their holdings. They must have just finished construction fairly recently, because there was still a stack of lumber over to the side of the house, half covered with a plastic tarp.

The builder had been justly proud of his work. At the entrance to what would be the front yard, now taken up with stacks of sod and rows of burlap-balled trees and shrubs, he'd erected a large cutout wooden sign in the shape of the Dobbs mansion. CUSTOM HOMES BY CUTLIP & SONS, the sign said. I jotted down the builder's phone number. Zack would be very pleased.

I parked the van way over to the side, under some trees, hoping it might be inconspicuous if anyone came calling.

Then I walked briskly up to the front porch. My cover story, if anybody showed, would be that I owned a cleaning business and had heard the new owners might be interested in hiring help.

I peeked in through the front windows. The hallway was done in green marble, with a huge crystal chandelier and a curved staircase rising up through an atrium-style space to the second and third floors. Inside I could see some furniture, most of it still draped in the plastic from the store, and a scrap of

muddy carpet where the owners had been wiping their shoes after walking through all the construction muck.

The porch wrapped all the way around the house. I moved on to the side, looking in at a dark-paneled study where cartons of medical texts were still being shelved. A big mahogany desk took up one corner of the room. The only things on it were a sleek black telephone and one of those pouty glamour-shot photos of Suzanne Shaddeau in an ornate silver frame. Oh yes. I had the right house.

At the back of the house I found what had to be the master suite. They hadn't had time to put up what Suzanne would undoubtedly refer to as "window treatments" here, so somebody had tacked a bedsheet across the window. Fortunately, the window was grander than the sheet.

Inside I saw an immense carved four-poster bed. A rug was rolled up against one wall, and a welter of paint cans, brushes, and ladders took up the other wall. The bed had linens on it though, and I could see large unopened cartons marked "clothes" in the center of the room. The house was still being worked on, but it looked like Carson and Suzanne had moved in, at least temporarily.

If I looked away from the house and the clearing around it, I could see a glimpse of water through the trees. It was a pond. I walked a little ways through the woods and saw a corner of what looked like a large new barn, with an enclosed riding ring. Some spread for a doctor teetering at the edge of poverty.

I was peering in at the kitchen through a set of French doors when I heard a car drive up around front. My heart was beating fast, but I tried to calm myself, reasoning that it was probably just one of the contractors. I could recite my story and make a quick but decent exit.

I tiptoed around the corner of the house to see who the company was. Bad news. Suzanne was climbing out of one of those

huge Ford Explorers suburban women have taken to driving lately. She was dressed in her idea of country casual: tight jeans, high-heeled boots, and one of those expensive shearling coats.

The driver of the Explorer looked like she'd dressed for lunch at the club. She was middle-aged, with the kind of hairdo more properly called a coiffure, and she wore a calf-length dark fur coat. She frowned at the muddy drive, but reached back in the car for a bolt of fabric and a book of wallpaper samples.

It was a designer visit. This could take hours. I sighed and tried to plot my escape. The van was parked around front, under some trees not terribly far from where the designer was parked. There was no way Suzanne could have missed seeing my van.

I hopped off the porch and made for the tree line. The plan was for me to skirt the house through the woods, come back around the front, and make a dash for the van.

And it almost worked. I was a few yards away from the van when the voice pierced the autumn quiet.

I looked up. Suzanne had come out onto the front porch and was heading down the steps, hands on hips, looking una-mused.

"Excuse me," she called. "What are you doing on my property?"

My face burned. The price you pay when you do as much sneaking around as I do is that sometimes you get caught.

Immediately I ditched the cleaning lady pretext. "I was looking for the Carroll place," I said. "I feel so stupid. Must have made the wrong turn."

"Wait a minute," Suzanne said, stepping into the mud bath of a front yard. "I know you. You were in our office the other day. With an older lady. You took up all Carson's time, and then you didn't even have insurance."

The mud was slimy and slippery. It was slowing her down, but she was making a determined advance toward me. And I was making just as determined a retreat, backpedaling as fast as I could, a stupid feckless grin on my face as a disguise.

"Hey!" Suzanne said. "You were at Whitney's funeral too. With that goddamned lawyer who's suing us. Hey you. Stop right there. You're trespassing. I'm calling the police. Hell, I'm calling our lawyer. You can't come sneaking around out here . . . "

I took the last few yards at a flat run. Fortunately, I'd left the keys in the ignition. I started the motor and began backing away from the trees. And backed right over something fairly sizable. A rock or some lumber, I didn't know and I didn't care. I threw it in forward and jerked the steering wheel to the right. The tires spun in the mud, so I backed again, hit the rock again, then put it in forward and floored it.

I could hear the rear tires spinning mud as they tried to gain traction. Suzanne was screaming something at me, but I couldn't make it out. Finally, the van shot forward and I sped up the rutted dirt road as fast as I dared.

When I was back on dry paved road again I allowed myself a small smile of satisfaction. I'd found the house. And it was a nice one. Worth hiding. I wondered idly how much it had cost. A million or two? It would be a nice place to raise a child. Lots of trees to climb, horses to ride, a pond to fish in. Of course, if one of your parents had killed somebody in order to be able to give you all this, it could take away some of the luster. But what the hell, Carson was a doctor. And psychiatrists give professional discounts.

Escapes always make me hungry. Part of my original plan had been to visit the restaurant where Bollinger had staked out Carson and Suzanne. But the restaurant was useless now. I'd found what I was looking for.

I had another idea. This was a familiar neighborhood. Just a couple miles up the highway there was another dirt lane leading to another horse farm. And a log caretaker's cabin.

Mac's place. Somehow I'd avoided coming up this way for months and months. After the breakup, he'd kept calling for a while. I knew Edna and C. W. and Linda kept in touch with him still, but I hadn't laid eyes on the man since the morning after I'd caught him cheating on me. With his ex-wife.

It had been a long, lonely old year since then. I'd ignored the advice of my shrink, my family, and my friends, and refused to take him back. I was still hurting, still missing him. I'd gone to a Braves game once, back in early summer, and at the concession stand I thought I saw the back of his familiar salt-and-pepper hair. I'd walked straight back to my seat without the beer or the hot dog I'd gone for.

The misty cold rain that had turned on and off like a faucet all week was off at the moment. The sun seemed to wash the surrounding hillside in soft Renaissance golds and ambers. It was the middle of the afternoon. Why not take a run past the cabin? No harm to it. Maybe I'd stop and say hello to Rufus, Mac's clownish black Lab.

There was a mom-and-pop country store on the way to Mac's place. Beer and bait and canned biscuits and cigarettes. But they've also got a small deli counter in the back. You wouldn't want to see what they consider salami, but they do make a mean pimento cheese on white bread. I got a sandwich, a bag of potato chips, a cold Diet Coke, and a small box of Milk-Bones for my buddy Rufus.

When I pulled into the yard, Rufus recognized the pink van at once and came bounding out to greet me. He nearly knocked me over as I got out, jumping up, licking my face, wagging his tail in a joyous nonstop frenzy.

Of course, he could have smelled the Milk-Bones. I pre-

ferred to believe it was me that he was delirious about.

"Hiya boy, hi boy," I crooned, kneeling down to scratch his ears, cradling his muzzle between my hands. I didn't even flinch when he licked my face. "That's right. It's Callahan. But it's a secret, remember?"

I looked around cautiously. No sign of Mac's Blazer. Rufus ran ahead of me to the cabin.

I picked a sunny spot on the front steps for my picnic, unwrapped the wax paper covering my sandwich, and stretched. I had to throw Rufus a couple of Milk-Bones to get him to stop sniffing at my pimento cheese.

I'd demolished the first half of my sandwich and I had a mouthful of salt-and-vinegar potato chips when I heard the creak of the front door opening.

I froze.

A pair of boots walked slowly across the wooden porch floor. I didn't turn around to see whose they were. I didn't need to. He sat down on the steps beside me. He whistled softly, once, and Rufus abandoned his treat and trotted obediently forward. Mac nudged the dog with the toe of his boot and Rufus flopped over on his back to have his belly scratched. "Well, look what the dog dragged in," Mac said quietly.

I didn't say anything at first. After all, I had a mouthful of salt-and-vinegar potato chips. I took a long sip of Diet Coke and considered my options.

Caught trespassing twice in the same day. If the state licensing board for private investigators got word of this they might make me turn in my X-ray glasses and my secret decoding ring.

Life was no fair. Mac had gotten sexier. I had gotten— what? Tired?

"You shaved," was my brilliant opener.

His chin had half a day's stubble, but the full gray Papa Hemingway beard was gone. It made him look ten years younger than his real age, which was pushing fifty.

He rubbed his jaw. "Yeah. Corporate life. They make me wear a suit and tie and carry a briefcase too."

"That sucks," I observed.

"Pay's not bad," he said. "I bought the cabin, you know."

I didn't know. He'd rented this deluxe caretaker's cottage for at least eight years from the wealthy family who owned the horse farm. Once upon a time, we'd discussed his giving up the cabin and moving into town to live with me. Both of us knew it wouldn't work. We'd blamed Rufus, who needed room to roam, but we'd both known that Mac needed the country as much as his dog.

I put the uneaten half of my sandwich back in the paper sack I'd brought it in. I crumpled the empty chip bag and added it and the Coke can to my litter sack. With as much dignity as I could muster, I brushed the potato chip crumbs off my lap and stood up. Rufus looked up at me, reproach in his soft dark eyes.

"Guess I'd better go," I said. "I've got a big case, been working nonstop."

"So that's what this was?" Mac asked, puzzled, but not angry. "A pit stop? Would you at least like to come in and use the bathroom?"

"Oh, no. No thanks," I said hastily. "See, I was just down the road working a case, and I hadn't eaten lunch and it's such a pretty afternoon, I thought I'd run by and see Rufus."

"Rufus," he said, his voice flat. "Not me."

"I assumed you'd be at work," I said. "There was no car. I didn't want to intrude."

"You're not," he said. "The Blazer's in the shop. I'm taking a vacation day. Sure you don't want to come in? I'm alone, if that's what you're worried about."

"I'd better go," I said. "Some people I need to talk to."

Mac took my hand for a minute, then let it go. "It was only that one time, you know," he said. "One stupid, drunken, it'll-never-happen-again time. She got married to that guy she was dating. They're moving to Houston after Christmas."

"My shrink says it's time to forgive and forget," I heard myself saying. "Time to move forward."

"Sounds like a smart shrink," Mac said.

"I don't know," I said doubtfully. "She's the one who talked me into going to work for Whitney Dobbs. Now Whitney's dead, and I'm up to my ears in this murder investigation, trying to run The House Mouse and keep tabs on Edna's health."

"I talked to Edna not long ago," Mac said. "Try not to worry too much about her, Callahan. Your mother's a tough old bird. She's a survivor."

"With a prolapsed mitral valve," I said. "She might have to have surgery. Did she mention that?"

He laughed. "She just called it heart trouble. Said it was heart trouble made her quit smoking."

"At least some good came out of it," I admitted.

"You're working too hard," Mac said suddenly. "Spreading yourself too thin, like always. Can't you slow down, Callahan? Maybe take on somebody to help with business?"

"I wish," I said fervently. "The business is at a critical stage right now. We've got to grow to make a decent profit, but I just can't find competent help."

"I wasn't talking about The House Mouse," Mac said. "Can't you scale back on this P.I. stuff? Edna's worried about you running around all hours of the night and day. She says you don't sleep."

I was fuming. What else had my darling mother been

telling Mac? "I can take care of myself, Mac. You of all people should know that."

"Yeah," he said, his jaw set angrily. "I forgot. Callahan Garrity can do it all."

Our conversation was starting to sound like a bad rerun. All the anger and bitterness came flooding back. A cloud scudded in front of the sun, and things went gray again. Back to November.

I leaned down and patted Rufus's head. "I gotta go," I said.

He didn't tell me good-bye, didn't follow me to the van. When I looked in the rearview mirror, I saw him standing on the porch, holding Rufus by the collar to keep him from chasing me down.

26

FOOD HEALS A BROKEN HEART, but all I had left was a soggy half sandwich, so I threw myself back into my work.

Cutlip & Sons Custom Builders were located about two miles away. Their office was a miniature mansion. As I pulled into the driveway, a tall blonde woman came out the front door of the office and turned to lock the door. She was getting into a pickup truck with the words Cutlip & Sons on the door when I pulled alongside of her. I honked to get her attention, and she looked up, startled.

"Hi," I said. "I'm looking for Mr. Cutlip?"

"Me too," she said. "He and our secretary went out for a sandwich three years ago and never came back."

"So you're the builder?" I asked.

"Now I am," she said. "My sons are Scott and Steve. I'm Lisa. Is this urgent?"

"Kind of," I said, smiling engagingly. "I just saw a house I

really liked. And it had your sign on it. Over on Bradford Ferry Road?"

She nodded and put her keys back in her pocket. "Mrs. Laidlaw's house," she said proudly. "It's great, isn't it? That was a custom job, but we can probably do something pretty similar if you've got the right lot."

"Mrs. Laidlaw?" I said, confused. "I thought that was Carson Dobbs's house."

"Nope," she said. "Doreen Laidlaw. And of course, Suzanne, her niece. Suzanne is who we dealt with."

"Suzanne Shaddeau?"

"That's right," Lisa Cutlip said. "Mrs. Laidlaw is her great-aunt. As soon as her hip's better, she'll be moving down here."

"Down here from where?" I asked.

Lisa Cutlip's gray eyes flickered over me, and then my pink van.

"You're not in the market for a house like that," she said quietly. "Why are you really so interested in that house?"

Lying takes a certain amount of energy, I've found. And at that moment, my energy level was about a quart low. "I'm a private detective," I admitted. "I'm interested in Suzanne Shaddeau and her fiancé."

"The doctor?" One of her pale blonde eyebrows shot up in surprise. "Why? What's he done?"

"Maybe you saw it on the news? Carson Dobbs's wife was murdered."

"I don't watch the news," Lisa Cutlip said. "I'm on the site at sunup and I generally stay until the subs leave at night. The only reason you caught me here is that we're between jobs right now, and I had a mound of paperwork to do. I was just leaving to go look at a lot."

"Carson and Whitney were in the middle of negotiating a divorce settlement when Whitney was shot to death," I told

her. "Carson was claiming he was broke. Whitney didn't believe it. I was hired to find out where he was hiding his assets. Now their daughter is my client. We think Carson's money paid for that house you just built."

"Not as far as I know," she said firmly. "It's Doreen Laidlaw's house. Suzanne had power of attorney, and we dealt mainly through her. But Mrs. Laidlaw's name is on the deed. And she paid cash. No mortgage."

Interesting. "Where did you say she was moving from?"

"Knoxville, Tennessee," she said.

"Did you ever meet her?" I asked.

"No," Lisa said. "Suzanne handled everything. She mentioned that she's her aunt's only living relative."

"How old a lady is she?"

She frowned. "I never asked, but I would gather she's at least in her seventies."

"Don't you think all of this is a little odd?" I asked. "An elderly woman with a hip injury, wanting to build a house that big—three stories—at that age? Aren't most people that age moving to a condo in Florida?"

"We designed a ground-floor master suite for her," Lisa explained. "Suzanne is going to live upstairs and look after Mrs. Laidlaw."

"Have you been over to that house lately?"

"I walked through with Suzanne last week," Lisa said. "We're essentially done over there."

I took a deep breath. "I saw the house today. Suzanne's stuff is in the master suite you described. And Carson Dobbs's stuff is there too. I don't suppose you'd be willing to save us both some time?"

"What do you mean?" she asked. "I've really got to get going. Like I told you, that deal is done. What they do with their house is none of my business."

"My client's attorney can get a court order to have you produce all the records pertaining to the house and Doreen Laidlaw," I told her. "You'll have to hire a lawyer. It'll be a pain in the ass neither of us needs."

She checked her watch. "Jesus. What is it you want?"

"A look at the sales contract for that house. Any of the paperwork pertaining to it. An address for Doreen Laidlaw. The name of the bank where her checks were issued."

"All right," she said, turning back toward the office. "But let's make it quick."

Half an hour later, I had what I needed.

When I got home, Ruby's car was in the driveway. It was only three-thirty. She should have still been working, unless her blood pressure was acting up. Or something was wrong at the house. I hurried in the kitchen door. Ruby was on the phone, her voice high and childlike, but polite. She sounded confused.

"No, I'm sorry," she was saying. "Callahan can't come to the phone. She's out on business. That's right. A cleaning business."

I stood in front of her and motioned for her to hand over the phone. "Here," Ruby said, covering the mouthpiece to avoid being overheard. "She won't tell me what she wants."

"This is Callahan Garrity," I said crisply. "What can I do for you?"

"You the detective?" Her voice was low, cautious. Hard to tell, but she sounded sort of young, maybe in her twenties.

"Among other things," I said.

"Say," she said. "You got some kinda assistance program for people giving you confidential information?"

"Sometimes. What's this about?"

"I could use some assistance," she said.

"What kind of information are we talking about?"

"Arliss Woods. I hear you're looking for him."

The old man in the shack. The Promised Land. "Yes," I said, trying not to sound too eager. "Have you seen Arliss Woods?"

"How much assistance we talking about?" she asked.

I opened my billfold and looked at my cash supply. I had three twenties. "How about twenty dollars?"

"How 'bout forty?" she shot back. "I got expenses."

"A phone call's only a quarter," I pointed out. "Thirty."

She thought about that.

"You know that house you come to the other day? Over in the Promised Land? That's my friend you talked to. He stays there sometime. You go back there, give the money to him, tell him it's assistance for Wanda. But you got to go right now."

"How do I find Arliss Woods?" I asked.

"He's gonna tell you that after he's got my money," she said. "You're a white lady, ain't you?"

"That's right. So what?"

"Arliss don't like white peoples," the young woman said. "A white man came over there one time acting all nice. Next thing you know, he stole all a Arliss's pictures."

I looked over at Ruby. It wasn't until then that I noticed the television was on in the den, and Baby and Sister were sitting in front of it, engrossed in their favorite soap opera.

"I'll get a friend of mine to talk to him," I assured her.

"Come right now," she repeated. "Arliss, he don't stay in one place."

"We finished up early," Ruby said after I'd hung up. "I brought Baby and Sister back here, to see if y'all had another job for us. But Edna's in the bed asleep. I hated to wake her up."

"Asleep?" Edna never took naps in the middle of a business day. At least, she hadn't up until now.

I went back to her bedroom. She'd wrapped herself in a knit afghan and she was asleep on top of the bedspread. I sat down on the edge of the bed and put my ear to her chest. She seemed to be breathing fine, snoring softly.

Her eyes flickered open. "What?"

"Nothing," I said, standing up. "The girls were a little worried about you, that's all."

She sat up slowly and patted her hair into place with one hand, with the other she seemed to be searching for something on her bedside table.

"Damn," she said. "I forgot. No cigarettes."

"That's right," I said. "Go back to sleep. I can take care of things around here."

"Like hell you can," she retorted, struggling to her feet. "I've got to get those girls back to work. Is Neva Jean back too?"

"Just Ruby and the Easterbrooks," I said. "Anyway, I've got a job for them."

"Ruby and Baby and Sister?" Her eyes narrowed with suspicion. "What kind of job?"

"Just a little missionary work," I told Edna. "Nothing you'd be interested in."

Fortunately, Ruby had her Bible and a cardboard box of gospel tracts in the trunk of her car.

"You never know," she said jubilantly, patting the box that now rested on her lap. "You never know when the time will come to tell the Good News."

"Amen to that," Sister called from the backseat of the van. "Spread the Gospel and get paid for being a detective."

"Tell us again, Callahan, what we're supposed to do," Baby said. "These two old fools think we're out to save souls."

"Read him all the Bible passages you want, if that's what it takes," I said, repeating my earlier instructions. "Then try to get him to talk about the day of the shooting. Ask him if he heard the gunshots, or saw the pretty woman in the baseball cap getting shot. Ask him if he saw somebody. Somebody in a green jacket running past in a big hurry. See if you can get a description. If it's going good, ask him if he'll talk to me."

"You say this man don't like white people?" Ruby fretted. "I've heard about this Promised Land. I know about that part of town, Callahan. Those people don't like strangers. I heard people get shot over there."

"It's all right in the daytime," I said, not too convincingly. "We'll be long gone before dark. You all are God-fearing, Bible-toting ladies. Nobody's going to mess with you."

"They better not," Baby said, raising a liver-spotted hand and making chopping motions in the air. "I know Joe-jitsu. Karate too. Somebody tries to mess with us, I'll whip their ass."

"Miss Baby," Ruby said, shocked.

"I will too," Baby promised. "Got me a can of Mace right here in my bosom."

"Leave off the Mace, Miss Baby," I advised. "I'll be right here. And my gun is right here under the seat."

We were in the Promised Land now. And it definitely did not live up to its name. The street was narrow, with potholed asphalt. A half block of storefronts made up the business district: a liquor store, video arcade, Laundromat, and fish market. Men and women stood outside the liquor store, drinking from bottles in brown paper bags. Across the street in front of the arcade, two teenage girls stood face-to-face, screaming obscenities we could hear through the van's rolled-up windows.

"Better take that gun out and get it loaded up," Sister said, shaking her head. "These people don't look like they're ready for salvation just yet."

27

WANDA'S FRIEND WAS FRIENDLIER the second time around. He answered the door before I'd finished knocking. The same sleepy baby was on his shoulder.

"You got something for me? Forty bucks?"

"For Wanda," I said. "Where can I find Arliss Woods?"

He poked his head out the door and looked up and down the street. "Yellow cab just dropped him off with a sack of groceries. Hour ago."

"Where?" I asked patiently. And stupidly.

He grinned widely. "His place."

I'd been had. I took a twenty and put it in his outstretched hand.

"Hey," he said. "We had an agreement."

"I got expenses," I said, turning to go. "Deal with it."

Ruby clutched her Bible tightly when I pulled the van into the dead end and pointed out Arliss's shack. "My goodness," she said. "You mean to tell me somebody lives in there?"

"He's an artist," I said.

"He's crazy," Baby said.

"You got that movie camera?" Sister asked. "I could use that purse. Hit that old man if he tries something sneaky."

"Yes," Ruby chimed in. "It's my turn to take the movie, isn't it, Callahan?"

"Afraid not," I said regretfully. "I gave it back to the lawyer."

It wasn't a bad idea. If Arliss Woods had seen something important, I could turn the tape over not just to Zack, but to the cops. If everything went well, I promised myself, I'd bring it next time.

Ruby got out of the van first and helped the Easterbrooks sisters disembark, each with a fistful of Ruby's Gospel pamphlets. I watched as they approached the shack, arm in arm, looking around doubtfully at the mound of trash that surrounded it. They managed to climb up on the porch and I held my breath as the little building listed to one side under their combined weight.

Baby stepped boldly up to the door and knocked. From where I sat, slumped down in the van, I couldn't see who answered. But a moment later, she took a half step backward, turned, and gave me the okay signal. Then all three of them went inside.

For the first five minutes or so, I kept my eyes glued to the shack. Nobody approached. Once, I saw something stirring at the edge of the trash heap and I tensed, leaning forward to get a better look. It was a rat. The biggest, ugliest rat I'd ever seen. I swallowed hard and hoped he shared Ruby's low opinion of Arliss Woods's home.

When the rat scampered off into a pile of old tires, I relaxed a little. Then I got bored. I glanced over at the notebook where I'd written the information I'd gleaned from Lisa Cutlip's file on Suzanne Shaddeau's house.

All the checks to Cutlip & Sons were drawn on Cumberland Savings and Loan of Knoxville, Tennessee. The account was in the name of Doreen Laidlaw and Suzanne Shaddeau, the address a post office box in Atlanta. Lisa Cutlip had told me that the checks had cleared her bank without a hitch.

It was four-thirty now. Late, but I decided to try calling the bank anyway. As I'd halfway expected, I got a recording telling me to call back between business hours, nine to four, Monday through Friday.

I watched the shack for a few more minutes. No more rats. Then I called Knoxville directory information. There were six Laidlaws listed in the greater Knoxville area. No initial D. I dialed three numbers, found somebody home at the third. She sounded young and out of breath.

"My husband is Pete Laidlaw, there's only two Laidlaws in town who aren't related to us," she said. "And I never heard of a Doreen. Must be from the Arkansas branch."

I called Zack next and told him I'd found the house—and Suzanne. He copied down the information I gave him about the bank in Knoxville.

"But they're not going to give me anything without some kind of an order from a judge," he said. "You got any contacts in Tennessee?"

"Don't think so," I said gloomily.

"We're close," Zack said. "If I could just get some elbow room from this damn judge."

"I could take a run up to Knoxville," I said. "It's what, four or five hours by car?"

"Not without more to go on," he said. "You'd just be spinning your wheels. What else have you got?"

I told him about Arliss Woods.

"The neighbors say he's crazy?" Zack asked. "How crazy?

Would he make any kind of a witness even if he did see something?"

"I don't know yet," I admitted, watching a skinny yellow cat picking its way across the trash pile. I hoped he was a good mouser.

"Hey," Zack said. "Talked to your mother a while ago. That was good work."

"What?"

Suddenly I saw all three girls step out onto the front porch. Ruby was still facing the door and talking animatedly.

"Gotta go," I told Zack, and I hung up.

Now Baby and Sister were on the porch, pulling Ruby by her arm. And then a fourth person stepped out.

Arliss Woods was tall. He was so skinny he reminded me of a cartoon figure. Maybe six foot four, and his faded blue overalls and green work shirt flapped on his frame like the clothes on a scarecrow. He was nearly bald, with a little cloud of fuzzy white hair that clung to the very back of his head. He flapped his arms as he spoke, obviously agitated about something. And he held something in one hand, a board or something, that he kept gesturing with.

I rolled the window down to try to hear what he was saying, but the words were too faint.

Ruby was making good-bye gestures, talking and edging away from him. She and Baby stepped down off the porch and then proceeded to haul Sister down like a sack of potatoes. Arliss Woods didn't seem to notice they were leaving. He kept shouting and flapping his arms.

"Mercy," Ruby said as she approached the van. "Have mercy."

"That old man is sure enough something," Sister said as I helped her into the backseat.

"Something?" Baby echoed as she followed Sister in. "You

could hear him shouting clear to Jerusalem. He's crazy."

Ruby got in the van and fanned herself with her Bible. Her face was shiny with perspiration, and she was winded, from excitement or fear—which one I wasn't sure.

"That man is a powerful Gospel man, Callahan," she said, when she could finally talk. "He knows his Book."

I started the engine and headed out of the cul-de-sac.

"All right," I said. "That's a start. He knows the Bible. Does he know anything about who killed Whitney Dobbs right here in his own backyard practically?"

"He saw something," Sister said. "He kept pointing to those walls with the pictures on them. He wanted to show us. I couldn't make it out too good."

"That's 'cause it didn't make no sense," Baby said. "I'm not blind and even I couldn't see nothing that made sense in there."

"Did you get him to talk about the day of the murder?" I asked.

Ruby coughed apologetically. "You see, he doesn't really answer questions. Not directly. And he doesn't talk like we're talking now. It's all Scripture. And it's all mixed up, like a riddle. And he's shouting and waving his arms all the time."

"I had to get out of there," Baby vowed. "He liked to knock me down with that psalm-singing of his."

"What was that he was trying to show you, out on that porch when you were leaving?" I wanted to know.

"Oh that," Ruby said. She laughed nervously. "It was one of his pictures he made. He wanted to sell it to us. For a hundred dollars!"

"Everybody in this place wants money," I said. "They still believe that Promised Land bit."

"Moses led his people into the desert," Ruby mused. "I wonder who in the world led these people into this mess?"

"Wasn't no prophet," Sister said.

"What makes you think he saw something?" I asked Ruby.

"He got all excited when we asked him about the blonde lady being shot," Ruby said. "That's when he started talking about Cain and Abel. That's a murder in the Bible."

"Yeah, I remember them vaguely from Catechism," I said dryly. "But weren't Cain and Abel brothers?"

"That's right," Sister said encouragingly. "Cain was the farmer and Abel was the shepherd. And Cain, he was jealous of his brother. So he tricked him into going out into a field. Then he jumped out and bashed Abel on the head with a rock. Killed his brother. Killed him dead."

"And God, he saw it," Ruby continued. "He called to Cain and asked him where Abel was at."

"That's right when Cain smart-mouthed God," Sister jumped in again. "He told God, 'Am I my brother's keeper?'"

I had to smile at that one. How many times, baby-sitting for my bratty little brothers, had I asked Edna a version of that same question. And how many times had she rewarded me with a pop to the butt for smart-mouthing back to her?

"God threw Cain out," Ruby said. "He gave him a mark on his head, so that everybody would know who he was," Baby said, finishing the story.

It was growing dark now, and as we passed through the Promised Land's wind-whipped streets, I leaned over and locked Ruby's door, and then my own.

"Do you think Arliss Woods would talk to me?" I asked her. "Maybe if you were there, we could ask him some more questions, pin him down a little."

"I don't know," she said, snapping the wide rubber band that held the pages of her worn Bible together. "He saw you out in the van when he was out on that porch. And he was calling you the devil, and serpent woman, and I don't know what-all."

"Maybe you ought to buy one of those pictures of his," Sister said. "Or one of those doohickeys he makes out of junk."

"You talkin' bout those sculptures of his?" Baby asked loudly. "Look like all the stuff I ever found under a sofa cushion glued all together. Ain't nothing I want on my coffee table."

"A hundred dollars," Ruby said in disbelief. "Just looks like paint smears to me. My little grandniece can do better than that with a jar of finger paint."

"I'm interested in art," I said. "I'd like to see his paintings. Real soon."

I fixed dinner that night. That is, I opened the Ragú jar and burned the garlic bread. I never can make our broiler do right.

Edna coached from the sidelines.

"Turn down the heat on that sauce," she said. "You'll burn my best pan."

I poured her a big glass of the cheap Chianti I'd picked up on the way home. "Drink this," I said. "It's good for your heart."

When I turned away from the stove to get the lettuce out of the refrigerator, she got up and peered into the pot of water I was trying to boil for the pasta.

"Put a little olive oil in there," she said. "Did you already add the salt?"

"Yes and yes," I said, taking a long gulp from my own wineglass. Now I remembered why I never cook with my mother around.

She watched me closely while I made the salad.

"I think I made some progress on the case today," I said, trying to distract her. "But the more I find out, the more I need to know. Where's Ben Dwyer, Carson's business manager? He can't have dropped off the face of the earth. And what kind of fiddle are Carson and Suzanne pulling? And where is Doreen Laidlaw? And Bryant Mayes. Where does he fit into this whole thing? Could Bucky be right? Maybe he really did kill

Whitney, and we're just chasing our tails."

I whacked away at the salad vegetables with the biggest cleaver in the kitchen as I ran down my list of frustrations.

"Bucky called and left a message on the machine," she said, examining the lettuce. "Dwyer doesn't have a criminal record. And neither does Suzanne Shaddeau. Her most recent address is in Sandy Springs. And that lettuce has brown spots on it."

I held the knife up and made a slashing motion in her direction.

"I'm just trying to help," she said innocently.

"Why don't you set the table and leave me alone?" I suggested. "Before I do you bodily harm."

"Fine," she said. But instead of going to the cabinet where we keep the dishes, she walked into the den and came back holding out a slip of paper.

"You want me to tell you what kind of game that Carson Dobbs and Suzanne Shaddeau are playing?" she asked.

"Yeah, I do." I splashed a little of the wine from my glass into the pot of spaghetti sauce. I'd seen a chef do that on a television cooking show once.

Edna slid her bifocals down to the end of her nose and looked at the paper. "Farmers Trust," she said. "You ever heard of it?"

"No."

"I hadn't either," she said. "So I called Amy Fritz, my little teller friend at the bank. You know, the cute one with the freckles on her nose? I asked her if she could see if that check you wrote for Dr. Dobbs had cleared yet."

"It's only been two days," I reminded her.

"Electronic banking," Edna said smugly. "Amy explained it to me. Guess where that check was deposited?"

"Farmers Trust?"

"It's new," Edna said. "They've only got the one office. Guess where that is?"

"Right beside Carson Dobbs's office?"

"Try right *inside* his office building," Edna countered. "It's in the lobby. I remembered the name because it was so odd for Buckhead."

"You've got to admit, it's handy," I said.

"That lawyer fellow thought so too," Edna said smugly.

"Who?"

"Zack Alexander. Whitney Dobbs's lawyer."

Was that what Zack had meant when he mentioned talking to my mother?

"You? You called Zack? Mom, you can't go around calling my clients, fishing for information."

"I do it all the time."

"When I ask you to."

"He thinks you asked me today," she said calmly. "I told him you wanted to know where all the bank accounts for Cardiovascular Associates of Atlanta were. And he was real happy to help out. NationsBank. That's where the accounts were that he knew about. He got even happier," she added, "when I told him Dr. Dobbs had opened another account and had deposited our check there."

She handed me a photocopy of the front and back of our check.

"And I've got an idea about where to find Doreen Laidlaw, too," she said.

"No," I said. "I don't want you doing this. You're sick. You've got a leaky heart valve, remember?"

We argued about Edna's medical condition through the salad and the spaghetti and the whole bottle of cheap wine. Then I got out a boxed mix and started to make a pan of brownies. This is how she drives me to chocolate.

We were arguing about whether I should add pecans when C. W. Hunsecker showed up.

28

WHAT'S WRONG?" I asked quickly. "Linda? The baby?"

"Calm down," he said, easing down into a chair. "I guess you didn't see the news, huh? You didn't hear about Deavers?"

"What happened?" Edna asked, beating me to the punch. She'd always had a soft spot for Bucky, even after it became apparent that our friendship would always be platonic.

"It's that goddamned Justice Department investigator," C. W. said. "He issued a preliminary report today. Saying Deavers has a history of race bias. And that the finding of that rifle in Bryant Mayes's truck was questionable."

"Questionable?" I repeated. "What's all this supposed to mean?"

"He's accusing Bucky of planting that rifle. Of setting Mayes up."

"Bullshit," I said. "That's just bullshit. Bucky's no racist. You know that, C. W."

"Tell it to City Hall," C. W. said. "The mayor had a joint

press conference with that Justice Department guy at five o'clock. The mayor announced Bucky's been suspended."

"Lloyd Mackey suspended Bucky?"

"Chief's orders. By way of the mayor," C. W. said. "I talked to Mackey a little while ago. He's torn up about it, but what could he do? It's politics."

"What about Bucky? Have you talked to him?"

"He's holed up with the lawyers," C. W. told me.

"Who's paying for that?"

"Police Union," C. W. said.

I pushed the pan of brownies to the back of the counter. I'd suddenly lost my taste for chocolate.

"This sucks," C. W. said. "I trained Deavers. Held his head while he puked his guts out the first time he saw a maggoty corpse."

"You did the same thing for me," I reminded him. "So why the visit?" I wanted to know. "You could have called with the news."

"You still working for Whitney Dobbs?"

"Her daughter," I said. "Alison's lawyer is filing a wrongful death suit against Carson Dobbs."

C. W. took off his glasses, wiped them on the tablecloth, and then put them back on again. "I got no dog in this hunt," he said. "My disability leave is subject to a city review board. More politics. If I rock the boat, I'll get pushed off. And there's Linda's career too. She's up for sergeant. You know how vindictive people can be. But you, you're a private investigator. Got a bona fide client."

"True."

He raised himself out of the chair by grabbing the back of the chair I was still sitting in. I thought briefly about his upper-body strength.

"Let's go for a ride," he said. "Go talk to Bryant Mayes."

* * *

The ride was quiet. After he got rid of his wheelchair, he'd
bought himself a big second-hand Mercedes. I worked things
around in my head while C. W. drove. How to approach
Bryant Mayes. How to ask what I needed to know without
antagonizing him. I wished I had my yellow legal pad.

C. W. got bored and started playing spin the dial with the
radio. He switched stations every minute or so, listening to a
few bars of a song, a tidbit of news, some fan chatter on the
all-sports call-in show. When he switched again and Ellis
McIntyre's voice oozed out of the speakers, I winced and
reached for the dial. "Not this jerk again."

C. W. pushed my hand away. "What's the matter? You
don't like Atlanta's Voice of Reason? I listen to him all the
time."

"Are you serious?"

He nodded. "What? You didn't know you could be black
and conservative?"

"Ellis McIntyre is a hatemonger," I said. "He hates blacks.
Hates women. Hates welfare."

"Hates crime," C. W. said calmly. "He hates government
bureaucracy, Band-Aid social programs that are nothing but
handouts. He makes some good points, you get past the cracks
he makes about 'Third World mentalities.'"

"That's the kind of stuff I can't get past," I said. "I'm sur-
prised you can."

"Now you sound like Linda," he said. "She can't stand the
guy either. Only place I can listen to him is right here in this
car."

McIntyre's voice was positively quivering with indignation.

"And now," he was saying, "you've got some pinhead from
Washington, probably got a law degree from Tuskegee
Institute, someplace like that . . . "

"See," I said. "Racist."

"Shut up," C. W. warned.

"This pinhead comes down here with orders from our esteemed lady attorney general. 'Get me a cop.' We don't care about the truth. Or justice. Or that a woman has been shot to death by some blood-hungry *outlaw*. We just don't want to *trample* this *criminal's* civil rights."

McIntyre paused for three beats. Trained at the Paul Harvey school of broadcasting.

"Folks," he pronounced. "We've got the gorillas running the zoo."

That's when I put my fingers in my ears. "I can't listen to any more of this," I told C. W.

After a minute or two, he tugged at my arm. "Show's over," he said. "Anybody ever tell you you need to lighten up?"

"Maybe once."

We'd been on the expressway for about ten minutes when C. W. got in the lane for the Central Avenue exit.

"You never told me where we were going," I pointed out.

"Firehouse," C. W. said, making a left at the bottom of the ramp. "The Double Deuce."

"You think Mayes might show up there tonight?"

"He's there," C. W. assured me.

"How do you know?"

"I worked the arson squad for a year, back in the early eighties. They had a deal then, you were attached to the firehouse, instead of working out of the precinct. I was attached to the Double Deuce."

"Did you know Mayes?"

"He was around," C. W. said. He slowed the car and leaned forward in his seat, looking for the right street. Two more blocks, he made a left and then a quick right. The firehouse was on the left, on the corner.

"Been a long time since I've been down here," C. W. said. "Age hasn't improved it."

The Double Deuce had been built in the early sixties, when somebody somewhere had decreed that all civic architecture should be blonde brick, with brushed aluminum windows, square and squat, bargain-basement Bauhaus. The engine house sat out front, with the house itself off to the side. The windows were lit up. It looked like the guys were at home.

C. W. parked next to a familiar-looking pickup truck. "He's here," he said, nodding at the truck. "Mackey had to let his truck out of the impound lot. You got yourself set on what you're going to say?"

"Sort of. How about you?"

"I'm just out for a ride, getting some fresh air," C. W. said. "Remember that, and don't be dragging me into anything."

"Who dragged who?" I wanted to know.

We entered the house through a small office area. Four desks, some computers, and file cabinets. From an open door at the far end of the room, I heard voices.

"Let's go," C. W. said.

His metal canes made a clacking noise on the linoleum floor.

The residents of the Double Deuce—six men, four black, two white—were sprawled on sofas and recliner chairs, watching a movie on television. Bryant Mayes was sitting on a weight bench, dumbbells in hand, watching instead of exercising.

"Y'all still watching *Backdraft*?" C. W. said loudly. "Isn't that tape worn out yet?"

A muscle-bound white guy with a gray crewcut sprang out of his recliner. "You're in the way, Hunsecker, you asshole." He came over and slapped C. W. on the back.

"Looking good, Hunsecker," he said. "Looking good." He gave me a good-natured leer. "Your old lady know you got a white girlfriend?"

The other men in the room hooted and hollered. "That Linda Nickells. She'll kick your ass, man," somebody warned.

"Naw, man, nothing like that," C. W. said. "Callahan. This is Freddie Walker. Used to be a friend of mine."

Walker shook my hand. "Callahan and Linda are old running buddies," said C. W. "Callahan used to be on the job. I told you about her."

"Burglary squad," I said.

C. W. lowered his voice so the others couldn't overhear. "You think Mayes is in the mood?"

Walker glanced at Mayes, who was openly staring at me.

"Ask him," he said.

Walker put his hand on C. W.'s shoulder. "Come on out in the kitchen. We'll fix you up with some coffee."

I pulled a kitchen chair up next to Mayes.

"Bryant?"

He picked up a magazine and started to read. "Yeah."

"You know who I am—right?"

"That's right." The magazine was an old copy of *Sports Illustrated*, from before the Super Bowls went into double digits.

"Look," I said. "Can we cut the crap for a few minutes? I'm not after you. I'm just trying to do my job. My client is Alison Dobbs. Whitney's daughter. She's convinced her father had something to do with her mother's murder. Her lawyer is going to sue Carson Dobbs for wrongful death. I think we could help each other."

"I don't think so," he said, looking up at me. His eyes were red-rimmed, with deep rings of sagging flesh beneath them. His face was round, with surprisingly high cheekbones.

"My little girl is dead. Faneeta. Whitney Dobbs took care

of that. My wife kicked me out. I been arrested, lost my job, dragged through the mud." His hands tightened on the magazine, crumpling the edges.

"So you were set up," I said, still unconvinced, but working the witness, like I'd been taught. "Maybe I can help you prove it."

"You think I'm stupid? You're friends with Deavers. The cop who set me up and then busted me."

I glanced around. The other firefighters were all listening in, pretending to be engrossed in *Backdraft*.

"Can we go somewhere else and talk?"

Mayes heaved a sigh and threw the magazine down on the weight bench. "In the office," he said.

The outer office was half-lit and chilly. Mayes sat behind a desk near the front door. "This was my desk," he said. "Before the shit came down."

I took a rolling chair from a typewriter stand and scooted it so that I was across from him.

"Tell me about that afternoon," I said. "Everything."

He picked up a pencil and began bouncing the eraser on the desktop.

"What? So you can get your buddy off the hook?"

C. W. had warned me on the way over. "Mayes is a big baby. Got a king-size chip on his shoulder."

"Deavers was suspended today," I said. "He can take care of himself. I want to find out who killed Whitney. If it wasn't you, it was somebody else."

"This is stupid," Mayes said. "My lawyer's gonna kill me if I talk to you."

Fred Grossbart, Mayes's lawyer, had been in the newspaper, on television, and on the radio every day since Whitney Dobbs was murdered. I'd even seen Grossbart on one of those television tabloid shows, spouting off about police corruption in Atlanta.

"Your lawyer has had the kind of publicity money can't buy," I pointed out. "He should be paying you."

"That's what Janie says," Mayes said. "She doesn't trust him either."

"What happened?" I prompted.

"After Faneeta, my little girl, got killed? Everything fell apart. I got pretty messed up. Me and Janie, we were fighting a lot. I been staying with friends. I got suspended. It was all that bitch's fault."

"Whitney. Tell me about the day she got killed. Where were you?"

"At the park. I go there a lot. There's a place you can sit. Sometimes I take notes and leave them. To Faneeta."

"Did anybody see you that day?"

"I don't know. I took a bottle of José Cuervo with me. Ask José. He'll tell you." Mayes laughed at his own joke.

"You stayed there all day?"

"Most of it. Drove around. Went past that bitch's house."

He buried his head in his hands. "You know what she told the cops when they stopped her that day? She said she thought she hit a speed bump. A fuckin' speed bump," he said, his voice cracking. "Janie saw it happen. She gets nightmares."

The newspaper photos, the ones the paper had run again and again, flashed in my mind. The one of a shy little girl. And the one of Whitney, highball in hand, laughing out loud. I shuddered involuntarily.

"I was going to kill her," Mayes said. He was bouncing the pencil again, beating a tattoo on the desktop. "Janie found out where Whitney lived. After the trial, she made these signs and she'd go over and just stand there, staring at the house. Messing with her head."

"And you made the phone calls," I said.

"One of Janie's friends from church works for Southern Bell.

She got us the number. Whitney told you about those, huh?"

"Yeah. And you followed her?"

"I had my gun loaded. Not the rifle. That's a hunting rifle. I got a forty-five, that's what I was going to use."

"Why didn't you?"

He shrugged. "It was easier to get high, drive around, think about how good it would feel."

"If you had the forty-five, why was the rifle in your truck?"

Mayes just stared. "It wasn't. I told the cops that. That was my dad's rifle. I never kept it in the truck. Where I live? Somebody would have ripped it off. That rifle was in my garage."

"You didn't know it was missing? Didn't report it stolen?"

"Faneeta was killed last summer. I ain't done any hunting in a year. Anyway, I wasn't living at home. So I didn't know it was gone."

"What about Janie? Did she notice the rifle was missing?"

His head jerked violently and he dropped the pencil. "She doesn't know nothing about that rifle. It's mine."

He was lying. And doing a bad job of it.

"Does she know how to use a gun? Ever take her hunting?"

"I don't know," he mumbled. "Maybe her brother took her when she was a kid. They lived over in Madison. It was a long time ago. Janie hates guns."

But Janie Mayes had access to that rifle. Her motive was obvious. But the means. Had she known where to find Whitney? Could she have been the person Billy Tucker saw running through the woods?

"Does Janie have a green jacket? One with a hood?"

"I don't know," he said sullenly.

"Did she ever go with you to Brown's Mill, to the golf course?"

"Cut this shit out," he said abruptly. "We're talking about

me. Not her. You think Janie killed Whitney Dobbs? You're crazier than the cops. Janie never did anything like that. Thought you told me that doctor did it."

"Did you ever meet Carson Dobbs?"

"I don't remember."

"His wife hit and killed your daughter," I said. "That seems pretty memorable to me."

"My lawyer took me to see him." Mayes didn't look up.

"For what?"

"To talk about a settlement."

Jesus Christ. Circles in circles. "When was this?"

"Right after the trial started. Dobbs was going nuts because of the bad publicity. Me and my lawyer, we thought Dobbs should make us a cash settlement. Pain and suffering. Faneeta was our only kid, man. Janie can't have any more kids. But nothing happened."

"Why not?"

"Fuck!" Mayes said, snapping the pencil in two. He heaved the pencil halves at the glass door. "That lawyer. Alexander. He came up with the part about how the arresting officer denied Whitney proper medical attention. What a crock. Dobbs's lawyer couldn't believe it. He hadn't even thought about that. But as soon as it came out, Dobbs told us to fuck off. So there went our settlement. We didn't get a dime."

Between all the lawyers, Mayes had been tricked out of the only restitution anybody had offered for the loss of his daughter. He was more bitter than even I had expected.

"I'd like to talk to your wife," I said. "Do you think she'd agree to it?"

He laughed. "She can't not talk about it."

29

"WHAT DO YOU WANT?"

Janie Mayes clutched at the collar of her bathrobe, even though the chain lock was on and we could only see six inches of her.

Bryant leaned in, his voice persuasive.

"Open up, Janie. This lady is a detective. The man too. She says they can help us."

"I know who she is, fool," Janie said. "I've got nothing to say to her. You neither. Now go on, before I call the police." She tilted her chin defiantly. "This is East Point right here. Not Atlanta. You can't fix things to go your way down here."

"Janie," Bryant said. "Come on, honey. You want people to go on thinking we did this? Killed that Whitney Dobbs?"

"We?" she cried. "What's this we business?"

"That's what we'd like to talk to you about," I said.

*　　　*　　　*

The room was small, with heavy rose brocade drapes, swagged and cascaded over a small picture window. The sofas and chairs were covered with clear plastic, the tables made of imitation pecan-wood, protected with doilies and lace runners. There was nowhere you could look in that room and not see Faneeta Mayes.

There was a small fireplace with a mantel, and across it marched a pictorial parade of Faneeta Mayes. Infant pictures, toddler pictures, stiffly posed family portraits, school pictures, and family snapshots. There was a recent dance recital photo of Faneeta in a spangly black cat costume with a little headband with white-tipped cat ears. She had drawn-on whiskers and she was posed to prowl. It broke my heart, that picture. At the edge of the mantel was a clumsily executed airbrush caricature of Faneeta, the kind you get for ten bucks at an amusement park.

The coffee table and end tables held more photos.

Janie Mayes sat down on an armchair and the plastic covering made a funny fart kind of noise, but nobody laughed or even smiled. I got the impression that this was no longer a home where that kind of tastelessness was tolerated.

Bryant sat in a matching chair, but on the edge, as though he knew the meter was running. C. W. and I sat on the sofa.

"What do you people want?" Janie Mayes said. Her hair was skinned back, like she'd been washing her face. She sat ramrod straight.

"Bryant tells me he never kept that deer rifle in his truck," I said. "How did it get there the night Detective Deavers found it? How was it used to kill Whitney Dobbs? That's what we're wondering."

Her hands were folded in her lap. Neat. "I told the police. I don't know how that detective did what he did. I don't know how he got hold of that gun. It was my husband's. I never paid any attention to it."

"You never noticed it missing?" C. W. asked. "You folks have a burglary recently? Have you noticed anything else missing?"

"No," Janie Mayes said.

"But people knew Bryant had a rifle, right? Knew he did some hunting?"

I looked at Bryant. "You told me you had a forty-five too. What happened to it?"

Janie bit her lip. "I threw it in the river. After they arrested Bryant. You want to arrest me for that? It was his gun. He had a license for it."

"Lots of folks knew about my rifle," Bryant said. "So what?"

"Maybe somebody knew you'd moved out of this house," I suggested. "You said the rifle was kept in the garage. Was it locked up?"

"Last time I checked," Bryant said, glancing sideways at his wife.

"I wouldn't know," Janie said. "I don't mess with his things."

"But you knew how to use a rifle—right? Didn't you do some hunting when you were growing up?"

"Who told you that?" she asked angrily. Bryant looked away. "That was a long, long time ago. I was a little bitty girl. I never killed anything. Nothing. Just shot at some tin cans with my brother."

She was twisting the corded belt of her bathrobe, corkscrewing it, till it looked like it might cut her in two.

Janie looked accusingly at her estranged husband. "You think I had something to do with killing Whitney Dobbs?"

"No," he said quickly. "But the rifle. I been thinking about it too. How would that cop get it? If he planted it in the truck?"

"I was at work," Janie said. "At the Comfort Inn on Camp Creek Parkway." She was really steamed now. "That's where I

work. Somebody around here has to pay the bills. Maybe that detective came in here while I was at work and stole the rifle."

Why? I was on the verge of asking. But before I could, C. W. was talking.

"Could we just see where the rifle was kept?"

Janie Mayes was ready to send us packing then, but Bryant didn't give her the chance.

"Out in the garage," he said. "I'll show you."

The garage was a small detached cinder-block affair, with a window on one side and a pull-down metal door. The door was closed. Janie's white Ford took up most of the room. There was a workbench at one end. Tools hung in their appointed place from a pegboard rack and cans of paint were stacked neatly on a shelf beside it. There was a cupboard beneath the bench.

"Where's the padlock?" Bryant asked his wife.

"I never saw a padlock," she replied. "That's your stuff. Not mine."

Mayes opened the cupboard. The top shelf was bare. The bottom held gun-cleaning supplies and a box of shells. He knelt down and peered inside the cupboard, as though he expected the missing rifle to reappear.

"There was a padlock," he said, shaking his head. "You know, with Faneeta and the neighborhood kids around, I didn't want to take any chances. Kids see guns, they get curious. But not Faneeta. She didn't like me to go hunting. Tender-hearted. My baby was tender-hearted."

He turned around to seek agreement from his wife, but she was gone. Her slippers made a soft slapping sound against the soles of her feet. "I'm going to bed now," she called. A moment later, she was inside. We heard the clicking of the lock and a few seconds later, the outside light was snapped off.

"Guess that's it," I said.

"That gun was locked up," Bryant said. "I know it was."

"Anybody could have gotten in that garage," I said to C. W. We followed Bryant Mayes back as far as the interstate. He headed back to the firehouse, I guess. We headed back home.

"That door only had a little push-button lock," I said. "Edna could open that. Hell, Baby and Sister could open it. And even if Mayes was telling the truth about there being a padlock, somebody could have cut that off, if they wanted the rifle bad enough."

"Bolt-cutters hanging right there on that pegboard," C. W. agreed. "Be no problem."

"Funny that the wife never noticed anything about that rifle. She knew he had guns. With a kid around, you'd think she'd pay attention to that kind of thing."

"But their kid is dead," C. W. said bluntly. "She's been gone since June. They're heartsick. So they let things go."

"Did you see that house? Spotless. And the garage. Not even an oil dripping on the floor. Not even a stray newspaper. The woman's compulsive." I shuddered. "I'd hate to have her as a House Mouse client."

"She's got an alibi," C. W. said.

"How do you know?"

He kept his eyes on the road. "Mackey told me tonight. Off the record. He gave me a look at the case file."

Why should I be surprised? It's a man's world. Mackey wouldn't give me, a mere chick, the time of day. No. But to Hunsecker, a member of the He-Man Woman Haters Club, the clubhouse door was always open.

"You want to tell me about the alibi?" I asked. "Or is this a boy-type secret?"

"Janie Mayes was at work until five P.M. that day," C. W. said, ignoring my gibes. "Deavers got a copy of her time card. She works in the accounting office of that motel."

"Camp Creek Parkway isn't even ten minutes from the golf course," I said. "Did anybody talk to somebody else who saw her in that office every minute of the day?"

"Just the supervisor," C. W. said. "He told Deavers she's a good worker."

When we got back to my place, the driveway was full.

"Busy place," C. W. said, pulling up to the curb.

"You don't even know," I told him.

"What's the plan for tomorrow?" he asked. "I think we need to talk to everybody who was at that crime scene that night. Get witnesses who can prove Deavers never got near Mayes's truck until he went to drive it to the station. And you're right about talking to Janie Mayes's co-workers. We should do that too."

"Don't you have a business to run?" I asked pointedly.

"My partner can handle things for a day or so," C. W. said. "What's wrong? You don't want to help Deavers?"

"I do want to help," I said, eyeing the cars that had my van blocked in. One was Neva Jean's. The other was my sister's. "But I've some new developments in the case that I need to check out. For my client—remember? If that pans out, all this other stuff with Deavers will go away by itself."

"I'll call you tomorrow," C. W. promised.

The smell of warm brownies and hot coffee greeted me in the kitchen, along with the sight of the party of four at the kitchen table: Edna, Maureen, Steve, and Neva Jean.

"Hi!" Edna said brightly. "Ready for some dessert?"

"No thanks," I said, glancing pointedly at the kitchen clock. It was nearly eleven. "I'm tired. I think I'll go to bed."

Maureen coughed delicately. Steve dug into a slice of brownie à la mode.

"The carpenters found more termite damage. Can you believe it? All the floorboards in the bathroom and the hall are like sawdust. We had the place inspected six years ago. Steve thinks we should sue."

"I've got a termite certificate," Steve said. The corners of his mustache were coated with vanilla ice cream.

"You should probably sue," I said amicably.

Neva Jean got up and opened the refrigerator door. She took a can of Mountain Dew from the bottom shelf. A twelve-pack. It didn't take a detective to figure out she was planning an extended stay.

She popped the top and took a long swig. "I told Swannelle tonight. Told him plain. It's me or them emus. You know what he wants now? He wants to get a pair of breeding ostriches too."

"You should probably sue," I told her.

I went into my bedroom. Maureen's suitcase and makeup case were on my bed, along with a dry cleaner's bag containing Steve's EMS uniform. I swept it all up in my arms and carried it into the kitchen, where I dumped it on the floor.

The brownie eaters watched me in silent disbelief.

Then I went to the linen closet in the hall. I got an armload of pillows, three blankets, and a wad of sheets. These I took back to the kitchen and dropped on top of the heap of luggage.

I took a brownie and put it on a plate. Then I poured myself a glass of milk, emptying the gallon. I was ready to make my announcement.

"Until somebody else volunteers to pay the mortgage or the utility bills or the taxes, I'm sleeping in my own bed," I told them all. "Edna is not a well woman, mentally or physically, so she's not giving up her bed, either. You three can fight it out for the couch in the living room or the sleeper sofa in the den. But this is the last night. You hear? After this, termites and

emus be damned. I'm putting up the no-vacancy sign."

I was watching Letterman's monologue when the knock came. He was doing the thing with the monkey-cam again. Cute monkey.

"Go away," I called.

Edna came in anyway and closed the door behind her.

"I wasn't going to let them have your bed," she said.

"Good," I told her. "I wasn't going to let you let them."

"Maureen is so pissed at you she cleared out and went to the Motel Six," Edna said, unable to suppress a grin. "Steve said she's throwing good money away. I think he's planning on sleeping in the car."

"I guess she's done ovulating, then."

"I didn't ask," Edna said.

"So Neva Jean got the sofa bed by default?"

"She feels real bad," Edna said. "I think she's out there hatching up a plan to poison Swannelle's emus."

"Maybe she'll spray them with Raid," I suggested. A couple of years ago, during a tiff over a bass boat purchase, Neva Jean had nearly killed Swannelle by spritzing him with a can of roach spray. They'd made up again, but Swannelle still doesn't sleep easy if there's insecticide in the house.

"You got a phone call tonight," Edna said. "Maureen took the message. Somebody named Wanda. Who's that?"

"Part of the Callahan Garrity Witness Assistance Program," I said, yawning. "She probably wants thirty bucks to tell me where Jimmy Hoffa is buried."

The yawning was contagious. Now Edna was doing it too. "Maureen said this Wanda person said somebody wants to sell you a picture. Does that make sense?"

Arliss Woods. If it was true, which I doubted, I'd have to deal with it tomorrow. The Promised Land could wait. Right now, it was Dreamland I was interested in.

30

NEVA JEAN GOT HER COFFEE and sat down, uncharac-
teristically quiet. Edna read the paper, removing the crossword
puzzle and handing it over to me without a word. The silent
treatment, the crossword puzzle, it was all a plot to make me
feel guilty about closing down the bed-and-breakfast. And it
worked.

"I'm sorry I was irritable last night," I told Neva Jean.

"She's probably in her period," Edna said helpfully.

Neva Jean reached in the pocket of her pink smock and
pulled out two ten-dollar bills. She put them under the edge of
my coffee mug. Like a tip. "I'm no freeloader," she said.

"Keep your money," I said, pushing the bills back toward
her.

Edna scooped the money up. "Our heating bill is gonna be
something, with all this company," she said.

"You and Swannelle need to get this emu thing worked
out," I said. "You can't go on like this."

Neva Jean put her coffee mug down. "I got me a plan. Anonymous phone call to the county health department. Complaining about Swannelle McComb keeping livestock inside the city limits. What do you think?"

"Brilliant," Edna said. "Can I make the phone call? You know I do that cranky old lady voice real good."

"Dame Edna," I said. "The crankiest."

"Since I'm doing you a favor, Neva Jean, I need you to do me a favor," Edna said. "Ruby called last night and canceled on me. Her blood pressure's up. Can you take her houses today?"

Neva Jean got up, reached in the supply closet, and got a pink smock. "Make the phone call right away, okay? I want them emus out of there by tonight."

The phone rang then. I could tell from Edna's voice that it was Jackie, and that she was wanting to switch her schedule around.

"Absolutely not," Edna said. "That'll throw the whole week off. You know you need to give me more notice than that."

Edna looked glum. "She's job-hunting. I just know it."

"I'll talk to her," I promised.

We spent the next hour or so working the books and the phones, rearranging the day's schedule.

"Too bad about Ruby," I said, after we'd lined everything up. "I was going to take her with me to talk to that crazy artist."

I flipped open my case file on Whitney Dobbs. It was fat with notes about leads I needed to follow up on. People I needed to talk to.

"You never let me tell you my idea about finding Suzanne's aunt," Edna said.

"Go ahead," I said, still reading over my notes.

"The nurse, the one from Dr. Dobbs's office? The one you met at Whitney's funeral? She worked with Suzanne. Maybe Suzanne talked about her aunt around the office."

"Maybe," I said, hating to admit her idea had merit.

I called Alison Dobbs anyway, to get Carol Steiner's home number.

"Zack says you found my dad's new house," Alison said. "My dad called and left a message on the answering machine. He was yelling, saying awful stuff, calling me names. So I guess he knows about the lawsuit. Zack says I should probably sell the house, after this stuff is all over."

"It's pretty big for just one person," I agreed. "But I wouldn't rush into anything. Have you thought about going back to school?"

"Maybe spring quarter. Or summer. When this stuff is all over."

We talked a little more, I got Carol Steiner's number, and then we hung up.

It's never going to be over, I thought. If she didn't believe me, she could call Janie and Bryant Mayes. They could tell her.

Before I could call Carol, the phone rang again. Edna got it and then handed it over. "It's that lawyer."

Zack was pumped. "That checking account information you came up with was golden," he said. "And the judge was furious when he heard. We're talking fraud now. Dobbs has got to produce everything related to that account. We've got him by the balls now, Garrity."

At least one thing was going right.

"I'm working on locating Suzanne's aunt in Knoxville," I said. "But I found out something else last night. Were you aware that back during the trial Dobbs was ready to pay off Bryant and Janie Mayes? A big cash settlement?"

"Says who?" Zack shot back. "We never authorized that.

In fact, Whitney wanted to do something like that, but I made her listen to reason. It would have made her look guilty as sin."

"Maybe that's what Carson intended," I said.

"What kept him from forking over the money?" Zack asked.

"You did. That last-ditch stuff about Whitney's not being allowed to seek medical aid. Once that came out, Carson's lawyer knew you'd get her off. They told Mayes to get lost."

"Son of a bitch," Zack said. "You know this proves a prior connection between Dobbs and Bryant Mayes, don't you? Either he paid Mayes to kill Whitney, or he did it himself and set Mayes up to take the fall. Either way works for me."

"Janie Mayes may play into it," I told him. "She had access to the rifle, knew how to use it. And by the way, Mayes admitted last night that he was the one making the phone calls and following Whitney."

"Not the wife," Zack said.

"Why not?"

"A woman drives by Whitney, pulls over and pops her, and then pops the homeless guy too? No."

"It sounds far-fetched," I agreed. "But I've met Janie Mayes, Zack, and I wouldn't rule her out."

"I got five bucks says it isn't her," Zack said.

"I'll take it." Big-time gambler, that's me.

"Hey!" Carol Steiner said when I called. "I was going to call you. This is so funny. I was just telling my friend, I need to call that investigator Alison hired."

"What's up?" I asked.

"It might be nothing," she said, hesitating. "That's why I didn't call right away."

"Well, let's hear it," I suggested.

"I think I saw Ben Dwyer," she said.

"Where?" I got my pencil and started making notes.

"I've been working for a temp agency, a special one for nurses. The other day I was working on the urology floor at this little hospital out in Canton. Western Regional. The hospital shares a cafeteria with an office building next door. I was just going in for a sandwich and guess who I think I saw leaving? Ben Dwyer."

"Are you sure?"

"He was on the other side of the cafeteria, and I only got a glimpse, but it really reminded me of him. He's got a funny walk, he hunches his shoulders and pokes his head forward. Like a turtle."

"That's great," I told her. "Maybe he works in the building. Do you have any idea what kind of offices they are?"

"All kinds," she said. "There's nothing else around out there. It's the only high-rise in the county, as far as I can tell. Five stories. Now, why were you calling me?"

"I found Suzanne's dream house," I told her. "But the builder says the house is in the name of Suzanne's aunt, up in Knoxville. She's going to move down here and Suzanne will take care of her."

"Hah!" Carol said. "Not unless she has hooves and a tail and a mane."

"I need to find the aunt," I said. "It sounds phony to me too. Did you ever hear Suzanne mention a rich aunt? Doreen Laidlaw is the name."

"If she'd had a rich aunt she would have let us all know about it," Carol said. "As far as I know, Carson was her main meal ticket."

"Did she ever mention any relatives at all?"

"There was somebody," Carol said. "Let me think. I remember, Suzanne had a family emergency, last spring. She

was supposed to get out the payroll, but she didn't. Carson had to write our paychecks himself, and he made a big deal about what a hassle it was."

"Was she going to Knoxville?"

"That could be right. Seems like she had to switch somebody from a house to somewhere else. Some problem like that. We thought about sending flowers or something, but it never got off the ground."

"Can you remember anything else about an aunt?"

"Sorry. That's it."

I thanked her again for her help.

"How's Alison?" she asked.

"She's coping. But she sounds kind of lonely. I think things are getting pretty ugly with her father."

"I'll call," Carol said.

"Feel up to a little detecting?" I asked Edna.

She'd been listening in on my calls, of course.

"Does it involve a lot of walking?"

"Forget it," I said quickly. "You're not feeling well. Let's call Jeanne."

"I'm just a little short of breath," Edna said. "It's the change of weather. The rain. A little asthma maybe. I've got that inhaler. That helps. Now what about the detecting?"

We'd located Ben Dwyer. At least we had the right county, I thought. I could do the job myself. But Edna could do it just as well, and it would free me up for some more phone calls tracking Doreen Laidlaw. And to visit Arliss Woods.

"Promise you'll call Jeanne if the inhaler doesn't work," I said.

"I promise," she said, raising her hand in a scout's oath. Only it was her left hand.

I recounted what Carol Steiner had told me. "The building

is in downtown Canton. It shouldn't be hard to find. It's the only five-story one in the county."

"Five stories? You expect me to search five stories for this man?"

I opened the file folder and gave her the photo of Ben Dwyer that Zack had given me.

"You don't have to go door to door. Hang out in the cafeteria," I suggested. "There can't be that many places to eat lunch out there. If you see him, just follow him back to his office. Don't talk, just follow."

"And if I don't see him? What if he orders out today?"

"Find the building manager. Get a list of tenants. We're interested in medical, dental, insurance, anything like that. That's what Dwyer has experience in. Once we've got a handle on the list, we just start working the phones."

She got up and headed for the bedroom to change. She paused in the kitchen doorway and looked down at the photo of Dwyer. "He doesn't look like any kind of financial genius. He doesn't look like a criminal. He just looks like a nerd."

"He walks with his shoulders hunched and his head stuck out," I told her. "Think turtle."

For some reason, I was itching to get out of the house, to do something. Go see Arliss Woods. Last night's phone call was probably bogus, I kept telling myself. Probably.

I made a deal with myself. If I worked the phones diligently for one hour, I could leave and go look for Woods.

Without a Knoxville business directory, finding Doreen Laidlaw would be slow, slogging work. I could go to the library downtown and use their Yellow Pages, but parking was a pain down there and it would tie up at least another hour of my time.

Try again, Garrity, I urged myself. Work it from another angle. But which one? I went back to the case file.

Doyle Bollinger's business card was paper-clipped to my notes. I'd never asked him about a background check on Suzanne. Maybe Whitney had gotten him to run one for her when she first suspected what Carson was up to. Calling the other P.I. was the easy way out, but I'm not necessarily opposed to that.

"Oh yeah," Bollinger said, after I identified myself. "How's the case going? I heard on the news that they're going to drop charges on that fireman."

"They might," I said. "Things are complicated. More stuff involved than I realized."

"You'll get paid for your time, though," he said. "Even if you can't come up with the goods."

"I found their house," I told him. "And it was pretty close to that restaurant you told me about. So thanks. The deed to the house is in Suzanne's aunt's name, though. It's a scam, I'm pretty sure. But I need to track down the aunt. When you were working for Whitney, did you do any kind of background check on Suzanne? Find out any family names or addresses?"

"An aunt," Bollinger said admiringly. "Not bad. You wonder if they teach this stuff in med school, don't you? But no, Whitney fired me before I ran any checks or anything like that."

I felt a twinge of guilt about the way things had worked out.

"I'm going to ask Zack to bill the estate for four hours of your time," I told him. "Without that tip about the restaurant, I might not have found the house."

"That's decent," Bollinger said. "Not necessary, though. I got paid."

"I mean it," I told him. "The house led to the aunt. Doreen Laidlaw. Now I've got an idea Carson may have been funneling money through her. I can go back and do another deed

search, this time using her name. God knows what we'll find."

"Happy hunting," he told me.

Thinking about the house again made me think of Lisa Cutlip. She still didn't like talking to me, but she gave me what I wanted. The name of the lawyer in Knoxville who'd drawn up Suzanne's power-of-attorney papers.

"Fentress, Boyle, Hanlon, and Reardon," the receptionist in Knoxville chirped. "This is Karen."

"Hi, Karen," I chirped back. "This is Myra in Zack Alexander's office, down in Atlanta." I didn't think Myra would mind loaning me her identity for one phone call. "Is Mr. Hanlon in?" I asked.

"Sorry, he's not," she said.

This was not surprising. All law firm receptionists are trained to keep most phone calls away from the lawyers. Actual human contact cuts down on billable hours.

"Oh," I sighed. "That puts me in a bind. We're doing a lease purchase arrangement for Suzanne Shaddeau on some land adjoining her property. And Mr. Alexander needs to be sure our files are current on Miss Laidlaw's address. I called the number we have for her, but I keep getting a recording saying the number has been disconnected."

"Miss Laidlaw?" Karen said. "Let me just see if I can find the file."

I heard the sound of keyboard clicks.

"I'm going to put you on hold," Karen said. "We've got new software and it's driving me nuts."

She switched me to the Muzak mode. It being Tennessee, though, the law firm had cannily invested in an all-country Muzak flavor. Not bad. I whistled merrily along to "Motel Room in Dallas" while my fellow secretary did battle with the new software.

We were halfway through a particularly string-heavy ver-

sion of "Release Me" when Karen came back on the line.

"Good thing you checked," Karen said. "There's a new address as of last April. Twelve-oh-eight Valleyvue, right here in Knoxville."

"How about the new phone number?" I asked hopefully.

"Sorry," she said. "It's not in our files."

I got a ticket for parking in the loading zone at the library. But it was worth the trouble. According to the crisscross directory, Doreen Laidlaw was currently living at the Knox County Nursing Home. I had the phone number scribbled on a scrap of paper.

The call would have to wait until I got out of downtown. Half the streets were closed because of construction, the other half had gone one lane and one way, overnight, it seemed. They'd never get it all done in time for the Olympics.

Once I was on the expressway, I dialed the nursing home.

"Knox County Nursing Home," a woman's voice said. The drawl was thick, much thicker than an Atlanta accent.

"I'd like to speak to Miss Doreen Laidlaw," I said.

"I'm sorry," she said. "You can't talk to Miss Doe-Reen."

Had Suzanne moved her aunt? Maybe the secretary at the law firm had given me the old address by mistake.

"Can you tell me where she is?" I asked. "I really need to talk to her."

"Oh, she's right here," the woman said. "She ain't going nowhere. Didn't nobody tell you about Miss Doe-Reen?"

"No," I said. "I'm an old family friend. We lost contact. Is she sick?"

"She did have pneumonia," the woman said. "After she fell out of bed and broke her hip. Now it's just her mind. She wanders. Senile dementia, it says on her chart. You coming for a visit? She loves company."

"Not too soon," I said. "Give her my regards, will you?"

Now I knew how they'd worked it. They'd taken Suzanne's aunt, a senile old lady who was in a nursing home, and had Suzanne's name put on her checks. It wouldn't have been hard. Carson was a doctor. He'd probably signed the papers. Then all he had to do was funnel his money through the aunt. Suzanne had become an instant heiress.

The morning's drizzle had turned into a steady drenching. Traffic was slow and heavy, so heavy I nearly got creamed by an eighteen-wheeler who didn't want to let me get in the right lane to get off at my exit.

My windshield wipers could barely keep up with the rain. A shiver ran down my spine thinking about what Arliss Woods's shack would be like in this downpour. Maybe he'd agree to talk to me in the van. If he really was willing to talk to me.

I found the right street and passed the house where Wanda's friend lived. The narrow streets were empty, and gray rainwater slopped up over the broken curbs and into the side-walks and yards.

The dead-end street that led to the junkyard was right where it had been on my last visit. The junkyard was there too, looking more gawdawful than it had in the sunlight.

But the shack was gone. All that stood where Arliss Woods's house had been were the concrete block pilings.

31

BANGED ON THE DOOR as hard as I could with my fists, but the sound of the rain drowned it out. Then I took off my shoe and banged on the door with it. Tennis shoes do not make a really effective door-banging device, but it was all I had. My foot got wet.

Wanda's friend finally opened the door. This time he was minus the baby. And a shirt. His jeans rode on his hips, exposing a soft roll of baby fat.

"I want to see Wanda," I said, elbowing my way inside. "Where is she?"

"She ain't here," he tried.

"Wanda," I yelled. "I want to talk to you."

There was no entry hall. Just a tiny living room with too much furniture. It stank of dirty diapers and dope smoke.

"Be cool, man," he pleaded. "Roseanne's asleep. Don't wake up the baby."

"Wanda," I screamed again.

She came plowing out from the back of the house, wild-haired, wide-hipped, sleepy-eyed. Stoned. She got right up into my face.

"What do you want? You can't come crashin' in here."

"I want Arliss Woods." I got right back in her face. She was older than the boyfriend, by at least five years, and she outweighed him by at least sixty pounds.

"You had your man here call me last night. Arliss wants to sell me a painting, he said. I was just over there. And the there isn't there anymore."

"What you talking about?"

I shrank away from the scent of garlic and beer and fried fish. Jesus. Her breath would melt paint.

"Arliss's house is gone. Knocked flat," I said. "Are you pretending this is news?"

She did a cartoonish double-take, the head zigging toward the boyfriend, then back at me, then back at him. "Nuh-uh," she said flatly. "That ain't right. Is it?"

The boyfriend hitched his pants and they promptly fell back down on his hips. "Some kids came by a while ago. Running at the mouth about a truck knocking the old man's place over."

"Knocked it down," she mused. "Huh."

"Where would he go?" I asked. "Where does he usually go when he takes off like this?"

Now she got dreamy-eyed. "Different places."

"I'm not giving you any more money," I said.

In fact, I'd stopped at the ATM and gotten my limit of cash.

"I don't know," she protested. "He just goes off. Who would knock that house down? Who would do him that way?"

"He's in trouble," I said bluntly. "He's been talking about seeing that woman killed, hasn't he?"

"I told you that," Wanda said. "He all the time talks that shit. Serpents and devils and fiery furnaces. Nobody pays attention to that."

Somebody had.

"When did you see him last? Don't lie, okay? I think he's in trouble."

She shrugged. "Last night. He had that picture he wanted to sell to the white lady. He saw you out in that van yesterday."

The boyfriend spoke up. "Arliss came over this morning while you were in bed. Had me call him a Yellow cab."

"When was this?"

He rubbed his eyes. "Nine?"

I took one of the twenties out of my pocket, and one of my business cards. I wrote the car phone number on the back. "Ask around. Talk to those kids. See if you can get a description of the truck, a description of the driver, anything like that. Call me at this number, or the one on the front. If nobody's there, leave a message."

Wanda studied the card.

"You still want to buy that picture?"

"You've got it?"

"Arliss, he gets a hundred dollars for a picture," Wanda said. "And this one's good. It ain't no box top. This one's wood."

I brought out the twenties and let her see them. "How do I know you'll give him the money?" I asked.

"He's my daddy," she said indignantly. "You think I'd steal from my own daddy?"

Wanda looked to be in her early twenties. Arliss Woods had to be in his eighties. She saw me doing the math and poked the boyfriend in the ribs.

"Arliss has lots of children," she said. "He says he's like

Abraham in the Bible. I got a half brother only three."

The boyfriend sniggered. "The old dude has staying power, that's what."

"Can I see the painting?" I asked.

She went into the other room, closing the door carefully behind her. When she came back, she was holding out a ragged-edged sheet of plywood.

"Ought to get a hundred twenty-five dollars," she said. "This one's a lot bigger than the other ones. See how good?"

If size and amount of paint counted, she was right. The painting was probably sixteen by twenty inches, if any one edge had been straight.

It reminded me of a child's Garden of Eden, with towering green trees, bright flowers, a lion, lambs, and gigantic red birds. The proportions were wildly out of whack, the vision chaotic and disturbing.

Lambs were frightened, the lion perplexed. The middle of the painting was dominated by three figures. The smallest was a pale golden doe. At least I think it was a deer. The features looked more like a dog's, except for the abbreviated white tail and the huge terrified brown eyes. The deer's mouth was open, as though it was crying out.

To the right of the deer was a prancing green devil, his tail curved over his head, pointed horns dripping blood. Instead of a pitchfork, the devil held a long gun in his hands, and a terrible menacing snarl on his lips.

Over in the far right corner, lying outstretched with a huge red splotch on his chest, was a black bear. Unlike the other two figures, the bear had no facial features at all.

And up in the upper left-hand corner, wrapped beguilingly around a bright yellow sun, was a coiled purple snake. Its eyes were green and it had a long flicking tongue curled around in a cruel laugh.

I handed over the money and Wanda smiled broadly. "All right now," she said.

"Has anybody else seen this painting?" I asked from the doorway.

"Don't know," Wanda said, bored now that the cash part of the transaction was over. "He gets done with one, he starts another. Especially right after he's had a vision."

It hadn't occurred to Arliss's daughter that this vision could get him killed.

I went back to the dump, just to see if there might be any trace of Arliss's home.

It hadn't taken much to flatten the shack. Pieces of twisted tin with bits of Arliss's murals were scattered amongst the tires and beer cans and mattresses, and there were some old paint cans, but that was it.

Bucky had his answering machine switched on, but I knew he was home. "It's Callahan, Bucky. Pick up, dammit."

"What do you want, Garrity?" he drawled. "Didn't you hear? I'm off the job."

"Get your head out of your ass," I told him. "We're trying to help you."

"Who's we?"

"Me and C. W.," I said. "I told you before. There's a witness to these murders. An old man who lives in a junkyard. He's been telling everybody he saw what happened. He's been making paintings of it. I've got one. And I think you people need to talk to him. Maybe have him look at a photo lineup."

"Why call me?" Bucky asked. "Call Mackey. Have one of his good boys talk to the old man."

"The old man is gone," I said. "Somebody tore down his shack. I think whoever killed Whitney and Shawan got to the

old man. I know you, Bucky, you've got copies of everything in that case file. Let me come over and take a look, see if something connects . . . "

"No way," he said, cutting me off. "I'm already screwed. My lawyer says if I keep my head down we can maybe ride it out, prove how fucked up this Justice Department guy is. I can't give you nothing, Garrity. You know that."

Bryant Mayes's truck wasn't at the Double Deuce when I rode by, so I went back to his wife's house.

The garage door was closed. No pickup truck in the driveway. I hopped out and walked around to look in the window on the side of the garage. Janie's white Ford was parked in the same place I'd seen it last night.

She didn't answer the door when I rang the doorbell. And when I called her number at work the office manager said she'd called in sick.

"Did you talk to her?" I asked. "Did she say what was wrong?"

"She left a message on my voice mail. Said she had a migraine."

After I hung up I sat staring at the house for five minutes. The rain had stopped but a ground fog had settled in, shrouding everything in a sick milky white haze. I backed the van out of the driveway and parked it across the street.

There was a small wooden deck at the back of the house, and a door leading into what looked like a laundry room. I don't have a real official set of lock picks. But I do have a slender little wire gizmo I sent away for from a mail order "personal security" catalogue. Thirty dollars and it probably wouldn't work on anything too elaborate. It worked fine on the door to Janie Mayes's laundry room.

Once I figured out that nobody was home and my heart-

beat settled down to startled squirrel level, I roamed around the house, looking for . . . something. I was sort of hoping to find Arliss Woods in a closet, bound and gagged, but otherwise fine, like they always find witnesses in the movies.

The closets and drawers and cupboards were all neat and tidy, just like the owner. I sat down on the bed in Janie's bedroom and pouted about that. Which is when I noticed that the mattress was slightly crooked on the box spring. Not a very Janie thing at all.

I flipped the mattress off, bedspread, pillows, blankets, and all.

The file folder was in a white pillowcase. There were newspaper clippings from every day of Whitney's trial. And a sheaf of literature from Mothers Against Drunk Driving, and photocopies of letters Janie had written to some state legislators, urging them to toughen Georgia's drunk driving laws. There were notes, too. Whitney's address, her unlisted phone number, Zack Alexander's number, the name and address of the trial judge who'd presided over Whitney's trial and eventually set her free.

There was an odd sheet of paper too. It looked like a schedule of some sort. MTWTFS were the headings. No problem. Days of the week. There were numbers under each heading: 10–2, 12–4, 2–6. And abbreviations, like directions or something. There was a name too.

Colleen Danaher. I turned it over in my mind. I'd seen that name somewhere before, and recently. It had something to do with Whitney, I knew. But I'd talked to so many people.

I went back over the schedule. Not a full work week, certainly. But it wasn't supposed to be, I realized. It was Whitney's schedule. Her public service hours. And Colleen Danaher was her parole officer. Janie Mayes wouldn't have to follow the road crew van. Neither would Bryant. They knew in advance where she'd be.

I searched the rest of the house hurriedly, but compulsively neat people don't leave a lot of clues lying around. There wasn't even any trash in the house. Trash. I thought again about Whitney and Shawan Taylor, buried in a pile of roadside trash.

C. W. met me back at the Double Deuce.

His friend Freddie's face lost all its animation when I told him what I'd found at Janie's house, and what I suspected.

"Hell. You sure? Janie too? C.W?" Walker's bright blue eyes searched Hunsecker's face for some sign that this was all just a misunderstanding.

"They'd been following Mrs. Dobbs. Stalking her. Making harassing phone calls, threats," C. W. told him.

He turned to me. "This morning I talked to the woman who works the front desk at that Comfort Inn. She was scared, but after a little bit, she admitted she clocked Janie out the afternoon Whitney was killed. Janie was worried about Bryant. He'd been drinking, she said, and she wanted to check up on him. Janie called her right before five, and had her clock her out."

"Whitney and Shawan were probably killed around four-thirty," I added.

"God," Walker said, rubbing his jowls.

"Bryant said . . . we all thought . . . you know, police harassment. We thought the cops were making him a whipping boy. 'Cause he's black."

"Not this time," I said.

"There's a witness, Freddie," C. W. said. "An old man. He's missing. Janie and Bryant are gone too. Janie's car is at the house, and she called in sick today. We think they've got that old man. Where would they go, Freddie?"

Walker looked stricken. "Hell, I don't know."

"We heard he'd been staying with a friend after Janie

kicked him out. Who was it? Could they be over there?"

"No," Walker said. "Lewis's wife kicked him out too. Mayes slept here after that. Except for last night."

"Someplace else then," C. W. said. "A hangout, place he liked to be alone when he was drinking?"

"Piedmont Park," Walker said. "He'd take a bottle of tequila and sit up there on that little hillside and stare at the place his little girl got killed. I told him it was sick."

"The park's too public," I said impatiently. "Where else?"

"Family?" C. W. asked.

"I don't think they live around here," Walker said. "Or he would have gone there after Lewis's wife kicked him out. There was a hunting cabin," he said haltingly. "Down south of here. In Henry County. Belongs to a retired cop. Mayes and some of the other guys used to go down there, get boozed up, and pretend to be hunters. I think Mayes just liked to get off in the woods away from Janie."

"Where is it?" I asked. "How far from here?"

"I only went the one time," Walker said. "I don't like it when people mix booze and bullets. You got people falling out of deer stands, shooting at shadows. Not for me."

C. W. went to a desk and got a piece of paper. "Come on, Freddie. Think about it. See if you can draw us a map."

Walker sat down and chewed at the end of his pencil. He drew a little, scratched it out, started over. One time, he got up and walked over to a wall-mounted map of Georgia and traced a line with his finger. Then he sat down and drew some more.

C. W. watched over his shoulder. I borrowed a phone and called the house. The answering machine picked up. There was one message. A crisp female voice asking Ms. Garrity to call Westside Regional Hospital. Edna must have started working the phones. Maybe she'd found Ben Dwyer. Zack would be pleased.

"You sure that's it?" C. W. said, looking at the finished sketch.

"Should be pretty close," Walker said. "There's a liquor store right there at the turnoff from Georgia 308 onto the county road. I don't remember the name of the road, but you can't miss that liquor store. They've got a big concrete deer head sticking out of the front of the store. Big Buck Beverages. That's the name. Turn there."

"You carrying?" C. W. asked when we were in the van.

I got my nine-millimeter out from under the seat and showed it to him.

"Good," he said, nodding. He took his service revolver from a holster inside his jacket. "Lot of good it'll do, though," he said. "Right now I need both hands for the canes. I pick up a gun, I fall down."

"I've still got my little twenty-two," I offered. "It's so light, maybe you could use it. It's in the glove box right there."

"Never mind," C. W. said.

I glanced over at him. "You're not going to call Mackey? Let him know about this? Get some backup?"

"It's Henry County," C. W. said. "By the time they call down there, get it coordinated with the sheriff's office, that old man could be long dead. Bryant and Janie could be long gone. What's wrong? You don't like having a cripple for a partner?"

I tried not to take it personally.

"This wouldn't have anything to do with you being afraid of getting crossed up with the disability board, would it? Or maybe you just need to prove that a cripple can still pull his own weight? Is that's what's going on, C. W.?"

"Just drive," he growled.

The rain and the fog had lifted, blown off by a stiff wind coming in from the west. It pushed the van around the road a lit-

tle and whistled where there was a tiny hole in the back window.

When the car phone rang, it startled me so badly my hand jerked and the van drifted into the left lane. I jerked it back hard to the right and was rewarded with a long angry horn blast from a little red sports car behind me.

Zack Alexander wanted to brag on himself.

"The courier just came with the printouts from that checking account we found," he said. "Carson must have moved at least two million dollars through that one account in the last couple years. And he's been spending it on real estate. I had Myra run Doreen Laidlaw's name through a deed search on the computer. They've got holdings all over the place. Some raw land up there near the new house, two units in Carson's town house complex, an office complex on Peachtree-Dunwoody . . . "

I hated to give him the bad news, but since he represented my client, I had a responsiblity.

"Zack," I said, interrupting. "I can't talk now. You've got a good case of fraud against Dobbs. Doreen Laidlaw's in a county nursing home. She's senile and bedridden and penniless. The money's definitely not hers. But the wrongful death thing might not work out."

"Why not?"

"Bryant Mayes and his wife have disappeared. I think they've grabbed Arliss Woods. We're . . . I mean, *I'm* looking for him now."

"You sure?" Bryant asked, sounding disappointed.

Up ahead I saw the exit sign for State 308. "I'll let you know how it turns out," I said.

"Probably for the best," he said. "Wrongful death is a bitch to prove. We'll get them on fraud." He hung up.

"You didn't tell him you had help," C. W. said.

"Didn't want to get you in trouble with the big bosses," I said.

He nodded approval, but shifted uncomfortably in his seat.

"Mayes doesn't have to know we don't have help on the way," I suggested. "He probably doesn't even know you're on leave. Have you got your shield and your cuffs?"

"Always," C. W. said. "Habit."

"If Arliss is still alive, I think they'll give it up," I reasoned. "Bryant may be dumb, but Janie isn't. If Arliss is alive, they can both claim diminished capacity. They were crazy with grief. The system shafted them. Maybe they'll rat on each other."

"You believe that?" C. W. demanded.

"I'm trying to," I said.

The liquor store with the buck's head was right where Freddie Walker had said it would be.

I turned onto the county road and C. W. read the directions aloud.

"Four miles on this. Then there's supposed to be a big dead oak in a pasture full of horses. We make a left there, go another mile, and start looking for a dirt road with a post with a bunch of mailboxes nailed to it. We follow that, then take the third right. Cabin is way back in the woods.

We were jouncing along on the dirt road after we passed the mailboxes, mud splashing up on the windows so bad I had to use the windshield wipers to be able to see. Most of the names on the mailboxes were illegible, faded from sun and rain. But the letters on one started me thinking.

"Did Walker say who owned this cabin?"

"Just a retired cop," C. W. said. "All these guys hang out together down here."

"Doyle Bollinger's a retired cop," I said. "Only now he's a P.I. Whitney hired him and fired him, right before I went to work for her."

"Bollinger? Used to work for City of East Point?" C. W. asked, puzzled. "So what? I don't follow."

"Zack just told me that Carson and Suzanne own an office complex on Peachtree-Dunwoody. Doyle Bollinger's office is in a building on Peachtree-Dunwoody. Surrounded by medical offices."

"I used to know him," C. W. said.

"He said he knew you," I said.

"I knew him from when I worked a second job as a security guard at Grady. I quit after I made captain, but Bollinger worked there a long time."

"Where at Grady?"

"The emergency room," C. W. said. "I saw him sometimes after that, when we were down there working a case. I didn't know he had a P.I. license."

My stomach was getting queasy.

"Did you ever know any of the rooters that hung out at the E.R? A skinny black guy named Harold Eaves? He was friends with Shawan Taylor."

"It's been eight years," C. W. said. "All the rooters I knew are probably long dead."

"But Bollinger knew them both," I said. "He's a friendly guy. He made friends with Shawan Taylor. Shawan was still wearing a Grady bracelet when he was killed. That's why he was sticking so close to Whitney. Doyle Bollinger paid him to. Then he killed him. Like he killed Whitney."

C. W. was counting the turns. When we came to the third one, I stopped the van. The wind was gusting hard now. Bits of leaves and twigs swirled and whizzed by the windows.

"Call for backup," C. W. said.

For once I didn't argue with him.

32

THE SHERIFF'S DISPATCHER SOUNDED DUBIOUS.
"You're where?"

"I don't know the address," I said. "It's off in the woods. There aren't any road names. But it's about five miles from Big Buck Beverages."

The phone crackled and the dispatcher asked me to repeat the directions again. "It's a cabin that belongs to a man named Bollinger. Doyle Bollinger. He's a retired East Point police officer. We have reason to believe he's holding a hostage, a witness to a double homicide up in Atlanta."

The crackling noise again. "Spell Bollinger, please, ma'am?" she said.

Just then we heard a shot. There was a pause and there were two more shots.

"Send the damn car," I yelled. "We just heard gunfire. We're going in."

* * *

I jumped out of the van and landed in ankle-deep mud.

C. W. opened his door and took a look. "I can't get through this stuff with those canes," he said. "Can you get us in closer?"

"Bollinger knows the van and he knows I'm involved," I said. "Stick tight here. I'll try and sneak up on the house, see what's going on."

The road was too mucky to walk on. I tried to stick to the side, but it was overgrown with a tangle of waist-high kudzu vines and prickly shrubs that snagged and slapped at my face and arms. Twice I tripped and slid into the mud of the road.

After three hundred yards or so I saw where the road came to a turn-in. Through the screen of trees I saw wood smoke curling up from the chimney of an old cabin. It was made of weather-beaten logs with a tin-roofed cedar porch running all around the side. Everything about the cabin seemed to sag. The only vehicle in sight was Bryant Mayes's white pickup truck. Except for the wind, the cabin was quiet. The windows were curtained and no lights shone through.

I slipped and slid back to the van. C. W. was just hanging up the phone.

"I called Mackey. He's out. Everybody in the unit is down at the Five Points Marta Station. Gang shooting. Two dead, three injured. I left a message. Tried Deavers too. Left another message."

I didn't like the way this thing was shaping up.

"Bryant's truck is parked in front of the cabin. No other cars. They've got a fire going inside."

"Which means what?" C. W. wondered. "Mayes is working with Bollinger?"

"Don't know," I said. "The only way to find out is for me to go back down there and take a better look."

"Not by yourself," C. W. protested. "You get in trouble, how am I going to get to you?"

"We can pull the van in closer," I said. "There's a turn-around, maybe fifty yards from the cabin. Heavy underbrush. You can keep sight of the cabin from there, use the car phone if anything comes up."

"If anything comes up, I'm coming in," C. W. said. "Ten minutes then. You take a look, see what the situation is, then get back here. We've called for backup. Let's wait before we go in."

"Three gunshots," I said. "Arliss Woods could be dead or dying."

"If he's dead, there's no hurry. If he's dying, he'll have to wait," C. W. said. "You know I'm right."

Time was too precious to spend it arguing strategy. We coasted down the road in neutral, and I maneuvered the van into the little clearing.

I'd worn a yellow sweatshirt and jeans when I left the house, but now the yellow left me feeling as vulnerable and exposed as the deer in Arliss's painting. So I dug around in the back of the van until I found something to afford me protective coloration. The best thing I could find was a baggy black sweater that smelled like cough drops and powdered cleanser.

"Ten minutes," C. W. reminded me.

There was a little footpath that led through the woods from the turnoff. Bollinger and his hunting buddies obviously weren't ones for nature hikes. It was impossibly narrow and overgrown with fallen limbs and shrubs that had sprung up in the middle of the track so that I had to detour into the woods, resorting to a crawl in some places.

When I came to the cabin I skirted around it, staying in the woods until I came out parallel to the truck. Then I darted to

the side parked away from the cabin. I crouched down and duck-walked to the front of the truck.

I stuck my head up to take a look. The cabin was still, and then the front door opened and he stepped out onto the porch.

Doyle Bollinger was dressed for action. Old green army fatigues, a green hooded jacket, and high lace-up hunting boots. The green jacket. It must have been the same one Arliss had seen the day Whitney and Shawan were killed. Bollinger's beautiful silver hair shone in the dimness of the overhanging porch. He looked warily around and then strolled off the porch in the other direction.

I half stood to see where he was going. There was a shed off to the right of the house. It was made of the same weather-beaten boards and blended perfectly into the woods.

Before I went back to my hiding place, something in the truck cab caught my eye.

Bryant and Janie Mayes were in the truck, leaning close together, slumped over sideways toward the passenger door. There was blood on the side of Janie's face. Not much was left of Bryant's. Neither one was moving or breathing.

I sat on the mud and clamped my hand over my mouth to keep from screaming, biting into the flesh of the palm. It was an old trick one of my brothers had taught me as a kid. Good for situations that called for taking things like a man.

I crept around the edge of the truck. Bollinger came out of the shack. He was carrying a red plastic one-gallon gasoline jug and he was whistling. It sounded like that song from *The Bridge Over the River Kwai*. The song the American prisoners whistled while they were being worked by the Japanese soldiers.

When Bollinger got to the door of the cabin he set the jug down and went inside, closing the door behind him.

I looked in the bed of the pickup truck. Clean and neat, the

way Janie Mayes liked things. No sign of Arliss Woods. He had to be in the cabin. There had been three shots. One each for Bryant and Janie. They were past help. Had Arliss been shot too? Was he still alive?

The edge of the porch was maybe ten yards from my hiding place. I decided to try for it, angling away from the front door and over to the right side. As I crept along the back wall of the house, I could still hear the whistling inside. Bollinger was clearly a man who enjoyed his work.

There was another door at the back of the cabin. A torn screen door opened onto a battered wooden inner door with a small window. I edged over and peeked in the window.

It was dark on the porch and dark in the house. There was a single naked lightbulb in the kitchen. I could just make out the edge of a refrigerator and what looked like a stack of firewood. And the back of a head.

The whistling had stopped. I turned. Doyle Bollinger's gun was pointed at my face. It was then that I noticed his boots were rubber-soled.

"Now, now, now," he said. "You know, I come out of that shed, concentrating on what-all I've got to do, and I saw a little bit of pink paint back over there in the woods. And I said to myself 'Doyle, do we know anybody pathetic enough to drive around in a pink car?'"

I couldn't see his eyes behind the tinted aviator glasses, but the twist of his mouth said he was amused.

"And then I said, 'Doyle, that girl detective is not half as stupid as we thought.' So I stood right by that window inside, and I waited, and you know, when I saw you come running out in broad daylight like that, I'll admit, I said, 'Doyle, you were wrong. That girl is way too stupid to be a private detective.'"

I left my hands jammed in the pocket of the sweater, my hand resting lightly on my nine-millimeter.

"Give me your gun, please, ma'am," he said pleasantly.

Reluctantly, I handed him the gun.

"Come on in the house," Bollinger said, poking me in the ribs with his gun. He walked me around to the front of the cabin, but paused at the door, his head cocked, listening.

Then he turned to me, and he wasn't smiling anymore.

"You brought a helper. Didn't you?" he asked. "You're a woman of surprise and mystery, Miss Callahan. I like that."

Before I could answer, he whipped a set of handcuffs out of one of the pockets of his baggy fatigues. He pushed me over toward a porch railing, forced me to wrap my hands around it, and then handcuffed my hands together. I was trying hard not to think about the wire gizmo in the pocket of my jeans. But he found it and laughed. "Breaking and entering. I like that." He added the picks to his collection of my belongings, then he retrieved the gas can.

He stood at the edge of the porch and cupped his hands, like he was calling the hounds home for supper.

"Hey, out there," he hollered. "I got your friend, Miss Callahan Garrity, here. And I got a gun and a gallon of gasoline right here. You don't come out right now, and I mean without a gun, I'm gonna have me a barbecue. You can watch if you like."

He opened the gas can and started sprinkling gas on the wooden porch floor, whistling again. I kept my eyes on the van, hoping C. W. would have the sense to stay put. If we stalled long enough, Deavers or the local cops would show up. Bollinger stood beside me and poked me in the shoulder with the gun. He had my pistol tucked into one of the pockets of his pants.

"Where's your friend, sugar dumpling?"

"No friend," I said casually. "Just me."

He smacked me so hard I banged my head hard against the porch post. I blinked to keep back the tears.

"Sorry," he said. "It's not normally my way to hit a lady.

But we got to move things along now. And your friend needs to know how serious I am."

He took out my nine-millimeter, cocked it, and put it up against my cheek.

The ploy worked. C. W. emerged slowly from the screen of trees, leaning heavily on the canes, which were sinking with each step into the softened ground.

"Hurry up now," Bollinger called. He put his other hand on my shoulder and pinched the nerve there. I cried out, and C. W. stopped, then moved forward at an even more determined gait. He was at the porch now, his teeth gritted with the effort of moving up the steep steps. I closed my eyes. I could not watch. But Doyle Bollinger was enjoying himself.

"That's good," Bollinger coached. "One more step now."

When C. W. was beside us, Bollinger patted him down. He found the .22 right away and stuck it in another of his pants pockets.

He unlocked the handcuffs and gave me a little shove. "Inside. Both of you."

C. W. hadn't said a word. He was breathing heavily, his face shiny with sweat despite the cold and the wind.

The cabin was a wreck. Broken bits of furniture littered the floor, along with piles of trash, beer cans, and puddles of water where the ceiling had leaked in places.

Bollinger kicked at a rusty can. "Goddamn kids broke in and ruint the place," he said. "Come on in the kitchen and see who else is here."

C. W.'s canes made dull thuds on the wooden floor.

The kitchen was small. There was an old, rusted-out refrigerator, a stove with the oven door hanging off, and on the floor an elderly man, hands and feet tied tightly with rough brown rope. He lay on his side and there was a bloody gash on his forehead.

Arliss Woods was unconscious.

"Set right down beside him," Bollinger said, pointing the gun. He glanced at his watch, then he got out his handcuffs and handcuffed me to the cast-iron leg of the stove. He undid the old man's ropes and used them to tie up Hunsecker.

"I only brought the one set of handcuffs," he said apologetically. "But I don't believe Mr. Woods is going to be making any sudden moves." He took Hunsecker's canes and set them up in the corner of the room.

"Don't go away," he said, waggling a finger at us. He was whistling again, and then he was gone. We heard the front door open, and then his heavy boots were walking around on the front porch. He passed the kitchen door once, and the smell of gasoline wafted under the doorsill. The front door opened, and we heard him coming back our way. The gasoline smell was more intense. He came into the kitchen and knelt down and unlocked the handcuffs.

"Can't leave these here," he said. "When they find the bodies, it won't look good if there's handcuffs. Might give somebody the wrong idea."

"What's the idea?" C. W. asked. "You think they're not going to know what happened here? It's your cabin, Bollinger. You're all over this thing."

"What's the body count now?" I asked. "Whitney. Shawan. Bryant. Janie. Mr. Woods here, he looks like he might be number five."

"It's excessive," Bollinger said with a trace of regret. "And I'll admit, I'm not happy about that."

"How's your client feel about it?" I asked. "Hard to believe Carson Dobbs wanted all this left at his doorstep. Just to get out of paying alimony."

"Old Doc, he pretends he doesn't know about anything," Bollinger said. "That's called deniability. Another thing they

teach these doctors in medical school. Nobody's responsible for nothing. He forgets he's working with a professional. If it ever comes down to that, I got the proof I need."

"Who hired you?" I asked. "Was it after Whitney fired you? Did you get mad, Doyle? Call up Carson and offer to turn the tables? Offer to shortcut the property settlement? Dead women don't cash alimony checks, do they?"

Bollinger looked at his watch. "The stall. That's real good. I can't sit around here and discuss the details though. Let's just say Miss Suzanne recognized an opportunity when I dropped back by that restaurant and told her who I was and who I'd been working for. The Doc, he gets squeamish about this kind of stuff. Funny for a man who likes to cut open hearts, isn't it?"

"Did they pay you to kill Bryant and Janie too?"

"Mr. and Mrs. Mayes?" he said, pretending shock. "Oh, nooo. Noo. That's not how it's gonna look at all. See, Bryant Mayes, he was the one who killed poor Mrs. Dobbs and that wino. And it's y'all's fault all of this happened today.

"Last night, after y'all rattled his cage, he decided things were getting too messy. So he abducted this crazy old man here and brought him down to this old abandoned hunting cabin, broke in, and set it on fire. You two," he said, pointing to us, "showed up and got killed too.

"And then he got to feeling bad about things," Bollinger said. "Went home and got his wife and they drove over to Piedmont Park, and he shot and killed her, then turned the gun on himself. Tragic," he clicked his tongue. "Just tragic."

Before I could ask any more questions, Bollinger reached over with the butt of his pistol and clubbed me squarely on the base of the neck.

33

AS A KID I LOVED THE SMELL OF GASOLINE. It meant Sunday drives with the family, a trip to the beach, a sunny Saturday jumping rope while my dad mowed the lawn. And when I was a teenager a tank of gas was magic—the keys to the kingdom. Five bucks worth of gas and off I'd go, Miss Independence. When you're a grown-up, gas is just another necessity, an inconvenience really. Now it smelled deadly.

My own choking woke me up. White smoke roiled in under the kitchen door. I could see the flames from the windows, working at the wooden porch posts. My head felt like it had been used as a battering ram. Warm, sticky blood oozed down my neck. I tried to stand, but had to sit down quite suddenly, the nausea and pain were so intense.

"C. W.?" I called.

He was leaning on his canes, looking out the tiny kitchen window at the fire. "You okay?"

"Headache," I said. I leaned over and touched Arliss's

throat. He was breathing, but just barely. His skin was cool and dry to the touch, his breaths wheezy and erratic.

"Arliss? Mr. Woods?"

He didn't respond. "He's alive," I said, coughing. "Can we get out?"

C. W. shrugged. "He untied me after he hit you. This door here is nailed shut. He said he'd be out front, waiting, if we tried to get out. It's his idea of hunting, I guess."

I took a deep breath and stood up slowly. My head spun, but I was upright. It felt better.

Outside the fire crackled and roared, punctuated by loud pops from the resin in the old pine boards.

"We've got to get Arliss out of here," I said.

After I steadied myself, I went to the front of the house. Flames licked at the front door, and the heat was searingly intense. I could see a flash of white paint through the flames. Bryant's truck. So Bollinger hadn't left.

There was a tiny bedroom off the living room, but it was filled with smoke, and flames had crept in through a window. I slammed the door shut and went back to the kitchen.

C. W. was at the sink, messing with a faucet and a wadded-up strip of cloth he'd torn from his flannel shirt. The smoke was thicker now. "The water's turned off," he said, his voice emotionless. "The door won't budge. I tried. Anyway, the porch is nearly gone. No way out that way."

He let himself down awkwardly to the floor. "Get down," he said. "The hot air and gases rise. Fresh air's down near the floor."

I lay flat on my belly and pressed my battered face against the grit-layered linoleum. It had been tacked down over the original wooden floor and it was chipped and worn in places, exposing the boards beneath.

I could hear Arliss struggling for breath. He coughed feebly. I

took off the sweater and put part of it under his head, draping the sleeves lightly across his nose and mouth to filter the smoke.

"Floor stinks," I said idly.

C. W. put his face to the floor. "Smells like old rotten potatoes," he said, sniffing. "Old cabin like this, there's probably a root cellar under here, where they kept apples and carrots and potatoes, stuff like that. Before refrigerators."

"Great," I said, pulling the neck of my sweatshirt over my lower face. "We'll have baked potatoes later on. If we're alive."

"Fresh air," C. W. said, pulling himself forward on his elbows. "If there is a cellar, it's below the ground. We could wait out the fire."

There was a pop then, and the glass in the small kitchen door shattered into a million pieces. Flames licked at the door frame leading onto the back porch and more smoke billowed in through the broken window.

"My grandma had a root cellar," I said. "Hers had a door from the outside too."

The kitchen was small, maybe eight by eleven. You could tell where the heaviest traffic had been in the room. The linoleum in front of the refrigerator and the stove and the sink was worn clean through.

I crawled over to the sink and felt the floor. Nothing there but filthy old boards.

The worn place in front of the refrigerator was smaller. I worked at the edge of the brittle flooring with my fingernail, managing only to chip away a small piece until my nail broke.

"We need a tool," I said, looking in the cabinet beside the refrigerator, hoping for a knife or an icepick. But the cupboard and the drawer were empty.

Somebody had cleaned the kitchen out. The drawers were all empty, except for two yellowed cardboard Roach Motels. In the last cupboard I checked, I found a battered red-and-

white enamel saucepan and a rusty metal beer can opener.

"Look," I said, holding it up triumphantly.

We took turns hacking at the linoleum with the pointed end of the opener. After five minutes we'd pried away enough linoleum to see part of the outline of a door.

Another five minutes and we could see most of it. Four feet wide, with a curved groove cut into the wood for a handhold. But only eight inches of the door protruded in front of the squat, rounded-edged refrigerator.

C. W. grabbed the edge of the trap door and pulled, grimacing with the exertion, but the door opened only half an inch.

"We've got to get this refrigerator out of the way," he said.

Using the handle of the refrigerator, he pulled himself upright and wedged the canes at an angle under his armpits. We got on the same side of the refrigerator and pushed. It was an old behemoth and it felt like it was made of lead. We pushed and groaned and managed to move it maybe a quarter of an inch.

"Goddamn," C. W. said. "Let's try again.

We heard a great splitting noise from the other room. I crawled to the doorway and saw that the living room roof had burned through and caved in. Huge beams dangled down from the ceiling, and the freezing wind whipped the flames, feeding it oxygen to continue its path.

Smoke swirled around us and the heat in the room was becoming intense. I kept having to stop and put the sweatshirt over my nose and mouth.

"We've got to tip it over," I said finally, as flames licked at the ceiling line of the far wall.

"One. Two. Three." I took a lungful of the roasting air into my lungs and pushed for me, and for C. W. and Arliss Woods. Then I pushed for Jesus, Mary, Joseph, and all the saints. It was our last chance.

I didn't see the refrigerator start to tilt and then fall. My

eyes were squeezed shut, my energy focused on muscle moving mass.

The refrigerator made an echoing metallic crash as it hit the floor, splintering it on impact.

Both of us fell to the floor to see what we had achieved.

With our hands, we felt rather than saw the door. C. W. grasped the handhold and yanked. The door flew open, releasing a cloud of dust and sour, moldy air.

"Get the old man," C. W. said, letting himself down through the hole in the floor. He clung with his hands to the edge of the opening. "It's shallow," he reported, "Maybe five feet deep."

I gave him the canes and felt my way through the smoke to Arliss. Where the back wall of the kitchen had been was now a vertical sheath of flame. The smoke was black now, and chunks of charred wall and roofing paper fell into the room in a shower of sparks.

With Arliss hooked under the arm I managed to scramble on my hands and knees back to the trapdoor, chunks of burning wood falling all around us.

C. W. reached up and pulled Arliss down into the cellar and I followed after him, dropping down into the foul-smelling hole, landing hard on my butt on the earth-floored cellar. A jolt of pain went up my spine.

There was a loud popping noise then, and the sickening sound of a wall falling in. More chunks of burning wood fell in, one burning me on my right hand.

"Pull the door, for Christ's sake," C. W. screamed.

I reached up and yanked the trapdoor shut, plunging us into cool inky darkness. I thought of Alice in Wonderland falling down, down, down through the rabbit hole and instantly, the blackness seemed to press in on me, suffocating in a way that was just as bad as that smoke-filled room above us.

I sucked the burned place on my hand.

"The old man's bad," C. W. said. I reached out and touched him. It made things better, having C. W. there.

"Head injury," he said. "Maybe a skull fracture. Something like that. How about you?"

I laughed shakily. "Broke my butt when I hit the dirt. What about your own self?"

"I'm in one piece."

We could hear the fire roaring overhead, timbers falling. I got to my knees and reached up to touch the trapdoor. It was red-hot to the touch. "We've got to find a way out of here," I told him. "Can you pull yourself up?"

"Not without a handhold," he said ruefully.

The darkness in the root cellar was total. On my hands and knees, I crawled around, feeling to see what the space was like. It was rectangular, with walls that sloped up. My hand touched something rough, burlap maybe, and then something else, soft and shriveled. I jerked my hand back and backed away until I was up against the wall.

There was a skittering noise in the opposite corner.

"Do you think there are rats down here?" I asked.

"Probably."

I swallowed and inched sideways. My hand touched more burlap, and then I heard the sound of glass clinking against glass. My fingers found an object. A glass jar full of some kind of sloshing liquid. There was a metal screw-on cap. I sat back on my heels, unscrewed the cap, and sniffed. The smell brought tears to my eyes.

"Guess what else they kept down here besides roots," I said.

"Onions and apples," C. W. said.

"Corn likker," I corrected him. Nestled in a rotted burlap bag I felt three more jars like the one I held. Quart bottles, they felt like. Old, dust-filmed Mason jars. My grandma had

kept jars like this in her root cellar, but hers were always full of fig preserves or canned tomatoes.

I passed the jar over to him and heard him inhale deeply.

"Oh, yeah." He chuckled. "White lightning. The good stuff."

I put the jar down and ran my hands up the sloped walls, toward where the ceiling should be. It sloped too. Finally my fingers touched wood.

"I found it," I said.

If I kneeled and pushed straight up, I could feel the door move, just slightly. With both hands I traced the outline of the door, felt the rusted metal hinges. The door gave a little, but it didn't open.

"It's warped shut," I said, trying to hide my disappointment.

"Push harder," C. W. said. "Smoke's coming in."

I glanced upward. The air in the cellar was hot and getting hotter, and I could see the glow of flames on the trapdoor.

I heard a scraping noise and grunts, and then C. W. was right beside me.

"Lay on your back and kick," he said. "More strength in your legs than your arms."

Rat droppings. I'm lying on rat droppings, I thought. My hair will never be clean again. But I did as he suggested.

"On the count of three," he said.

"One. Two. Three." We counted together, and on three, I kicked with all my might. The wood was soft, waterlogged. It gave slightly, but not enough.

"Scoot your butt as far forward as you can," C. W. said. "Tuck your knees in to your chest, all the way up toward your chest. Now flex your foot so you strike with the flat of your foot. Brace your hands on the ground, close to your side. On three. And put your whole butt into it, Garrity.

"One. Two. Three."

I screamed like a banshee and kicked like a mule. The door

sprang open and flew all the way off. I stood up and popped my head out of the opening, taking in a lungful of the outside air. It was cold and smoky, but the bouquet was infinitely better than what I had been breathing.

"Good work," C. W. said as I helped him to his feet. "Let's get the old man out of here."

Between us, we managed to push and pull Arliss out of the door, dragging him away from the fire and into a clump of soot-blackened rhododendrons. We covered Arliss with my sweater, and C. W. wrapped his windbreaker around his legs. "He's in shock," he said. "His age, if we don't get him to a hospital, he won't make it."

The wind had died down a little. I kept to the woods on the edge of the clearing, circled halfway around until I was parallel with the house. By myself, maybe I could have made it to the van, and C. W.'s gun. But C. W. and Arliss were going nowhere in a hurry.

I hid behind an oak tree and willed myself invisible. The white pickup truck was there. And I thought, despite the wind and the roar of the fire, that I could hear him whistling. Bollinger was seated on the hood of the truck, a rifle laid across his knees, whistling and basking in the warmth of his bonfire.

"He's out there," I told C. W. when I got back. "Watching. Waiting for us to burn to death. And he's got a rifle."

C. W. had Arliss gathered into his lap. His fingers probed the ropy flesh at the base of the old man's neck. "His pulse is weak," C. W. said.

My eyes wandered to the cellar door. If I stood around and thought about it too long, my instincts would take over and I'd go anywhere but back into that dank, smoke-filled cellar.

I didn't think about it. The heat near the house was so intense I had to shield my eyes with my arm. I hopped into the hole. The trapdoor in the ceiling had burned almost all the

way through, and the ground was covered with chunks of smoldering wood. I grabbed two of the quart jars and scrambled back out.

C. W. didn't look surprised when I showed him the jars of moonshine. The liquid wasn't quite clear; it had a slightly yellowish cast.

"You got a match?" I asked, taking off my white cotton tube socks and putting my sneakers back on.

I unscrewed the lid of each jar, wadded up the socks and stuck one in the mouth of each jar, letting the toe soak down into the moonshine.

"You know I don't smoke," C. W. said.

I looked over at Arliss. A mashed-up soft pack of Camels stuck out of the breast pocket of his shirt. "Check the patient," I suggested.

C. W. turned Arliss Woods's pants pockets inside out, finally coming up with two wooden kitchen matches.

He handed them to me carefully, then took off his own socks and gave me them too. I stuffed each one down into the jar. It made a tighter fit.

"Molotov cocktails," C. W. said approvingly. "Can you throw that far?"

"Probably not," I said. "I throw like a girl. I'll get as close as I can without risking him seeing me, then I'll make a toss. If the first one misses, it'll at least make a commotion, maybe I'll have time to throw the second one before I run for the van."

"Throw underhanded," he suggested. "You try and throw overhand, the liquor might spill out and come back on you."

I nodded and made for the woods, creeping slowly so the moonshine didn't slosh out. It took a while to circle around through the woods in back of the house. The terrain was rough and crisscrossed with creeks. My sneakers were soaked through, my bare feet inside them were freezing. The fire lit up the sky around the cabin, smoke billowing up through the

treetops. I could see the back of the house; two walls had caved in, and the other two were crumbling bit by bit. Surely, I told myself, someone will see the smoke. Surely, somebody will come looking.

The fire was so spectacular that Doyle Bollinger couldn't keep his eyes off it. He'd set the empty gasoline can on the ground, near the back of the truck. As I came around the back of the house, I moved faster. There was a clump of trees only a few yards from the back of the truck.

I crouched there and waited. Still too far to throw with any accuracy. I cursed my parents for letting me play with dolls when I could been practicing the inside curveball. I could only see Bollinger's back from where I was. He was relaxed, having a good time. Once he picked up the rifle, sighted it at the house, then put it back down again. His shoulders shook with laughter.

It was all I needed. I tucked a jar under each arm and scuttled to within five yards of the truck. Not close enough. I crept closer, until I was within two yards. I'd never played much baseball, but I had done some time on the APD bowling team. I got out the kitchen matches and lit one sock, then the other.

I stood up, swept my right arm back and sent the first jar spinning, rolling toward the underside of the truck. Then the other.

The first one stopped two feet away from the truck's tailpipe, the other came to rest against the plastic gasoline can. For a maddening five seconds nothing happened.

"Cocktail time," I whispered. Then I ran like hell.

When the boom came, the impact knocked me backward. The truck was a fireball. Then another explosion. The truck's gas tank.

Pieces of metal and glass rained down around me. I got up and ran for the van and I didn't look backward. I didn't let myself think about the bodies in the truck. Not then, anyway.

EPILOGUE

HE'S ALIVE," C. W. said, looking up at me with a grim smile. "He's like a cockroach. You can stomp him, but you can't kill the son of a bitch."

Doyle Bollinger's flight had only been stopped by a sapling oak. No telling where he would have ended up otherwise. His body lay limply, like a discarded toy, his left leg turned back on itself. Otherwise, he was curiously unmarked.

"Let's get Arliss to the hospital," I said. "I'll bring the van as close in as I can get."

We heard cars then, sirens wailing, two different kinds. A blue Henry County sheriff's vehicle came plowing toward us, mud flying. Two more sheriff's cars were followed by a fire truck and an ambulance. Bucky Deavers's two-tone aqua Studebaker brought up the rear.

I showed them where to find Arliss. One of the deputies was insisting I tell him what the hell had been happening. A

288

fire, pieces of bodies flung all over the place. Hunsecker lost his cool.

"Damn idiots," he shouted. "Don't know your own county? Somebody calls and tells you shots have been fired, you wait two hours to check it out?"

Deavers strode into the middle of the mess and flashed his badge. "Atlanta homicide," he said in a surprisingly commanding tone. Captain Hunsecker here can give you a statement. Miss Garrity has a family emergency."

He hustled me off toward his car. The adrenaline had started to wear off, but now I felt my heart lurch.

"What is it?" I asked, knowing already. "Edna?"

"Heart attack, they're saying. She's stable," he added quickly. "When the hospital couldn't reach you, they got your sister Maureen. She's there."

"It's my fault," I said. "There was a message on the machine. Western Regional? Edna went over there to look for Carson Dobbs's missing business manager. We got a tip he'd been spotted there. I thought they were returning one of Edna's phone calls."

"I didn't get the whole story," Bucky said. "Apparently she thought she saw the guy and took off after him, up a stairwell. Two flights, and she collapsed. Lucky for her, an office worker was sneaking a smoke one landing up and found her. Lucky for her, she was in a hospital."

"Dear God," I gasped. And then I was biting the palm of my hand, trying to be a man about it, but the sobs came in great shuddering waves.

Maureen and Steve sat huddled together on a plastic sofa in the waiting room. They both had Styrofoam coffee cups in their hands. Maureen glared when she saw me.

"This is your fault," she started in.

"It is," I agreed. "One hundred percent. Can we discuss what a shitty daughter I am later? What's the deal? How bad is she?"

"She infarcted," Maureen said.

"What's that mean in English?"

Maureen rolled her eyes. "She had a heart attack. They got her down to the emergency room and got her resuscitated. Jeanne's with her now. That's all I know. Where the hell have you been? You smell like a weenie roast."

I looked down at myself. My clothes were torn and filthy, my feet so wet they'd left puddles where I walked. There was blood all over my neck, more on my hands and face. My hair was singed where burning pieces of wood had fallen on my head.

"It's a long story," I told her.

Jeanne Payne came through the door from the emergency room.

"She's going to make it," Jeanne said, giving me a hug. "Her vital signs are stable. They're moving her to the cardiac intensive care unit right now. I called the cardiologist I told you about. Tomorrow, if Edna's up to it, we'll have her moved over to Piedmont. Dr. Soong wants to look at her tomorrow."

"What about the surgery?" Maureen wanted to know. "Dr. Dobbs said she'd need surgery. Right away. Callahan wouldn't listen. She never listens."

Jeanne sighed and rubbed the small of her back. "I haven't seen the results of the tests Dr. Dobbs did, but yes, from the EKG they ran on your mother, and what I observed, I believe she does have mitral valve prolapse and some signs of coronary artery disease, which caused her heart attack. Dr. Soong can tell us more after she's seen your mother."

"What kind of surgery?" Maureen asked. "Is she going to need a valve replacement?"

Jeanne shook her head. "That's for the surgeon to decide. They'll do a cardiac catheterization first, probably tomorrow, and if she sees a blocked artery they'll do a balloon angioplasty."

"Can we see her?" Maureen asked.

"She's sedated," Jeanne warned. "She won't know you're there."

"Just for a minute?" I begged.

Western Regional was brand-new, squeaky, sparklingly efficient. The cardiac intensive care unit was two floors up. A circular nurse's station was opposite the elevator, and eight glass-walled rooms radiated out around it, like the spokes on a wheel. Behind the counter, monitors and dials gleamed in the fluorescent light. Western Regional's nurses wore what looked like white pantsuits, with white blazers and emblems on their pockets. "Looks like a damned yacht club," I muttered.

"Give it a rest," Maureen said sharply. "She could have died, you know. She still could."

The nurse took us in and let us look at our mother. They had an oxygen mask strapped onto her face, and I could see the adhesive patches from the electrodes attached to her chest under her hospital gown. There was an IV tube attached to her arm, and another tube running under the sheet. Somewhere under there was my mother, Edna Mae Garrity.

Maureen caught her breath. Maybe she reached for my hand first, or maybe I was the one who reached out to her. We stood like that for a long time, Maureen and I, listening to the monitor bleep, watching the wavy line draw pictures of our mother's weakened heart, my sister's hand clutched tightly in mine.

"Don't die," I whispered. "Please don't die."

They moved Edna to Piedmont Hospital the next day and did the procedure the day after that.

You're supposed to grow closer when there's a family crisis, but Maureen and I did not become best friends because our mother was sick. We fought over everything, from the kind of nightgown to take to the hospital, to the decision to do the angioplasty, to whether or not to guilt-trip our brothers into coming back home. "She could die," Maureen kept saying. "It could be their last chance to see her. Mom wants to see them."

"She's not going to die, damn it," I said. "If they come back just for this, you'll scare her into thinking she is dying. Brian hasn't been home in eight years, Maureen. Kevin just started a new job. They can both come when she's better."

Once Edna's surgery was over, I went to an art supply store and bought a big boxful of oil paints and brushes and canvases, and I took them over to Grady Hospital.

Arliss Woods seemed to like the supplies. And he'd found Biblical precedence for his survival and recovery from the fire.

"Psalms: chapter one, verse three," he intoned. "Fear not the myriads of people arrayed against me on every side. Rise up, O Lord! Save me, My God. For you strike all my enemies on the cheek; the teeth of the wicked you break. Salvation is the Lord's. Upon your people be your blessing!"

He was shouting and waving his arms. He got so carried away the nurses came in to quiet him down. "Eighty-two," one of them told me. "He's eighty-two years old and he's got girlfriends coming to visit."

They told me Doyle Bollinger was in Grady too, down in the prison ward, his good leg chained to the bed, his other one broken in several places. He had a shattered jaw and the explosion had knocked out his front teeth.

When I wasn't at the hospital, I was over at the homicide office, going over my statement with Bucky Deavers and Lloyd Mackey and various assistant Fulton County district attorneys and federal prosecutors.

Carson and Suzanne were arrested and charged with conspiracy to murder. The feds weighed in too, charging them both with mail fraud, tax evasion, and a lot of other stuff. Because she was pregnant, they let Suzanne out on bond. But the judge decided Dr. Dobbs was a flight risk. Bucky told me his office made arrangements to fax patients' charts to the doctor while he was in jail.

I also heard Carson hired a new private detective to look for the elusive Ben Dwyer. I never could find the man.

The girls sent flowers. Sister knitted slippers. Ruby came and sat long hours in Edna's room, reading Bible verses out loud. Edna made her read the Song of Solomon, just to see Ruby blushing.

Neva Jean and Swannelle showed up on the first Sunday Edna could have visitors, with a box of chocolates grown filmy with age. I was sitting in the room with Edna, having already delivered the requested *Soap Opera Digest* and Jergens lotion, when they came into the room holding hands and making googly eyes at each other.

"You two make up?" Edna asked.

Neva Jean giggled and Swannelle ducked out to find a place to catch a smoke.

"Swannelle sold the emus," Neva Jean confided. "Right after the health inspectors showed up. You know what was wrong with 'em?"

"What?" Edna asked, sitting forward in the bed.

Neva Jean glanced around to make sure she wouldn't be overheard. "Gay as a goose."

"Animals can be homosexual?" I asked. "That doesn't sound right to me, Neva Jean."

"Well they were," she assured us. "Swannelle had his doubts. He just didn't want to admit it. The new owners had somebody draw blood and they sent it off in the mail. DNA

testing. That's the only way you can tell for sure. And it come back that Nancy shoulda been named Nathan. We had to give back some of the money."

"Well I swannee," Edna kept saying.

Jackie came on a Monday to tell us both that she was quitting.

"It's not because of the black thing," she said, right off the bat. "I've been thinking about it. I guess what I resented wasn't so much working for a white woman as it was working for anybody."

Edna wasn't quite ready to forgive. "You said some hard things to us, Jackie," she said. "We were good to you, and you never appreciated any of it."

I saw Jackie's back stiffen. "I'm going to start my own business," she continued. "Me and my cousin. We're starting our own maid service. But I won't try to take my clients with me. That wouldn't be right."

She and I shook hands. Edna gave her a curt, dismissive nod. When Jackie was gone I picked a fight with Edna over her harsh treatment of Jackie. "They must have ripped your heart all the way out when they did that surgery," I said accusingly. "I'm gonna make them give us our money back. There's no heart at all." We fussed back and forth like that for thirty minutes and I knew then that my mother would get better.

When I went back on Wednesday, a technician was hovering over Edna, drawing various vials of fluids. I went out to the waiting room.

Mac sat on one of the couches, flipping through a magazine.

"She call you?" I asked, sitting down on the same couch, a safe distance between us.

"C. W. called. And I've talked to Edna on the phone a few times." He grinned. "She didn't want me to come see her until

she could get her hair done. Vain old biddy. C. W. told me what happened out at that cabin. He said you saved his life. And the old man's life."

"We saved each other," I said haltingly. "If I'd been in that cabin by myself, I would have died in the fire. We were trapped. And I was starting to panic. I don't know what I would have done." I swallowed hard. "I was terrified. And when we were in that hole, for a minute, I was so frightened, I forgot he was there with me. And I felt so damned alone. The fire would have been better. Better than dying alone in the dark like that."

"Alone's not good," Mac said.

"I've come to the same conclusion," I said. "You want to get a cup of coffee?"